HEADS—YOU LOSE

The headless horseman's wild laughter echoed through the night.

A whip cracked. Tillotsen screamed with pain, clutching at his face. The black horse reared up and the whip cracked once again. It snaked around Chilton's throat and pulled him to the ground. A club flashed and Crenshaw fell, unconscious. The rider swung the club again and Johnny Long crumpled to the street . . .

The next morning, all four men were discovered hanging from the Liberty Tree in Boston Common. Pinned to each corpse was a placard reading, "Hellfire to the Sons of Liberty!"

10 TIMEWARS

THE HELLFIRE REBELLION

SIMON HAWKE

ACE BOOKS, NEW YORK

A CHRONOLOGICAL HISTORY OF THE TIME WARS

April 1, 2425: Dr. Wolfgang Mensinger invents the chronoplate at the age of 115, discovering time travel. Later, he would construct a small-scale working prototype for use in laboratory experiments specifically designed to avoid any possible creation of a temporal paradox. He is hailed as the "Father of Temporal Physics."

July 14, 2430: Mensinger publishes "There is No Future," in which he redefines relativity, proving there is no such thing as *the* future, but an infinite number of potential scenarios, which are absolute relative only to their present. He also announces the discovery of "nonspecific time," or temporal limbo, later known as "the dead zone."

October 21, 2440: Wolfgang Mensinger dies. His son, Albrecht, perfects the chronoplate and carries on the work, but loses control of the discovery to political interests.

June 15, 2460: Formation of the international Committee for Temporal Intelligence, with Albrecht Mensinger as director. Specially trained and conditioned "agents" of the committee began to travel back through time in order to conduct research and field test the chronoplate apparatus. Many become lost in transition, trapped in the limbo of non-specific time known as "the dead zone." Those who return from successful temporal voyages often bring back startling information necessitating the revision of historical records.

March 22, 2461:	*The Consorti Affair*—Cardinal Ludovico Consorti is excommunicated from the Roman Catholic Church for proposing that agents travel back through time to obtain empirical evidence that Christ arose following his crucifixion. The Consorti Affair sparks extensive international negotiations amidst a volatile climate of public opinion concerning the proper uses for the new technology. Temporal excursions are severely curtailed. Concurrently, espionage operatives of several nations infiltrate the Committee for Temporal Intelligence.
May 1, 2461:	Dr. Albrecht Mensinger appears before a special international conference in Geneva, composed of political leaders and members of the scientific community. He attempts to alleviate fears about the possible misuses of time travel. He further refuses to cooperate with any attempts to militarize his father's discovery.
February 3, 2485:	The research facilities of the Committee for Temporal Intelligence are seized by troops of the TransAtlantic Treaty Organization.
January 25, 2492:	The Council of Nations meets in Buenos Aires, capital of the United Socialist States of South America, to discuss increasing international tensions and economic instability. A proposal for "an end to war in our time" is put forth by the chairman of the Nippon Conglomerate Empire. Dr. Albrecht Mensinger, appearing before the body as the nominal director of the Committee for Temporal Intelligence, argues passionately against using temporal technology to resolve international conflicts, but cannot present proof that the past

can be affected by temporal voyagers. Prevailing scientific testimony reinforces the conventional wisdom that the past is an immutable absolute.

December 24, 2492: Formation of the Referee Corps, brought into being by the Council of Nations as an extranational arbitrating body with sole control over temporal technology and authority to stage temporal conflicts as "limited warfare" to resolve international disputes.

April 21, 2493: On the recommendation of the Referee Corps, a subordinate body named the Observer Corps is formed, taking over most of the functions of the Committee for Temporal Intelligence, which is redesignated as the Temporal Intelligence Agency. Under the aegis of the Council of Nations and the Referee Corps, the T.I.A. absorbs the intelligence agencies of the world's governments and is made solely answerable to the Referee Corps. Dr. Mensinger resigns his post to found the Temporal Preservation League, a group dedicated to the abolition of temporal conflict.

June, 2497—
March, 2502: Referee Corps presides over initial temporal confrontation campaigns, accepting "grievances" from disputing nations, selecting historical conflicts of the past as "staging grounds" and supervising the infiltration of modern troops into the so-called "cannon fodder" ranks of ancient warring armies. Initial numbers of temporal combatants are kept small, with infiltration facilitated by cosmetic surgery and implant conditioning of soldiers. The results are calculated based upon successful return rate and a complicated "point spread." Soldiers are monitored via cerebral implants, enabling Search and

Retrieve teams to follow their movements and monitor mortality rate. The media dubs temporal conflicts the "Time Wars."

2500–2510: Extremely rapid growth of massive support industry catering to the exacting art and science of temporal conflict. Rapid improvement in the international economic climate follows, with significant growth in productivity and rapid decline in unemployment and inflation rate. There is a gradual escalation of the Time Wars, with a majority of the world's armed services converting to temporal duty status.

Growth of the Temporal Preservation League as a peace movement with an intensive lobby effort and mass demonstrations against the Time Wars. Mensinger cautions against an imbalance in temporal continuity due to the increasing activity of the Time Wars.

September 2, 2514: Mensinger publishes his "Theories of Temporal Relativity," incorporating his solution to the Grandfather Paradox and calling once again for a ceasefire in the Time Wars. The result is an upheaval in the scientific community and a hastily reconvened Council of Nations to discuss his findings, leading to the Temporal Strategic Arms Limitations Talks of 2515.

March 15, 2515—
June 1, 2515: T-SALT held in New York City. Mensinger appears before the representatives at the sessions and petitions for an end to the Time Wars. A ceasefire resolution is framed, but tabled due to lack of agreement among the members of the Council of Nations. Mensinger leaves the T-SALT a broken man.

November 18, 2516:	Dr. Albrecht Mensinger experiences total nervous collapse shortly after being awarded the Benford Prize.
December 25, 2516:	Dr. Albrecht Mensinger commits suicide. Violent demonstrations by members of the Temporal Preservation League.
January 1, 2517:	Militant members of the Temporal Preservation League band together to form the Timekeepers, a terrorist offshoot of the League, dedicated to the complete destruction of the war machine. They announce their presence to the world by assassinating three members of the Referee Corps and bombing the Council of Nations meeting in Buenos Aires, killing several heads of state and injuring many others.
September 17, 2613:	Formation of the First Division of the U.S. Army Temporal Corps as a crack commando unit following the successful completion of a "temporal adjustment" involving the the first serious threat of a timestream split. The First Division, assigned exclusively to deal with threats to temporal continuity, is designated as "the Time Commandos."
October 10, 2615:	Temporal physicist Dr. Robert Darkness disappears without a trace shortly after turning over to the army his new invention, the "warp grenade," a combination time machine and nuclear device. Establishing a secret research installation somewhere off Earth, Darkness experiments with temporal translocation based on the transmutation principle. He experiments upon himself and succeeds in translating his own body into tachyons, but an error in his calculations causes an irreversible change in his subatomic structure, ren-

dering it unstable. Darkness becomes "the man who is faster than light."

November 3, 2620:   The chronoplate is superseded by the temporal transponder. Dubbed the "warp disc," the temporal transponder was developed from work begun by Dr. Darkness and it drew on power tapped by Einstein-Rosen Generators (developed by Bell Laboratories in 2545) bridging to neutron stars.

March 15, 2625:   *The Temporal Crisis:* The discovery of an alternate universe following an unsuccessful invasion by troops of the Special Operations Group, counterparts of the time commandos. Whether as a result of chronophysical instability caused by clocking tremendous amounts of energy through Einstein-Rosen Bridges or the cumulative effect of temporal disruptions, an alternate universe comes into congruence with our own, causing an instability in the timeflow of both universes and resulting in a "confluence effect," wherein the timestreams of both universes ripple and occasionally intersect, creating "confluence points" where crossover from one universe to another becomes possible.

Massive amounts of energy clocked through Einstein-Rosen Bridges has resulted in unintentional "warp bombardment" of the alternate universe, causing untold destruction. The Time Wars escalate into a temporal war between two universes.

May 13, 2626:   Gen. Moses Forrester, director of the Temporal Intelligence Agency (which has absorbed the First Division), becomes aware of a super secret organization within the T.I.A. known as

"The Network." Comprised of corrupt T.I.A. section chiefs and renegade deep cover agents, the Network has formed a vast trans-temporal economic empire, entailing extensive involvement in both legitimate businesses and organized crime. Forrester vows to break the Network and becomes a marked man.

PROLOGUE ═══════════════

Reese Hunter had never seen a nation being born before, though he had seen more than his share of nations die. He had seen Rome sacked by Visigoths and he rode with Alexander as the Macedonian had carved his way across the ancient world. He was with Cortez when the Spanish conquistadores had descended on the unsuspecting Incas and he had watched from the cockpit of a bomber while Dresden was reduced to rubble and the Third Reich burned. He had seen governments fall and empires crumble, but he had never before witnessed a nation being born.

The English colonies in North America were about to be reborn as a new nation, and in a sense, Hunter was about to be reborn, as well. He was about to start a new life in a new universe, one that was almost a mirror image of his own. In his own universe, he had been a captain in the C.I.S., the elite Counter Insurgency Section of the Special Operations Group. Agents of the T.I.A. had captured him and brought him through a confluence point into their timeline, anxious to question him about the operations of his unit and, in particular, to find out how the C.I.S. had broken into their top secret Archives Section data banks. But the T.I.A. never had a chance to question him, because Hunter had stolen one of their warp discs and escaped into their past. Now there was no way back.

In many ways, this universe was a familiar one. His cerebral implant programming gave him a detailed knowledge of this timeline's history. He knew, for example, that in this universe, unlike his own, the Americans would win their war for independence, not lose and later have it granted to them by the British in the middle of the 19th century. However, his detailed knowledge of this timeline's history would not enable him to get back home. He had been unconscious when the temporal agents brought him through the confluence, a point where their two timelines intersected, and he had no way of knowing how to find it once again. He was trapped here now and he would simply have to make the best of it.

He had carefully considered all his options. Though he would now be on his own, without any logistical support, he could continue to function as a covert agent of the C.I.S. and work to disrupt this timeline's continuity. Or he could simply quit, leave the war behind and start a brand-new life. A simpler life, uncomplicated by the Time Wars. It was a very tempting option. Hunter had grown tired of fighting. The temporal physicists back home believed that the way to overcome the confluence phenomenon was to create temporal disruptions in the opposing universe. They believed that a timestream split would separate the two congruent timelines, but that was no more than a theory. It was also possible that a timestream split in either universe would only make the situation worse, creating still more parallel timelines that would intersect with one another, a temporal disaster that could ultimately lead to entropy. Hunter did not want that on his conscience.

He did not know what the answer was. No one in his timeline had even suspected that a parallel universe existed until that parallel universe attacked. The agents of the T.I.A. had claimed that it was all a terrible mistake. Their explanation had sounded very plausible, but Hunter wasn't sure what the truth was anymore. He had been told that in this universe, a scientist named Dr. Robert Darkness had perfected a devastating weapon known as the warp grenade, a combination nuclear device and time machine. It operated on the same principle as warp discs. The device was hellish, a nuclear weapon capable of pinpoint adjustability, designed to use all of its terribly destructive energy or only a small fraction of it. It could be set to destroy a city, or a block within that city, or a building on that block, or just a room within that building. At the instant of the detonation, the surplus energy of the explosion would be transported by the weapon's chronocircuitry through an Einstein-Rosen Bridge—a warp in spacetime—to a point in outer space where it could do no harm. Or so the scientists had believed.

In practice, what had happened was that such incredible amounts of energy being clocked through warps in spacetime had brought about a shift in the chronophysical alignment of the universe. Instead of dissipating harmlessly in outer space, the nuclear explosions had been clocked through space warps directly into Hunter's timeline, where they had caused untold destruction. Hunter's universe and this one had been forced into congruence, so that a confluence phenomenon was brought about. The timespace continuum was rippling and two parallel timelines were intertwining like a double helix strand of DNA. At various points in space and time, they briefly flowed together, so that it was possible to cross over from one universe into another. The two timelines were at war and Hunter now believed it was a war no one could win. Nor was he the only one who felt that way.

In his own universe, as in this one, there were people who had fatalistically accepted the inevitability of an irreversible temporal disaster, so they had chosen to escape into the past. They had opted out of their society and gone over to the Underground, a loosely organized confederation of temporal deserters, fugitives from the far future. And Hunter had encountered yet another group at work throughout the past. It was called the Network, an offshoot of the T.I.A.—a secret agency within a secret agency. Only this group had its own agenda, independent of any government. These were renegade temporal agents, profiteers conducting the complex business of an underground, trans-temporal economy. And for all Hunter knew, there could be a similar organization in his own universe, as well. It was insanity. There was no way of knowing how many people in the past were really from the future, no way to measure how fragile the timestream had become—in either universe.

In such a chaotic situation, the actions of one man seemed very small, indeed. But Hunter knew that the actions of one man could often make all the difference in the world. And on the day that he arrived in Boston, the actions of one man, a man named Samuel Adams, were about to ignite a conflagration that would burn like hellfire as it spread throughout the thirteen English colonies.

Hunter had arrived in Boston unsuitably attired. He had hidden in an alley by the waterfront until an inebriated seaman of a convenient size had stumbled by, whereupon Hunter had rolled him and stolen all his money and his clothes. He then found a tavern called the Harp and Crown, where he had an inexpensive meal called an "ordinary," a set meal served at a fixed price, and picked up a copy of the *Boston Gazette*. The date was August 14, 1765, and according to the paper, it was the birthday of the Prince of Wales. But the most newsworthy event of the day had occurred too recently to make the paper and it was the topic on the lips of everybody in the tavern.

That morning, the citizens of Boston awoke to see two figures hanging from the elm trees in the Common. One was shaped like a boot, with a devil peeking out of it, a play on the name of King George's favorite advisor, the Earl of Bute. The other was an effigy of Andrew Oliver, a local man, identified by his initials and a sign that read, "What greater joy did New England see than a stampman hanging from a tree?" Beneath the figure was a placard with the warning, "He that takes this down is an enemy to his country!"

It wasn't difficult for Hunter to get into a conversation with a group of citizens engaged in a spirited discussion about the day's events. He approached their table and politely inquired what the fuss was all about. They stared at him with disbelief.

"Why, where've you been, man?" one of the men asked him.

"I've been at sea," said Hunter, his stolen clothing lending credence to the lie. "Ten long years before the mast. I grew tired of seeing other men grow rich upon the spice trade while I worked like a dog without a whit to show for it. I heard tell that a man could make a good life for himself in the American colonies, but I have only just arrived in Boston and I must confess that I know nothing of these matters you're discussing. What has this man Oliver done that his image should be strung up from a tree? And what exactly is a stampman, anyway?"

"A stampman, sir, is a plague upon our liberty," one of the men said, "and if you plan to settle down in Boston, he shall be a plague on yours, as well. Sit down, sir, and it will be our pleasure to enlighten you."

They made room for Hunter and he joined them at the table.

"What is your name, sailor?"

"I'm called Reese Hunter."

The man offered his hand. "Ben Edes is my name," he said, "and I am the editor of that newspaper you've been reading. These gentlemen are Jared Moffat, Thomas Brown, John Hewitt, and Grant Channing. And as you might have heard, not all of us are in complete agreement." He scowled at Moffat, Brown, and Hewitt.

"Some of us possess a bit more sense than others," Moffat said wryly. "And a bit more loyalty, it seems."

"I'll hear no more talk of that!" said Edes, sharply. "My loyalty is not for you to question, Jared Moffat! Besides, our friend has asked a question and we owe him the courtesy of a reply." He turned to Hunter. "The matter concerns taxes, sir. Unjust and ruinous taxes imposed upon us by greedy and unscrupulous men—"

"You call the king greedy and unscrupulous?" said Brown.

"I've not said a word against the king!" snapped Edes. "It is the king's ministers who are to blame for this! That has been my stand from the beginning, so kindly do not go putting words into my mouth, sir!"

"He has no need for that, Ben," said Moffat, dryly. "You have a surfeit of your own."

"Let him speak, Jared," said Hewitt.

"Thank you, John," Edes said, frowning at Moffat. He turned back to Hunter. "Where was I?"

"You were speaking of taxation," Hunter prompted him.

"Yes, quite," said Edes. "Revenue. The king's ministers want revenue." He grimaced and shifted in his chair. "You see, sir, the matter stands like this. The end of the Seven Years War, which we called the French and Indian War here in North America, has left England with a heavy debt of some one hundred and forty million pounds. A considerable sum, you will agree. And revenue is needed, not only to pay that massive debt, but also to provide for the garrisoning of troops here in North America to keep the French from regaining their newly lost possessions."

"And Lord Grenville thinks it's only reasonable that the colonies should share in the expense," said Moffat. "After all, the troops are here for our protection."

"We can rely on our *own* militia to protect us," Edes said. "Besides, have we not already paid our share? Or have you forgotten who financed Lord Amherst's campaigns during the war? The colonies bore that burden, sir, and it has not pleased Parliament to reimburse us. Yet it pleases them to dip their greedy hands into our pockets, to tell us how we may conduct our trade, and to deny us our own land—"

"Oh, Lord, are you on *that* again?" said Moffat, with exasperation.

"They took land from you?" said Hunter.

"Land that was never rightly his," said Moffat, before Edes could reply.

"I paid good money for that land!" protested Edes.

"Oh, admit it, Ben, you stole it," Moffat said. "Why not tell him the truth? What he means is that he paid for it with trinkets; bits of pottery and looking glass is what he calls 'good money.' That is the princely coin in which he and other enterprising men have paid the Indians for land on which they hunted."

"It was a fair bargain! They accepted it!" said Edes.

"Only because you pressed it on them," Moffat said. "You took advantage of them, Ben. The Indians know nothing of deeds and rights of purchase. They don't know what such things mean. I lived on the frontier. I know them better than you do. I understand the way they think."

He turned to Hunter. "They are a simple, savage people, Hunter. In many ways, they are no more than children. And throughout the colonies, speculators like our friend Ben Edes and men of means such as Ben Franklin in Philadelphia and Col. George Washington in the Virginia colony saw a way to make an easy profit from them. They bought up large tracts of land from the Indians for trinkets and then sold them for considerable gain to westward moving settlers. Only the Indians didn't really understand what they had sold, you see. They became alarmed at settlers pushing deep into their hunting grounds. Under Chief Pontiac, the leader of the Ottawa tribe, they rose up in rebellion and destroyed all the frontier settlements in Virginia, Maryland, and Pennsylvania. They were finally defeated by the British troops and our own colonial militia, but the ministry did not want a reoccurrence of the uprising, so they decreed that speculators could no longer buy land from the Indians, but only through officials of the Crown. And they further stipulated that no trading with the Indians could be conducted except with a special license from a royal governor. I think it was a very wise decision, made to keep the peace, but Ben and others like him have been resentful of it ever since."

"That was not the real reason for the proclamation and you know it," Edes said angrily. "He has merely given you the Tory version of the truth. The real truth is that our British cousins seek to keep us from prosperity. They know that if we are confined to the Atlantic seaboard, our cities will grow and attract skilled artisans from England. They are afraid that we would begin to manufacture and compete with their production. On the other hand, if we continue to push west, our spread will soon take us out of British jurisdiction and we will cease to be dependent on the mother country. So their solution is to suppress our growth by acting to protect the interests of the Indians over our own. And it's true that I am not the only one who is resentful of it. But they did not stop there, no, sir! They passed a law to keep us from our land and now they seek to stop our trade, as well!"

"The smugglers' trade, you mean," said Moffat.

"And whose fault is it that we are forced to smuggle?" Edes said. "Do not the distillers need molasses to make rum? Do not the farmers need markets for their grain and cattle? Do not the butchers and the bakers and the lumbermen need markets for their goods, as well? You know as well as I that virtually all the produce of New England is barred from Britain to protect home trade. Yet we must import everything only from them! Is that fair, I ask you? Why should we import European goods only from England when we can obtain them far more cheaply elsewhere?"

"He means that we've always sent much of our produce to the French West Indies," Moffat explained, "where it was traded for molasses and European goods. It's long been a common practice for the captains and the owners of the ships to falsify their manifests and bribe the customs officers, but it was illegal then and it's illegal now. The only difference is that now the Acts of Trade and Navigation are being rigidly enforced. Some people seem to think that it's an imposition to obey the law."

Ben Edes snorted. "You talk about legality," he said. "What about the old principle of English law that upholds the right of people to be taxed only by their representatives? The Sugar Act was passed without anyone in Parliament remarking upon that, sir! They seek to bleed us dry and make it all seem legal! Now anyone caught smuggling will have their ships and cargoes confiscated, and instead of being tried in our own colonial courts, with juries, as is a citizen's right, those cases are now heard in admiralty courts, which have no juries. Defendants are presumed guilty until innocence is proven, and even if a man should be proved innocent, he must still pay all the costs and cannot recover any damages. Meanwhile, the Royal Navy leaps at every chance to collect colonial prize money by seizing any vessel 'suspected' of being a smuggler, not only merchant ships, mind you, but smaller vessels, too, which are not required to carry manifests of cargo. The Acts of Trade and Navigation enable agents of the Crown to break into any ship, home, store, or warehouse suspected of containing smuggled goods. Where is the legality in that, I ask you? Where is the justice? And now they want to ram the Stamp Act down our throats!

"You want to know why Andrew Oliver was hung in effigy?" Edes asked Hunter. "It is because he has accepted an appointment as the local stamp distributor, to profit from this latest outrage visited upon us. Thanks to the Stamp Act, my newspaper must now be printed on stamped paper taxed at one shilling a sheet. A three-shilling stamp is required on any legal document. School and college diplomas are to be taxed two pounds and a lawyer's license bears a ten-pound tax. Any appointment to public office must now be written on stamped paper taxed at four pounds. Even playing cards and dice are to be taxed one shilling! I tell you, sir, it is outrageous! And Andrew Oliver has agreed to become a party to this affront against our rights, to distribute the blasted stamps in Boston!"

He took the *Gazette* from Hunter, opened it, and stabbed a finger at a drawing of a badge-shaped stamp. It had "America" lettered at the top and around a Tudor rose ran the motto of the Order of the Garter, *"Honi soit qui mal y pense."*

"Shame to him who thinks evil of it," Edes translated in a sarcastic tone. "An irony indeed, considering what most people in the colonies think of Parliament's new measure! You saw that opinion expressed today upon the Common, sir!"

"The opinion of Sam Adams and the Loyal Nine, perhaps," said Moffat. "But do not presume these radicals speak for everyone in Boston."

"Well, certainly not for Governor Bernard," said Edes, sourly. "But Adams speaks for many of us. The governor wanted the effigies removed at once, yet he was advised against it by the members of his own council!"

"Only because the council felt it would be wise not to provoke an incident," said Brown.

"Precisely my point!" Edes said. "No incident could be provoked if the public sympathy did not lie with the demonstrators! I heard that Chief Justice Hutchinson ordered the sheriff to pull the figures down, but Sheriff Greenleaf said he feared he'd be risking the lives of his men if he tried to go against the crowd! He saw their mood and knew better than to interfere!"

"Undoubtedly, our fearless sheriff saw some familiar faces in the crowd," said Moffat, "among them Ebenezer MacIntosh, that hard-nosed cobbler who leads the rowdy South End Gang, and Samuel Swift, the leader of the North End Boys, who like nothing better than to break a head or two. I saw them whipping up the crowd myself. And if those two rival, brawling gangs of hooligans have come together for this demonstration, then Greenleaf knows there could be hell to pay before this day is through. I am not surprised that he wanted no part of it."

At that moment, someone came running into the tavern to announce that the demonstrators were going to march on the stampman's office.

"This I'd like to see," said Edes, pushing back his chair and heading for the door.

Hunter followed with the others as they hurried toward the Common. It was growing dark as they arrived and the crowd had grown quite large. The demonstrators had pulled down the effigies and nailed them to boards. They hoisted them up onto their shoulders and paraded shouting through the town, followed by the growing crowd of onlookers. Hunter went along as Ebenezer MacIntosh led the noisy march to Kilby Street, where Andrew Oliver, the stamp distributor, had established his new office. It took them less than five minutes to demolish it completely.

"And they shout about liberties and rights," said Moffat, shaking his head as he watched the demonstrators ripping down the building. "Well, I've seen quite enough." He turned to Hunter. "I fear that you have not found Boston at her best, sir. Good fortune to you."

When the demolition was completed, the crowd moved on to

Oliver's home. The stamp distributor had fled when he heard the crowd approaching, but if he thought they would disperse when they didn't find him home, he was tragically mistaken.

The rioters used rocks and clubs to smash out all his windows of imported English glass, then they broke open the stables and vandalized his handsome coach. They tore down the garden fence and started a fire in the yard. Most of the onlookers just watched, but a good number of them joined the rioters as they stripped every single fruit tree on the grounds, tore off all the branches, and fed them to the flames. Then they broke into the house itself.

Hunter followed them inside, where they smashed all the furniture to kindling and scattered Oliver's possessions all about the house. Many of them helped themselves to whatever valuables they found, and not one to waste an opportunity, Hunter stuffed his pockets with jewelry and cash. When in Rome, he thought, do as the Romans do.

There was a lot of celebrating in the taverns on the waterfront that night and Hunter cemented some new friendships by standing men like Ben Edes and Ebenezer MacIntosh to drinks, in some cases with money he had picked from their own pockets. He took a small room at an inn and the next day he joined some of his new friends in a delegation of "concerned citizens" who went to visit Andrew Oliver in his shambles of a home, where they convinced him, "for the good of the public," to resign his royal commission as the distributor of stamps.

Buoyed up by their success, these concerned citizens then decided to further influence their local officials by trashing some more houses. They built a huge bonfire on King Street, the better to attract a crowd, and in a proper festive spirit, they then proceeded to lay waste to the home of William Story, an officer of the vice admiralty court. A few of the more festive souls among the crowd cried out for Story's life, but he had made good his escape, and they were forced to settle for burning the admiralty records and stealing all his valuables. After Story's house was burglarized, the mob proceeded to the home of Ben Hallowell, a customs official, where once again they smashed a lot of doors and windows, broke up a lot of furniture, scattered all the books and papers, helped themselves to the contents of the wine cellar, and took away whatever valuables they found. Hunter came away with about two hundred pounds in cash, which he had discovered locked in Hallowell's desk. He decided that things were going along quite nicely, but they went even better at the home of Chief Justice Thomas Hutchinson.

Hutchinson fled with his family just in time. Shouting "Liberty and property," the demonstrators demonstrated their respect of same by working diligently through the night to demolish the entire mansion. They first broke open the wine cellars, for it was thirsty work, and while most of them were busy getting drunk and smashing up the furniture, Hunter and MacIntosh made a quick search of the house. Their efforts rewarded them with some jewelry and nine hundred pounds sterling, which they divvied up between them.

"Patriotism is its own reward, eh?" said the grinning MacIntosh, clapping Hunter on the back. In the short time they had known each other, they had become fast friends. Amazing what a little civil disobedience and alcohol can do, thought Hunter.

After the mob finished demolishing the furniture and smashing out the windows, they started tearing up the floors. There was no stopping them. Sheriff Greenleaf arrived and made a token effort at exerting his authority, but a barrage of rocks and bricks made him decide that he had more important things to see to at the office. Having thus repulsed the sheriff, the rioters celebrated their victory by smashing all the dishes and the crystalware, then tearing up the library. They destroyed the books and ripped up all the documents, including the manuscript for Hutchinson's history of the Massachusetts colony, which he had been working on for thirty years. Throughout the house, the rioters were going berserk like piranhas in a feeding frenzy, slashing all the mattresses and pillows, tearing down the drapes, smashing through the walls, and ripping down the chandeliers. When the interior of the mansion was completely gutted, the rioters tore the slate shingles off the roof and even dismantled the cupola, which took about three hours, but provided them with no end of satisfaction.

At some point during the night, Governor Bernard had given the order for the drummers to beat the alarm for the militia, but Sheriff Greenleaf had to disappoint him once again. The drummers, he reported sadly, were all part of the mob. It was dawn before the last of the rioters finally dispersed, leaving behind an utter ruin. Nothing remained standing of Boston's finest mansion except a wall or two and a huge pile of rubble. It looked as if a tornado had touched down upon the spot.

The Boston riots touched off similar events in other cities. Throughout the thirteen colonies, stamp distributors were pressured to resign. With no stamps to pass out, ships whose papers were not stamped were suddenly engaged in smuggling. They could not unload in England without the risk of seizure. In Philadelphia, one hundred and fifty ships had jammed the port. Without stamps for legal documents, courts had no choice but to close down. Writs could not be issued. Land titles couldn't be conveyed. Trials could not take place. An enterprising man could profit from such a climate of confusion and Reese Hunter found himself among enterprising men.

They called themselves the Sons of Liberty and their leaders met in a tavern called The Bunch of Grapes. Bed Edes had joined the Sons of Liberty and the *Gazette* became the most radical newspaper in the colonies. Sam Adams used it as his forum. Writing under a wide variety of pseudonyms such as "Determinatus," "Brittanicus Americus," "A Son of Liberty," "A Bostonian," and "Candidus," Adams kept up an unceasing barrage of invective against the ministers of the Crown and even against King George, himself, which many citizens of Boston thought was going much too far.

It was one thing to speak out against the ministry and Parliament, but it was something else again when Adams dared to criticize the king, to lecture him in print like an impatient schoolmaster. But most of the citizens of Boston were still unaware that what Sam Adams really wanted was nothing less than total independence from Great Britain, an idea whose time had not yet come, though Hunter knew that it was drawing closer. In another decade, the colonies would declare their independence from the mother country. Hunter intended to be long gone by then. He had no intention of being caught up in the war. But in the meantime, Boston was a fascinating place to be. And Hunter was in no hurry to go anywhere. He had all the time in the world.

It was growing late when he arrived to meet the others at the tavern. The feisty MacIntosh was already reeling from the effects of all the wine he'd drunk and he was being twice as loud as usual, which made for a considerable amount of volume.

"An' I *still* say it was a mistake," he slurred angrily, his mind still relatively lucid, though his mouth lagged a bit behind.

He was referring to the collection that had been taken up to repay Thomas Hutchinson for the destruction of his mansion. It had been done at the instigation of Sam Adams, who had spoken out in the Assembly and expressed his outrage at the actions of the mob. Needless to say, the money would not replace the mansion or its precious contents, and Hutchinson was reported to be heartbroken over the loss of his priceless *History of Massachusetts Bay*, thirty years of work undone in just one night. The morning following the riot, he had appeared in court among his fellow red-robed justices, wearing only what he'd escaped in the previous night. He had borrowed an ill-fitting coat from the neighbors he was staying with and he was a pathetic sight, indeed.

Sam Adams, unlike MacIntosh, was fully able to appreciate how the sympathies of Boston would lie with a proud, distinguished citizen so humbled and he had sought to prove that the Sons of Liberty, while opposed to men like Hutchinson in principle, were not a ruthless bunch of thugs—which was precisely what many of them were. And despite the fact that he had organized the demonstration, something he prudently did not admit in public, Adams sincerely sought to make amends. Much like Col. George Washington of Virginia, whose family crest bore the Latin motto, *"Exitus Acta Probat"* (The End Justifies the Means), Adams was not above utilizing any means he felt were necessary to achieve the end he had in mind, but he fully understood the subtleties of propaganda.

MacIntosh did not appreciate such tactics. "We taught that royalist bootlicker a proper lesson!" he shouted, slapping his palm down on the table and upsetting his glass of wine. "I say he had it comin'!" And now Sam Adams goes to him with hat in hand and humbly begs his pardon, sayin' 'Please, Yer Worship, forgive us all the trespass and kindly accept these monies by way of reparation.' Apologizin' to the likes o' him!"

"It's not like that at all, Mac," Edes reassured him. "Sam Adams knows what he's about. What's the point of all we're doing if public opinion turns against us? This way, Sam, stands by his principles and the Sons of Liberty have demonstrated that while our zeal is undiminished, we still have a concern for justice. And the lesson on Tom Hutchinson isn't lost, believe me."

"Well, maybe so," MacIntosh admitted grudgingly, "but I still say we shouldn't give the bastard one damn shilling! Tom Hutchinson is Massachusetts born an' bred an' I say he's a traitor to his own! An' I dare any man who thinks I'm wrong to stand up an' say so to my face!"

At that precise instant, something came crashing through the window of the tavern, struck MacIntosh full in the chest, and knocked him and his chair backward to the floor. Stunned, MacIntosh sat up and stared at the object that had felled him. It was a pumpkin carved into a jack-o-lantern. Its smashed and pulpy pieces lay splattered all around him. Chairs fell to the floor as the Sons of Liberty leapt to their feet and a bellowing MacIntosh led the charge outside.

For a moment, they saw nothing, but then they heard the rapid beat of iron-shod hooves on cobblestones. A black-clad rider with a long, billowing cloak came hurtling at them from the shadows, scattering the group. He turned, reining in sharply, and the handsome, jet-black stallion reared up, its forelegs pawing at the sky as the rider's screeching laughter filled the air.

He had no head.

His keening laughter echoed through the night as he came thundering at them once again. His horse struck a gaping Jebediah Stiles and sent him sprawling as the rider plowed through them like a juggernaut, wheeled around, pulled in his reins, and reared up once again. Ransome Howard swore, pulled out his sheath knife, and hurled it at the horseman.

It went right though him.

With a maniacal screech, the rider bore down upon them once again and as the others scattered, Hunter stood and stared, astonished, as both the horse and rider vanished right before their eyes, leaving behind nothing but the echo of the horseman's wild laughter.

"Holy Mary Mother o' God!" breathed MacIntosh, his eyes wide with disbelief. "Is it the drink, or did I really see that?"

"I saw it, too!" said Dudley Brenton. "He had no head! *The rider had no head!*"

"Your knife went right through him!" Eli Cruger said to Howard.

"No, he missed," said someone.

"I didn't miss," insisted Howard. "I never miss." He swallowed hard and crossed himself. "It was a ghost, sure as I live and breathe! A demon straight from hell!"

"You saw it, Reese!" said MacIntosh, his eyes bulging. "You saw! He vanished straightaway, before our very eyes! That was no man, Reese! Men don't just disappear! It was a ghost! You saw!"

"Yes, Mac, I saw," said Hunter. He took a deep breath and slowly let it out.

"A haunting!" MacIntosh said hoarsely. "A haunting, that's what it was! You all saw it same as I did, every man jack of you!"

Hunter bit his lower lip. His fingers felt the warp disc on its bracelet, concealed under his left sleeve. He turned and started walking quickly down the street.

MacIntosh ran after him. "Reese! Wait! Where are you going?"

"Go back, Mac," Hunter said. "I have to go and see someone."

"I'll go with you!"

"No, Mac, I must go alone."

"You're going to tell Sam?"

"No, you go and tell him if you wish," said Hunter. "But you'd best take some of the others with you, for I'm afraid he's going to need a good deal of convincing. I have to go see someone else." He paused. "They'll take some convincing, too, but somehow I must make them believe me."

He turned and walked away from the bewildered, frightened MacIntosh and entered a dark and narrow alleyway. He looked around, pushed back his sleeve, and quickly programmed a sequence of transition coordinates into the warp disc. He took a deep breath and exhaled heavily.

"I sure hope I know what the hell I'm doing," he said.

A moment later, MacIntosh came running after him into the alley. "Reese, wait!" he cried. He stopped suddenly and looked around. "What the devil . . ."

The alley ended in a cul de sac, but Hunter was nowhere in sight.

1 ⸻⸻⸻⸻⸻

Lucas Priest was tired of being poked and prodded. For the past two weeks, he had been subjected to just about every type of medical examination known to man. He had been psychiatrically evaluated, biochemically analyzed, and holographically scanned until he couldn't stand it any longer. Tall, slim, handsome, and muscular, with a bionic eye replacement as a result of being wounded on a temporal adjustment mission, he was in excellent physical condition, but the tests had worn him out. It seemed to him as if his mind and body had generated enough medical and psychiatric data to keep an entire team of doctors busy for a month. But then, he thought, that's what you get for dying.

"Hey, Doc, are we going to be finished anytime this year?" he asked, wearily running his hand through his thick brown hair as he sat up on the lab couch.

"Well, unless someone upstairs thinks up anything *else* that we can put you through, that was it," said Capt. Hazen, entering some data into her hand-held terminal. "You're all finished."

"You're kidding. Really?"

"Really. You can put your clothes back on."

"You know, I never thought I'd be so glad to hear an attractive woman telling me to put my clothes back *on*," said Lucas, with a grin.

She arched an eyebrow at him. "You never know, I just might ask you to take them off again sometime." She grinned. "On the other hand, maybe not. I wouldn't want to be accused of necrophilia."

"Very funny."

"Sorry. It's just that I've never flirted with a dead man before."

He gave her a wry look.

She chuckled. "Okay, I'll stop, but you might as well get used to it. After all, you're the only soldier in the history of the Temporal Corps who ever came back from the dead. Something like that is bound to cause a little comment. Anyway, that's it for now. You're free to go. We should have all the test results in about another week or so."

"Just what do you expect to find?" asked Lucas.

"I haven't got the faintest idea," she said. "I'm just following orders. Maybe they expect me to tell them that you don't really exist, that you're nothing but a ghost."

"There's no such thing as ghosts."

"Tell that to your buddy Dr. Darkness," she said.

"There's a lot I could tell him," Lucas said, with a wry grimace. "That man's got a lot to answer for."

She gave him a questioning look. "Are you saying you're not grateful that he saved your life?"

Lucas shrugged. "I don't know. I wish it were that simple. I can't help having the feeling that maybe I was *supposed* to die. Sounds kinda crazy, doesn't it?"

"I don't know," she said. "A bit fatalistic perhaps, but crazy? You're one of the sanest men I know. People who have survived near death experiences have often come away feeling profoundly changed, sometimes even a bit regretful. Of course, this isn't quite the same thing, is it? You don't really remember the experience."

Lucas shook his head. "How can I? Darkness went back into the past and altered the conditions of my death. Or of my life. Hell, even the semantics of the situation are impossible. I can't remember something that didn't happen because the past was changed."

"I'm still not exactly clear on that," she said. "How could he have changed the past without bringing about a temporal disruption?"

"You're asking me to answer a question that's giving our top temporal physicists a lot of headaches," Lucas said. "One possible answer is that it wasn't a change significant enough to bring about a temporal disruption, though Lord knows, it was certainly significant enough for me! On the other hand, maybe it *did* cause a temporal disruption, only we're not aware of the consequences yet. That's one of the things that worries me. What if something terrible happens in the future simply because I didn't die when I was supposed to?"

"I never did hear all the details. What exactly happened?"

"Well, we were on a mission in 19th-century Afghanistan," said Lucas. "We were with the British headquarters command of the Malakand Field Force, standing on a rock cliff over-looking a valley where the Bengal Lancers were fighting with the Ghazis. It was a bloody slaughter. The commanding general was there, watching the action, as well as the regimental surgeon and a young war correspondent whose name happened to be Winston Churchill. We were on the lookout for a temporal disruption that we knew was going to occur and we expected it to center around Churchill, who was the most historically significant person there. The rock we were on had just been captured from the Ghazis. They had sniper nests all over it and the infantry had charged and driven them all out. Only they had missed one.

"While everyone was busy watching the fighting down below, this one Ghazi sniper got up from the rocks where he was hiding and drew a bead on the surgeon, whom he probably mistook for the commanding officer. I just happened to glance over and see him bringing up his rifle. I yelled, 'Hugo, look out!' The surgeon was a veteran who'd just spent weeks pinned down by severe enemy sniper fire and he reacted instinctively by immediately dropping flat to the ground.

"In an instant, I saw what I'd done by warning Hugo. The moment he dropped, he left Churchill directly in the line of fire. I made a dive for Churchill and at the same moment, the Ghazi sniper fired. Instead of hitting Churchill, the bullet struck me in the chest." He took a deep breath. "Now this is where it starts getting very complicated."

"I don't remember the bullet hitting me because, as a result of what Dr. Darkness did, that bullet never did actually strike me. The others saw the bullet hit me and they saw me fall to the ground with a big hole in my chest. Only it *wasn't* me. See, during that mission, we encountered a commando unit of

Special Operations Group from the parallel universe. They were the ones involved in the attempted temporal disruption. Among that unit was an officer who was my twin from the parallel timeline, my exact duplicate right down to the DNA. No way to tell us apart at all. Finn Delaney killed him, only that didn't happen until *after* I was shot. What Dr. Darkness did was go back into the past and snatch my double's corpse. He then clocked to the moment of my 'death,' and moving faster than the speed of light, he took me out of the bullet's path and teleported me away. Then he put my double's corpse directly into the path of that bullet, so that it would impact in the exact same spot left by the wound inflicted when Delaney killed him. An autopsy would probably have revealed that there were two wounds in the same place, but the point was that no one had any reason to believe it wasn't me. Darkness had snatched the corpse seconds after death; the blood hadn't coagulated yet and the body was still warm. And I was officially reported killed in action."

"So then you never really died at all," she said. "The past *wasn't* changed."

"Yeah, well, unfortunately that's the part no one can figure out," said Lucas, with a sigh. "Looking at it logically, I *did* die, because you'd think there had to be a moment when my death actually occurred, *before* Darkness went back and altered the scenario, but when it comes to temporal physics, all logic breaks down. By doing what he did, Darkness changed the past so that the bullet struck my double's corpse, not me, and *that* became the past. Or maybe it didn't *become* the past, maybe it *was* the past, because what Darkness did was part of the temporal scenario. Or maybe what he did was create a sort of temporal loop, in which there was a kind of . . . a kind of skip or something in my own personal history, but not the history of the timeline. Maybe, somewhere in time, there exists an instant in which I actually died . . . only nobody knows for sure and chances are no one will ever know, no matter how many damn tests they run on me. How the hell is something like that supposed to show up on some test?"

"Good question," she said. "But as the saying goes, why look a gift horse in the mouth? You're alive. That's all that matters, isn't it?"

"Maybe," Lucas said, "but how'd you like to go through life knowing that somewhere in time, there could exist a moment when you'd died, only you can't remember it because in a certain sense it never really happened? How'd you like to be the only person in the world who ever experienced a temporal paradox, but has no memory of the experience? And what if it's some sort of temporal ripple that could, at some point in the future, somehow catch up with me?"

"Do you really think that's possible?"

"I don't *know*," said Lucas. "That's the exasperating thing about it! I don't think even that Darkness knows and he understands temporal physics better than anyone alive. The thing that really gets me is that he didn't give a damn about me one way or another. He only did it because he'd implanted me with the only existing prototype of his new telepathic temporal transponder and he didn't want to lose the only working model. I've got what amounts to an ultra-miniaturized, thought-controlled warp disc implanted in my body, bonded to some molecule somewhere, and any stray thought is liable to send me on a trip through time. It's already happened several times. You have any idea what it's like to go to sleep and dream you're back in ancient Rome, then suddenly wake up to discover that you're actually *there*?"

Dr. Hazen shook her head. "Wow. I hadn't known about that. I can't say I envy you, Lucas. Frankly, I'm amazed they're letting you go back on active duty. I hate to say it, but after what you've just told me, I honestly feel that it's my responsibility to pronounce you medically unfit."

"You can't."

"I'm sorry, Lucas," she said. "Under the circumstances, I really have no other alternative."

"You don't understand," said Lucas. "I'm not *asking* you not to do it, I'm saying that you *can't*. Under ordinary circumstances, you would certainly have that authority, but then these aren't ordinary circumstances. By all means, do what you feel you have to do, but I'm telling you right now, if you order me removed from active duty, the brass will override you. I've got the only thought-controlled warp disc in existence. In effect, Darkness has turned me into a living time machine and the brass wants to see it tested in the field. They want to find out if it'll work over the long haul or if it will induce the same atomic instability that Darkness suffers from. He tried an earlier version of the same process on himself and it altered his atomic structure irreversibly. And his condition's getting progressively worse. Eventually, he's going to discorporate and depart at multiples of light speed in all directions of the universe. The brass would sort of like to find out if that's going to happen to me before they start to issue telempathic temporal transponders to the troops."

"I thought you said you had the only working prototype," she said.

"I do," said Lucas, sourly. "Darkness said it would take a bloody fortune to produce another one, and before anyone's ready to commit to that, they want to see if there are any bugs in mine. And since his own atomic structure is unstable, Darkness is on borrowed time, so the brass is anxious to get on with the field testing, which they can't do if I'm removed from active duty."

"I think that's inexcusable," Dr. Hazen said. "It's downright criminal. They're using you as a human guinea pig."

"So?" said Lucas. "What's the worst that could happen? I could die?" He shrugged. "Hey, it's not as if it's anything I haven't done before."

The comscreen in the lab emitted a short series of beeps and came on with an image of General Moses Forrester, the Director of the T.I.A.

"Dr. Hazen?"

"Yes, sir."

"Is Col. Priest still in the lab with you?"

"Right here, sir," Lucas said, stepping in front of the screen. "We just completed all the tests."

"Good. I need you up here on the double."

"I'm on my way."

The screen went blank.

"I'm still going to have to recommend that you be removed from active duty, Lucas," Dr. Hazen said. "I suppose the brass can override me, but I can't in good conscience go along with what they're doing."

"I understand," said Lucas, nodding. "And I appreciate your concern, but even if they did follow your recommendation—which they won't—you really wouldn't be doing me a favor. I'd go crazy if they put me behind a desk or, worse yet, confined me to a hospital for tests and observation."

"A man's gotta do what a man's gotta do, is that it?" she said, with a wry smile.

"No, not really," Lucas said. "It's not some macho thing.

Look at it this way, after all the years you spent to get where you are now, how would you feel if you were suddenly transferred to a national health clinic in Bakersfield?"

She sighed. "Yes, I'm afraid I see your point."

"I'd better go. When the old man says 'on the double,' it usually means something important has come up."

"Good luck."

He smiled. "Thanks. See you around."

She waited till he'd left, then added softly, "I sure hope so."

Finn Delaney, Creed Steiger, and Andre Cross were already there when Lucas arrived. Everybody jumped when the old man said, "On the double." Andre looked sharp, as usual, but Delaney, also as usual, looked sloppy and unkempt, his uniform unpressed and his boots unpolished. In any other outfit, such a turnout would have called for disciplinary action, but Forrester was an unusual commander. Ever since the T.I.A. had been combined with the First Division of the Temporal Corps and Forrester had been made Director, the agents of the T.I.A had not quite known what to make of their new leader. The men and women of the First Division, organized and led by Forrester, had grown accustomed to what many senior officers in the Temporal Corps felt was an overly casual brand of leadership. For the agents of Temporal Intelligence, men like Col. Creed Steiger, it was a completely new experience.

Forrester cared less about how his people looked on the parade ground than about how their performance measured up in the field. When he had organized the unit, he had hand-picked all the personnel, many of whom had less than favorable military records and were deemed misfits in their former units.

Finn Delaney was an excellent example. Large-framed, red-haired, and barrel-chested, with the appearance of an amiable bear, he had come within a hairbreadth of dishonorable discharge more times than he could count. His record was chock-full of infractions of just about every military regulation there was, from disobedience of orders to striking superior officers. He had spent his entire adult life in the service and his rank had fluctuated like the fashion industry. No sooner would he be promoted as a result of outstanding performance in the field than he would be busted for breaking some military regulation. He was on a first name basis with practically every officer who ever sat on a court martial. Indeed, he would have long since been discharged if it were not for the fact that he was an absolutely first-rate soldier, with a record of performance that was absolutely unsurpassed.

Clearly, Delaney was a problem, but unlike many other senior officers, Forrester had known that a man's worth as a soldier could not be measured by how snappy his salute was. Some of history's greatest fighting men, such as George Patton, Benedict Arnold, and Julius Caesar, had personalities that were ill-suited to military discipline. Patton had been egotistical and insubordinate; Arnold's unchecked ambition had led him to turn traitor; Caesar had been overly familiar with his troops and had seized power by turning his legions against Rome, but each man had been an unquestionably brilliant soldier on the field of battle. Delaney had a mercurial Irish temper and a contempt for what he called "military assholes," but with a commander such as Forrester, who knew the proper way to handle such a man, he had steadily risen to the rank of captain and his disciplinary problems had fallen off dramatically.

Creed Steiger, on the other hand, was the sort of soldier whose appearance would find favor with the most nit-picking commander. He was blond and gray-eyed, hook-nosed, slightly cruel-looking, and solidly built. Like Lucas Priest, he looked like a model officer, but there the similarity ended. While Priest's record was absolutely spotless, Steiger was a maverick. As the former senior field agent of the T.I.A., he had often bent the rules, only unlike Delaney, he was adept at covering himself. His mentor in the agency had been none other than the late Col. Jack Carnehan, a legendary temporal agent codenamed Mongoose, who had instructed him in the complexities of being a professional chamelion. Carnehan had been virtually uncontrollable, with an unshakable belief in the correctness of his actions, regardless of what his orders were. But Steiger had learned the hard way that in an organization as complex and devious as the T.I.A., with agents that were so deeply buried under cover that there was often no record of their existence, orders from the top were frequently not to be trusted.

The corruption in the T.I.A. ran deep. Steiger had never wanted any part of it, but when even the former director of the agency had been a secret member of the Network, there was no way of knowing if an order had been given legally or not. Yet now that Forrester was in charge, determined to root out the corruption and break up the Network, Steiger was finally able to do his job as he saw fit. Forrester had appointed him to organize and lead a special unit, the Internal Security Division, whose sole function was to police the agency and ferret out corrupt agents of the Network. It was a formidable task. Over the years, the Network had spread through the agency like a cancer, with its members both concealed within the agency bureaucracy in the 27th century and scattered throughout time, as well. Dealing with the threat posed by the parallel universe was difficult enough without having to battle enemies within their own organization. Both Steiger and Forrester had already survived several attempts upon their lives, in one case by a man Steiger had known and trusted for years. And many agents of the T.I.A. deeply resented having the I.S.D. constantly look-ing over their shoulders. Lucas did not envy Creed his job.

As for Andre Cross, seeing her now, it was hard for Lucas to believe that the first time they had met, he had thought she was a man. Born in the 12th century, she had been orphaned at an early age and had survived a life of almost intolerable hardship. While still a child, she had learned to pass as a young boy in order to decrease her vulnerability and as she grew older, she had perfected the disguise. In her early teens, she had fooled an English knight errant so completely that he had taken her on as his squire and trained her in the arts of warfare, so that by the time she reached adulthood, she was the equal of most any man in fighting ability and strength.

Her appearance was deceptive. Some young men were handsome to the point of being almost pretty and she had passed for one of those. She had worn her hair as men did and she had a compact and powerful athletic frame. She wrapped her chest to conceal her breasts, took the name of Andre de la Croix, and became a mercenary knight. It was in that guise that Lucas first met her on a temporal adjustment mission in medieval England, in the lists at the tournament of Ashby. In full armor and on horseback, they had jousted with each other and it was an experience he would never forget. When he thought of it, he could still feel the incredibly jarring impact of her lance. By the time they met again, several centuries had passed.

She had become a member of the Temporal Underground and was taken from her native time to 17th-century France, where their paths crossed once again. She had helped Lucas and Finn defeat a group of temporal terrorists who called themselves the Timekeepers and they had brought her back with them to the 27th century, where it was determined that her temporal displacement would not have a disruptive effect on history. She was given a cerebral implant, programmed with an education, and made a member of the First Division. Since then, she had been a valued member of their team and she and Lucas had grown extremely close.

They had become as intimate as two people could be without ever physically consummating their relationship. They had never said, "I love you," to each other, but it was not something that needed to be said. Both of them knew it, felt it deep down in their souls, and yet they had always hesitated to take that final step. It was something neither of them ever spoke about. In fact, the curious nature of their relationship was that it went largely unspoken, as if they unconsciously desired their love to be idealistically platonic, and were hesitant, even frightened, to take it any further. Instead, they cloaked their feelings for each other in military camaraderie, in awkward brotherly and sisterly affection, and in hard-drinking fellowship, not unlike two male friends who were emotionally repressed and expressed their feelings for each other in punching one another's shoulders and hearty slaps upon the back.

Perhaps part of their problem lay in the fact that Andre never had an opportunity to be raised as a girl child. She never had a female role model and she was inexperienced in relationships, unable to express her deepest feelings.

And though Lucas would never admit it to a soul—not even to his best friend, Finn Delaney, who knew it just the same—he had been painfully shy around women all his life. He could hide it well up to a certain point and he was not sexually inexperienced, yet in almost every case, it was the woman who had taken the initiative, often in exasperation. And those sexual relationships had been just that—primarily sexual. Stated simply, Lucas Priest, a soldier who had been decorated many times for bravery, was an abject coward when it came to love, as paralyzed with shyness and indecision as a young boy sitting alone in tortured agony for hours, trying to summon up the nerve to make his first call to a girl he had a crush on.

There were times when Finn Delaney wanted to take them both and shake them, force them to come out and admit their feelings for each other, but he was enough of a friend to both of them to know where to draw the line. There were some things that went beyond the bounds of friendship, some things people simply had to do all by themselves. Sooner or later, it would have to happen for them, because the tension was increasing. When she had thought Lucas had died, Andre had been grief-stricken beyond words. When he came back, she'd been so overjoyed to see him alive that she'd responded with her feelings before she had a chance to think and had thrown her arms around his neck and kissed him.

Afterward, Delaney found it almost comical to see their mutual embarrassment, but a large chunk of the barrier between them had been broken through and Finn knew that it would only be a matter of time before the remainder of their inhibitions fell away. Privately, he hoped they'd hurry up and get around to it, because lately they'd been using him as a reluctant chaperone, a convenient third party to keep them from being alone together. It made him feel uncomfortable and he wished to hell they'd both grow up and act their age. Two grown people, unable to express their feelings. He simply didn't understand it. But then, being an Irishman, he wouldn't.

They stepped through the weapons detector, then had their palm prints, voice and retinal patterns checked before being admitted into Forrester's suite of offices and, beyond them, his personal quarters. Forrester himself detested the security measures, but Steiger had insisted on them, especially after a recent assassination attempt that had cost the lives of several of the general's personal staff. It was solely for that reason that Forrester had agreed to have the security systems installed. He felt responsible for those deaths and he didn't want anyone else to die because he was marked for assassination by the Network. Forrester's orderly, who now always went armed, conducted them into the general's presence.

"Come in, people," Forrester said, as usual not standing on ceremony.

No one in the service knew his exact age—his personal dossier was classified—but Forrester looked ancient. His face was deeply lined, his hands were wrinkled and liver-spotted, and he was completely bald, yet his emerald-green eyes were bright and alert and his massive, six-foot six-inch frame was packed with two hundred and fifty pounds of solid muscle. He worked out strenuously for two hours every day and could curl an eighty-pound dumbbell as if it were a paperweight.

"Have a seat," he said gruffly. "Bar's open."

The last remark being a signal to Delaney, who usually did the honors, to help himself to Forrester's bar and pour drinks for them all—single malt Scotch for Lucas and Andre, vodka and soda for Steiger, Irish whiskey for himself, and for the old man a horrible concoction known as "Red Eye," a cheap, Old West rotgut whiskey Forrester had inexplicably picked up a taste for. The stuff could remove paint, but the old man tossed it back like it was water.

"Have the prisoner brought in," said Forrester to his orderly.

They all exchanged glances, but said nothing. Not until two armed I.S.D. men brought in their prisoner.

"Christ, it's Hunter!" said Delaney.

"Okay, as you were, men," Forrester said to the two armed guards, who had snapped sharply to attention with Hunter between them, restrained in magnacuffs. The bracelets around his wrists were locked together by magnetic force and as the guards snapped to attention, one of them used the remote key to bring Hunter to attention, too. The bracelets fastened around his ankles abruptly came together with a sharp click and Hunter almost lost his balance.

"Give me a break, guys," Hunter said. "I've got respect. I would've snapped to."

"Shut up," said the guard.

"I'll take that," said Forrester, holding his hand out. The guard gave him the remote key. "Okay, thank you, gentlemen. Dismissed."

The two guards came to attention, saluted, about-faced, and left the room, leaving Hunter standing stiffly in the center of the room, his wrists and ankles tightly locked together.

"Permission to assume the position of parade rest, sir?" Hunter asked wryly.

"I can do better than that," said Forrester, pointing the small remote control box at him and releasing both sets of bracelets. "Have a seat. Delaney, get the man a drink."

Hunter looked stunned.

"What's your poison?" said Delaney.

"Uh . . . got any beer?"

"Any preference? Light, dark, imported, domestic?"

Hunter shook his head. "I don't care. You're buying. Hell, if I'd known you treated your prisoners like this, I might've surrendered sooner."

"He *surrendered*?" Andre said, glancing at Forrester with disbelief.

"Clocked into base and turned himself right in," Forrester replied. "Wouldn't give a reason. He insisted on speaking only to you people."

"I don't believe it," said Delaney. "What the hell are you trying to pull, Reese? You had a warp disc. You were free and clear."

"But he couldn't find the confluence point," said Steiger. "That's what this is all about, right, Hunter? You think you can swing a deal with us to help you get back home?"

"Why don't we let the man tell us himself?" said Forrester.

"Thank you, General," said Hunter. He took a swallow of beer and sighed. "Ahh, I needed that. Sorry, my nerves are a bit ragged. Tell you the truth, I wasn't really sure what to expect. I figured on being interrogated, but I gambled that you'd give me a chance to talk before your people tried to break me down."

"That's still an option," Steiger said. "Your cooperation isn't necessary, Hunter. You've got nothing to bargain with. If we want to, we can open you up like a tin can."

"I know it," Hunter said. "And to a certain point, I'd spill everything I knew. But past that point, I'd slip into a coma. You see, pilgrim, C.I.S. agents all have subliminal triggers specifically designed to allow us to undergo a certain amount of interrogation, but there are certain things they wouldn't like us to divulge. Ask the wrong questions and we switch right off. And for obvious reasons, I'd sort of like to avoid that."

"If that's not a bluff, then you took a hell of a chance by turning yourself in," said Lucas. "Why?"

"I'll answer that question if you answer one of mine first," Hunter replied.

"You're in no position to make any demands, Hunter," Steiger said.

"As you were, Colonel," Forrester said. "This isn't an interrogation yet. The man turned himself in voluntarily, let's allow him some courtesy as a fellow officer. What's the question, Captain?"

"I'm not asking for any classified details, you understand," said Hunter. "But just tell me one thing. Have you got some sort of unusual temporal adjustment mission in progress in colonial Boston, around the 1760s?"

"If we did, then why should we tell you?" said Forrester.

"All right, I understand that. Let me put it another way," said Hunter. "Let's proceed, for the moment, on the assumption that you haven't. And let's also proceed on the assumption that if my people had crossed over and were attempting to create a temporal disruption in that time period, I'd know enough about your history and the way my people operate to recognize it going down. Okay?"

"Okay," said Forrester. "I'll accept that for the sake of the discussion. What's your point?"

"With your indulgence, sir, I'd like to make one more assumption before I get to it," said Hunter. "I know about the Network. I know they're a bunch of renegade agents, but they're basically into organized crime, temporal profiteering, right? I'm assuming they'd have no reason to create a temporal disruption that could endanger their own timeline and their money-making operations, correct?"

"Correct," said Forrester.

Hunter nodded. "In that case, General, there's something going down in colonial Boston and if it's not you, and if it's not my people, and if it's not the Network, then who does that leave?"

There was a brief moment of silence.

And then Delaney voiced what all of them were thinking.

"Nikolai Drakov," he said.

"Yeah, that's what I figured, too," said Hunter.

"I think you'd better tell us what you know, Captain," said Forrester, tensely.

Hunter gave him a steady stare. "Let's talk about a deal first," he said.

"No deals!" said Steiger.

"Colonel, I said *as you were*," snapped Forrester.

"Yes, sir. I'm sorry, sir."

"I'm listening, Captain Hunter," Forrester said.

"I appreciate that, sir," said Hunter. "And as Col. Steiger said, I realize that I'm in no position to make any demands, but

I'm asking you to consider that I came in voluntarily. I didn't have to do that. I was also in a position to create a temporal disruption of my own, but I didn't do that, either. Now I've already given you a lot for free." He glanced at Steiger. "I realize that you could probably get the rest of it out of me through your interrogation techniques, but on the other hand, you just might wind up setting off one of those subliminal triggers and that would be all she wrote. I'd be a vegetable and you'd be right back where you started. You know there's something going down in colonial Boston in the 1760s, but that still leaves you with a lot of territory to cover, doesn't it?"

"Very well, Captain," said Forrester. "What did you have in mind?"

"Safe conduct through a confluence point back to my own timeline," Hunter said.

"If your information's good, I think that might be arranged," said Forrester. "But not until your information has been thoroughly checked out."

"That's fair," said Hunter. "But I want one other thing."

Forrester raised his eyebrows. "You're already asking quite a lot, Captain."

"I want in on the mission," Hunter said.

"What?" said Steiger. "You're out of your mind!"

"Back off, Steiger," Hunter said. "I helped save your bacon in 20th-century New York, remember? You owe me. Nikolai Drakov poses a threat to both our timelines. Besides, this has nothing to do with the hostilities between us. This is strictly personal. I've got unfinished business with that man. And I've already established connections in that temporal scenario. I could make things easier for you. Without me, you'd be going in cold." He turned back to Forrester. "What's it going to be, sir?"

They all looked at Forrester expectantly.

The old man thought about it only for a moment. "All right, Captain," he said. "I'll take a chance on you. You've got a deal."

2 ⎯⎯⎯⎯⎯⎯⎯⎯⎯⎯⎯⎯⎯⎯⎯⎯⎯⎯⎯

The last time he had been to Boston was in 1867, but that time would not arrive for about another hundred years. Nikolai Drakov had known nothing about time travel then, only that his father, whom he hated, had come from the far future. Moses Forrester had met his mother, loved her, and then returned to the future once again, leaving her to give birth to their child alone as Moscow burned during Napoleon's retreat.

The infant Nikolai had survived the savage Russian winter while grown men around him died. His poverty-stricken mother married a kindly Russian army officer who took them in, but the man was a Decembrist and Nikolai was just thirteen when they were exiled to Siberia. He survived Siberia as well, only his family did not. His adoptive father had died of influenza in his prison cell and his mother had been murdered by a rapist. Nikolai had been too young to save her, although he had tried. He still bore the mark the murderer had left him with, a knife scar running from beneath his left eye to just above the corner of his mouth. In years to come, it would be taken for a dueling scar and thought quite dashing. In still later years to come, cosmetic surgery could easily have removed it, but Drakov chose to let it stay. He wanted to remember.

An old trapper took him in and Drakov learned to hunt and live off the frozen wilderness. Eventually, he made his way to the Russian settlements in Alaska. At the age of twenty, he was once more on his own and he took up the fur trade. He still looked very young. He could not have known back then that due to the advances of the future, he had inherited from his father an immunity to all known diseases and an extended lifespan that would be measured in centuries, not decades. He knew only that he had survived conditions that had killed ordinary men and he hardly seemed to age. He looked so young that many people tried to take advantage of him. He learned how to fight and how to kill. He had long ago learned how to hate.

He became a seaman and hunted seals in the Pribilofs. Before long, he had his own ship and the hardened sailors soon learned to respect their tough "young" captain. At thirty-eight, he still looked like a teenager, although his rough life had given him a powerful physique. After a while his constant youthfulness started to cause comment and people became too curious about him. It was time for him to move on.

He sold his ship and arrived in Boston a very wealthy man. He purchased a handsome mansion on Beacon Hill and invested in the stock market. Within a few years, he had multiplied his fortune many times. He was thought to be some European nobleman and he became much sought after in society. But notoriety soon led to curiosity and as the years passed, people again began to wonder why he never seemed to age. It was time to move on once again.

He was seventy years old when he arrived in London, though he did not look a day over twenty-five. He had no need of looking for an occupation. He had millions. He had everything a man could want. Everything but answers. And he found the answers when he found Sophia Falco, alias the Falcon, one of the leaders of the Timekeepers, a terrorist organization from the 27th century. When they found out whose son he was, they eagerly accepted him into their ranks. The irony of Moses Forrester's son becoming a member of the Timekeepers was too delicious to pass up and from that moment on, Drakov's life had taken on a whole new meaning.

He had joined the Timekeepers and traveled to the future, where a biochip had been obtained for him and he was educated via cerebral implant programming. With the native intelligence he already possessed, after the programming, he emerged a genius. He finally understood who and what he was and he was able to comprehend the convuluted principles of temporal physics. And he had made up his mind that he would devote the remainder of his life to destroying Moses Forrester and the perverse world that he came from.

Now he was the last one left. Sophia, Benedetto, Taylor, Singh, Tremain . . . all of them were dead. The Timekeepers were no more. But Drakov wasn't finished yet. With all time at his beck and call, he had infinite resources. He would stop the future, even if he had to destroy the world to do it.

It had been a long, unpleasant voyage across the North Atlantic. The bunks were damp, the bread was weevil-ridden, and the beef was tainted. The merchant ships of this day were like crude, ungainly barges compared to the sleek schooner he had sailed in the Pribilofs and there were far easier ways to make the passage. He could have simply used his warp disc to clock to 18th-century America, but that would not have fit in with his plans. It had first been necessary to establish an identity for himself in London, set up finances, and make the right connections with influential men such as John Wilkes, Sir Francis Dashwood, Lord William Howe, and Benjamin Franklin, one of the colonial agents in London. If anyone in New England was to inquire into his affairs, he wanted to make certain that he could easily account for how he had arrived in Boston, so the long sea voyage had been necessary.

The Boston of the 18th century looked very different from the Boston he had known. He stood on deck when the ship passed Castle Island, where Castle William stood, the British garrison in Massachusetts Bay. The Union Jack flew high over the fort. Sea gulls rode the wind currents over the ship, hoping for some scraps of garbage to be thrown overboard. The city of Boston was almost an island, attached to the mainland by a narrow, mile-long neck of land. The docks were crowded with a mass of piers and wharves and shipyards, stages for drying fish, distilleries and warehouses. All manner of sailing vessels crowded the harbor. There were merchant ships and schooners, sloops, whalers, ferries, fishing ketches and ship's lighters, and even a British man o'war, the *Romney*, with its seventy-four guns. They had passed her on the starboard side and just beyond her, Drakov had seen another British naval vessel, the schooner *Lawrence*. He smiled as he saw the Royal Navy ships. He had timed his arrival perfectly. Boston seemed a lovely, graceful, tranquil city as they sailed into the harbor, but it was a hotbed of rebellion, a powder keg just waiting for someone to ignite the fuse.

"Americans are the sons, not the bastards of England!" The words were William Pitt's, spoken in the House of Commons, and widely quoted three thousand miles away in Boston. Readers of the *Boston Gazette* hung anxiously on every word spoken in Parliament by men like William Pitt and Col. Isaac Barré, who had fought gallantly in the French and Indian War and was a good friend to the colonists. Drakov had seen Col. Barré take the floor in Parliament and reply to Charles Townshend in the debate over Lord Grenville's Stamp Act.

"Will these Americans," Townshend had said indignantly, "children planted by our care, nourished up by our indulgence until they are grown to a degree of strength and opulence, and protected by our arms, will they grudge to contribute their mite to relieve us from the heavy burdens which we lie under?"

To which Col. Barré had replied, "They planted by *your* care? No, your oppressions planted them in America! They fled from your tyranny to a then uncultivated and inhospitable country, where they exposed themselves to almost all the hardships of which human nature is liable, and among others, to the cruelty of a savage foe, and yet actuated by the principles of true English liberty, they met all hardships with pleasure, compared with those they suffered in their own country from the hands of those who should have been their friends! They nourished by *your* indulgence? They grew by your neglect of them! As soon as you began to care about them, that care was exercised in sending persons to rule over them in one department and another, men whose behavior on many occasions has caused the blood of those sons of liberty to recoil within them!"

Sons of Liberty! It had a ring to it. A small group of patriots in Boston known as the Loyal Nine had read that speech in the *Gazette* and from that moment on, they became the Sons of Liberty, an organization that would grow with each new outrage visited upon the thirteen colonies.

A large percentage of the colonists were still loyal to the Crown, but more and more were having second thoughts. They recalled the words of William Pitt, who had said in Parliament, "When trade is at stake, you must defend it or perish!" Nor was Pitt the only one in England sympathetic to the colonists. King George, however, was determined to be firm. If America successfully asserted its right to reject British taxation, might Ireland not be next? But as stubborn as King George was, the Sons of Liberty were equally determined.

At the urging of the Boston patriots, the Stamp Act Congress had been convened in New York City. It was the first real united assembly of the colonies. The representatives met to discuss a course of action and there was much talk about the Virginia Resolves, authored in the House of Burgesses by the brilliant young lawyer, Patrick Henry. The Resolves asserted that Americans had the same rights as Englishmen to be taxed only by their representatives. But Henry went still further, maintaining that only a colony's legislature, and not Parliament, could tax its citizens.

The next few years would mark an important turning point in history. The people of the thirteen colonies were not yet ready to accept the idea of independence, but the actions of Sam Adams and the Sons of Liberty would soon provoke a series of events that would work to change their minds. Only what would happen, Drakov thought, if someone were to stop them?

He stepped off the ship onto Boston's Long Wharf, which jutted out two thousand feet into the harbor, so that even the largest vessels could come in to its south side at low tide. On the north side of Long Wharf stood warehouses, shops, and counting houses. It was a small spit of the city running out into the bay. Drakov found a dock porter to see to the unloading of his trunks, then hired a carter to deliver them to the home of Jared Moffat on Newbury Street. No sooner had the carter loaded up and started off than the dock began to clear. A moment later, Drakov saw the reason why. A longboat with armed sailors from the *Romney* was pulling in. The word was quickly passed among the workers on the dock.

"Press gang! Press gang!"

Men often died at sea and the captain of the *Romney* was apparently shorthanded. He had sent a ship's officer and a party of armed men ashore with instructions to secure replacements. As the press gang came ashore, Drakov watched them form up on the wharf and march off toward the taverns on the waterfront. Curious, he followed them to a public house called The Bunch of Grapes.

The officer quickly scanned the tables in the tavern. The room had gone dead silent. There was a suspicious dearth of able-bodied seamen.

"You, there!" said the officer, pointing to a man slumped over in his chair, with his head down on his arms. The man did not respond. Two of the Navy men quickly made their way to him and dragged him to his feet. His head lolled and one of the men pulled it back up with a sharp yank on his hair.

"I said, *you!*" the officer said curtly, frowning at the drunken man. "What is your name?"

"F-Furlong, sir," the drunk stammered, and alarm showed in his face as he became aware of what was happening to him.

"You have the look of a seaman about you," said the officer.

There was utter silence in the tavern. Drakov leaned against the bar and watched. He was quite safe. No British officer would ever dare impress a gentleman.

"I—I already have a ship," said Furlong, looking around for help. None was forthcoming. "I—I serve aboard the *Boston Packet*."

"The *Boston Packet*, is it?" said the officer, with a smile.

Drakov noticed a small group of older men seated at a table in the corner. One of them nodded to the others and his companions quietly got up and left the tavern.

"Y-yes, sir," said the drunk, sobering rapidly as panic mounted. "Moored at Hancock's Wharf, sir."

"Hancock," said the officer. "I know that name. A notorious smuggler."

"I—I know nothing of smuggling, sir," protested Furlong.

"I'll warrant that you do," the officer replied. "Well, Mr. Furlong, your smuggling days are over. You have been impressed into the service of His Majesty's Royal Navy. We will conduct you to the *Boston Packet* and collect your gear."

"You will do no such thing," a soft voice said.

The officer spun around. *"Who said that?"*

"I did," said the man sitting at the table in the corner.

He was in his forties, of medium height and build, with bright blue eyes, a slight paunch, and receding brown hair. His dress, though somewhat sloppy, showed him to be a gentleman, but he had apparently gone out in public without his wig, a sign that he was either slovenly or absentminded. His red broadcloth suit was rumpled and his boots were unpolished. There were dark smudges of printer's ink upon his cuffs.

The officer glared at him. "And who the devil might you be, sir, to speak in such an insolent manner to an officer of His Majesty, the King?"

"My name is Samuel Adams," said the man. And looking past the officer, he added, "Take heart, Mr. Furlong. These men shall not take you anywhere against your will."

"Are you aware, Mr. Adams," said the officer, "that it is treason to resist impressment or to counsel others to do so?"

"And are *you* aware, sir," Adams replied calmly, "that since the time of good Queen Anne, by act of Parliament, it has been illegal to impress sailors in American waters?"

"We are ashore sir," said the officer.

Adams smiled. "I think the statute was intended to apply to those ashore, as well. You know that as well as I."

"Well, in that case, sir, you may complain to Parliament," the officer said, with a contemptuous sneer. He turned back to his men. "Take him."

The panic-stricken Furlong turned to Adams.

"Never fear," said Adams. "You have friends."

With a snort, the officer beckoned to his men and they dragged Furlong outside. Adams made no move to get up from his chair. Curious, Drakov followed the press gang as they frog-marched their captive to the *Boston Packet*, moored at John Hancock's wharf. An angry crowd was waiting for them there. The men of the press gang hesitated, looking to their leader.

"Go on," the officer snapped at them. "They dare not interfere."

He was dead wrong. A stone sailed out from the crowd, striking one of the sailors in the forehead. He cried out and brought his hands up to his face. Another followed and another and moments later, the press gang was rapidly retreating in a hail of rocks and bricks as the angry crowd pursued them to their longboat. Outnumbered as they were, the press gang knew better than to try to use their arms against the crowd. They piled into their longboat and quickly pulled away, their officer, blood streaming from his face, shaking his fist at them in fury. A cheer went up and the rescued Mr. Furlong was hoisted up onto their shoulders and carried to the tavern, where he happily celebrated his narrow escape. Drakov looked around, but there was no one at the table in the corner. Sam Adams had quietly disappeared.

The carriage let Drakov off in front of the Moffat residence on Newbury Street. A pretty young woman dressed in servant's clothes answered the door. Her eyes grew wide as she saw Drakov and she curtsied deeply.

"Welcome, Master," she said, looking down at the ground. She stood aside to let him in and shut the door.

"Do not address me as 'master,' Sally," Drakov said. "In private, you may call me Nicholas. In the presence of others, you will call me 'sir.' Is that clear?"

"Yes, Nicholas."

"Good. Go tell Moffat I am here."

"No need," said Moffat, from the stairway. He came up to Drakov and held out both hands. "Welcome, Father."

Drakov winced. "How many times must I tell you? You are not to call me that. Nor 'master,' either."

Moffat dropped his arms and looked stricken. "Forgive me. In my delight at seeing you again, I had forgotten."

"See that you do not forget again," said Drakov. "Remember that we are both gentlemen here, of equal standing. When the time comes, you will introduce me to your friends as Nicholas Dark, a gentleman of independent means whom you knew well in London."

"Yes, I remember," said Moffat. "I will not slip up again. I swear. Sally, brew some tea."

As Sally hurried to do Moffat's bidding, Drakov glanced around at the elegant appointments of the home. "You have done well," he said.

"I've followed all of your instructions to the letter," Moffat said.

"Excellent. Then the meeting place has already been secured?"

"A small country chapel in Cambridge, not far from Harvard College," Moffat said. "Well set back from the road and isolated."

"Good. We shall look at it tomorrow. In the meantime, you can bring me up-to-date. I'd like to get started as soon as possible. What about the horseman?"

Moffat smiled. "He has already made his first appearance. I'm pleased to report that it was quite effective."

"You had no difficulty with the fugue clocking sequence?"

"I did it exactly as you've taught me," Moffat said. "It worked perfectly." He smiled. "Even better than I expected. One of the Sons of Liberty actually threw a knife at me. I activated the preprogrammed sequence, clocked out for an instant, and it appeared as if the knife passed through me. You should have seen their faces!"

"Perfect," Drakov said. "Since they are so fond of terrorizing people, let's see how they respond to some of their own medicine." They sat down at the table as Sally brought in the tea and served them. "What is your assessment of their leaders?" Drakov asked.

"Well, their real leaders remain behind the scenes, for the most part," Moffat said. "John Hancock quietly pursues his shipping interests and thanks to all the money his adoptive father made in smuggling, he lives in regal splendor in his mansion up on Beacon Hill. 'King' Hancock, they call him. But while he remains essentially above it all, he funds most of the radicals' activities. James Otis is already beginning to show the symptoms of the insanity he will succumb to before long. He's a highly eloquent speaker in the Assembly, but his manic depressive tendencies are already very much in evidence. He succumbs to frequent mood swings and often has a tendency to rant for hours on end. He's alienated many of the others and though he recently won reelection, many of the citizens are starting to regard him as a fool. John Avery is less a leader than a follower. He's Harvard-educated, a merchant who's quite active in society, but not really a force to be reckoned with. Benjamin Edes and John Gill are chiefly propagandists. They publish the *Boston Gazette* and write whatever Adams wishes them to write, whether it has any bearing on the truth or not. Edes is rather temperamental, but like Gill and Avery, he, too, is more of an Indian than a chief. Joseph Warren's a good man and Josiah Quincy is one of their best speakers. He can really fire up a crowd. But the real power behind the Sons of Liberty is Samuel Adams."

"Yes, of course," said Drakov. "I saw him earlier today."

"Really?"

"We did not exactly meet," said Drakov, "but I saw him neatly foil the intentions of a Royal Navy press gang. Tell me more about him."

"There's quite a lot to tell," said Moffat. "His father, Deacon Adams, was a prosperous merchant who owned his own wharf and a brewery on Purchase Street. As a young man, Sam went to Harvard and lived rather elegantly. His classmates called him 'the last of the Puritans' because he was never known to smoke or drink, take snuff or consort with women.

He still likes to play up to that pious image, but the fact is that he can drink most men right under the table. Harvard ranks their students by their social standing and young Sam was ranked fifth in his class. He took his social standing very seriously. He didn't even eat with the other students in the dining room, but instead dined privately, like an aloof young gentleman. All of this changed for him practically overnight.

"Deacon Adams was the director of the Land Bank, which he and some of his associates founded in an attempt to give some stability to colonial paper currency. Thomas Hutchinson was against it from the start. He fought the idea of the colonies printing up their own paper money and he petitioned Parliament to outlaw the Land Bank, which they readily agreed to. A lot of people were ruined as a result and Adams himself lost everything. Sam was reduced to waiting tables in the student commons, serving the very boys he'd been too good to eat with. He never got over it. His hate for the Hutchinsons is pathological.

"Even in his student days, he was already a fervent follower of John Locke. Recently he wrote in the *Gazette*, 'It is the right of the people to withdraw their support from that government which fails to fulfill its trust. If this does not persuade government to live up to its obligation, it is the right of the people to overthrow it.' That's a direct quote from Locke. Sam was always more interested in politics than anything else. He has failed at absolutely everything he has ever tried. After he took his masters from Harvard, he accepted a position in a counting house under Thomas Cushing. He didn't last long. He then tried his hand at business and wound up in debt within six months. The Deacon bailed him out, though he could hardly afford it. Sam then went into the family brewery business and proceeded to run that into the ground, as well. It's still struggling along after a fashion, but I suspect it's only because Hancock keeps him afloat. His political career seems to have started purely out of spite. The governor had apparently promised the Deacon a place on the Council, but when a vacancy occurred, he gave it to Andrew Oliver, instead. Sam remembers things like that. First chance he got, he ran for the Assembly, just so he could work against the governor.

"He then started up a small newspaper he called the *Public Advertiser*. Wrote most of it himself. That's where he learned the fine art of propaganda. He would write inflammatory editorials and then, under different names, he would write 'letters to the editor' in support of the editorials he'd written. He still does that sort of thing, only now he's doing it in the *Gazette*. After he started publishing the *Advertiser*, all of his old classmates started to avoid him. He is considered something of a lunatic, dangerous and disrespectable. Sam doesn't care. He prefers the company of his lower-class friends down on the waterfront.

"He's been married twice," Moffat continued, "both wives named Elizabeth. The first one died of fever, leaving him with two children. He didn't know the first thing about raising them alone. The Deacon died and Sam inherited his debts. The brewery was going to hell in a handbasket and Sam was constantly in court, losing one suit after another for slow payment to the Crown. As I said, he remembers things like that.

"A few years ago, they made him a tax collector. God only knows why. He was constantly in arrears. The sheriff, Stephen Greenleaf, was finally ordered to put Sam's estate up for auction—the brewery, the house on Purchase Street, the wharf, everything. Incredibly, Adams intimidated Greenleaf by threatening him with a lawsuit. The auction was postponed twice and finally it never did take place. Greenleaf's been a little frightened of him ever since. Then Hutchinson charged Adams with malfeasance in his duties as a tax collector. Quite honestly, I don't think Sam ever actually embezzled anything, he was just incredibly inept. And softhearted, too. He couldn't find it in himself to bring charges against people who couldn't afford to pay, so he wound up paying the difference himself. But he never could catch up. They finally just gave up and kicked him out, appointed a new man to the job, and decided to forget the whole thing. He simply wore them out.

"He recently got married a second time, to a sweet girl named Elizabeth Wells, some twenty years his junior. She's the best thing that ever happened to him. She's bright, extremely lovely, takes good care of his children, and manages the money, what there is of it. So far as anybody knows, Sam is absolutely faithful to her, though he does enjoy the company of women. They must have a peculiar homelife. Beth has to be the most patient woman in the world. His cousin John came down to visit him from Braintree not long ago and he said that the moment the dinner conversation strayed from politics, Sam got disgusted and left the table to go down to The Bunch of Grapes and spent the night plotting with his friends. He's got some sort of nervous disorder. Sometimes he can't keep his hands from trembling, but it comes and goes. Aside from that, he has a healthy constitution.

"Still, he's not the sort of man you'd think capable of being a leader. I'm really not sure what it is about him, but he does have a certain charisma. Hutchinson calls him 'The Great Incendiary.' He'd like nothing better than to arrest him, but he can't get anything on him. His friends are absolutely loyal to him, Hancock in particular. You should see the two of them together. Sam looking his usual slovenly self, half the time forgetting to go out with his coat and wig on, that ridiculous red suit looking like he slept in it, and Hancock in his exquisitely tailored lavender suits and yellow carriage. They make quite a pair. I don't personally know Hancock very well, though I've tried to get close to him, as you wanted me to do. 'King' Hancock is very particular in his choice of friends, though what he sees in Adams is beyond me. But I know Sam quite well. He dearly loves to argue with me. I've often had him in for dinner. He'll come, so long as the food is good and the conversation sticks to politics. And he is very vulnerable, by the way. He never takes a carriage or a coach, except when he rides with Hancock. Walks everywhere, usually alone, often late at night. And he's usually off in his own world somewhere. He'll make a very easy target."

"Excellent," Drakov said. "You have done very well, indeed, Jared. You have lived up to all my expectations. I'm very proud of you. Very proud, indeed."

Moffat's eyes shone as he basked in the praise. "I can't tell you what that means to me," he said, his voice choked with emotion. "Ever since you sent me here, I've sought to prove my worth. And Sally—Sally has been a great help, too," he added, glancing at her. She looked down at the floor demurely.

"You've both done extremely well," said Drakov. "My confidence in you has been fully justified."

"Does—does that mean . . ." Moffat swallowed hard, struggling to get the words out. "Does that mean you will . . . perhaps . . . give us a child?"

Sally stood absolutely motionless, watching Drakov as if he held her very life in his hands. Which, in fact, he did. It was almost touching. It was so often the same with them. Because they were mules, they could not reproduce and they desperately longed to be allowed to raise a child. They so wanted to be human.

"When we are finished here," said Drakov, "if you continue to do so well, I will find a more suitable time and place for you where you can raise a child."

Sally fell on her knees, took his hand, and kissed it. "Oh, thank you! Thank you!"

Moffat's eyes were moist. "I—I had not dared to hope for such an honor," he said softly.

"You have earned it," Drakov said. "But first, we still have work to do. And now I'm tired. If my room has been prepared, I would like to get some rest."

He climbed the stairs to the bedroom they'd prepared for him, where his bags had already been unpacked for him. He went over to the window and opened it to let in the breeze. He looked out over the streets of Boston and smiled. He would be forever grateful to Dr. Moreau for teaching him the secrets of his special brand of genetic engineering. He had no need of the Timekeepers anymore. With the hominoids, he could create his own organization, seeded throughout time. And they were unquestioningly loyal, fanatically devoted to him, perfect parents for his replications of himself.

As he undressed, Drakov wondered, not for the first time, about the curious curse of his existence. He wondered if he, himself, was one of the replications he'd created. It was a fascinating idea. He knew himself to be the original Nikolai Drakov, but he had created the replications of himself as his crowning achievement, to be given to hominoid parents and carefully raised according to a detailed plan. Each of them, up to a certain point, would have their own individual memories of their existence, but past that point, their subliminal genetic programming would become activated and they would forget their past lives and remember only the life of the original Drakov, his memories and his experiences, his personality engrams down to the last detail. They would even scar themselves with a knife slash across the face. Each one of them would come to believe that he was the original, as he did. And each one would always puzzle over the same metaphysical riddle—did I create myself?

He got into bed and lay staring at the ceiling, lost in thought. He almost didn't hear it when the door to his bedroom opened softly and Sally entered. He turned when he heard the rustle of her dress falling to the floor. She stood there, completely naked, exquisitely formed and trembling slightly.

"What are you doing?" he asked.

She bit her lower lip. "I—I thought . . ."

"Get out."

She flinched, as if he'd slapped her. "Please, forgive me," she said, quickly stooping to pick up her dress and cover herself with it awkwardly. "I—I only hoped to please you . . . I—I only thought . . . I never meant to . . ." Her lips began to tremble and she was on the verge of tears. She quickly turned and bolted from the room. Drakov leaned back and sighed.

They so wanted to be human . . .

3 _____

They clocked in at Reese Hunter's Boston residence in Long Lane, a small rented two-story home just off Milk Street. Prior to leaving the 27th century, they had gone in for a refresher implant briefing and then drawn weapons and period clothing from Ordnance Section. Lucas, Finn, and Andre immediately started to search the house. Steiger had remained behind to coordinate the mission.

"What's the matter, don't you trust me?" Hunter said.

"No, not really," said Delaney, holding up a laser pistol he'd just taken from a drawer in Hunter's desk.

"There's a .45 semiauto under the pillow on my bed and a commando knife taped to the back of the headboard," Hunter said. "You'll find spare ammo and clips hidden in the breadbox in the kitchen and a brace of flintlock dueling pistols tucked under the cushion of the reading chair in the study."

They quickly appropriated the weapons.

"Sure you don't have a spare warp disc tucked away somewhere?" asked Andre.

"Even if I had, it still wouldn't get me home, would it?" Hunter said. "You people are the only game in town. You know about all the confluence points we've used before and your people are patrolling them. If any new ones have been discovered, it's happened since I got separated from my unit.

Besides, if I knew of any others, do you really think I'd still be here?"

"You don't mind if we look just the same?" said Lucas.

Hunter shrugged. "Help yourselves. Just try not to make a mess. The maid doesn't come in until Tuesday."

Delaney glanced at him.

"Just kidding, pilgrim," Hunter said. "Nobody comes to these digs but me. While you're tearing apart the house, I'll go and make some tea. We still drink tea in Boston. For a while, anyway."

He left the room and went into the kitchen.

"What do you think?" said Andre.

"I don't know," Delaney said. "He played straight with us before, when we went up against the Network in New York. Besides, like the man said, he's been here for a while and he's got connections. If he wanted to, he could've hidden ordnance all over Boston."

"He probably has," said Lucas. "Wouldn't you? Remember *our* Reese Hunter?" he said, referring to Hunter's twin from their own universe, who had deserted from the Temporal Corps to join the Underground and who'd been murdered by the Timekeepers in 17th-century France. "First time I met him in 12th-century England, he had an entire arsenal at his disposal, plus all the comforts of home. Sound system, classical record-ings, books, microwave oven, generator . . . had himself a modern bachelor pad all set up in a cabin in the middle of Sherwood Forest. Genetically, this Reese Hunter is identical. I wouldn't put anything past him."

"The question is, how far can we trust him?" said Delaney.

"About as far as his own self-interest is concerned," said Lucas as they continued their search. "But he did turn himself in voluntarily. He didn't have to. He could have chosen any time period he wished, set himself up comfortably, and retired. Or he could have gone underground and worked on his own to disrupt our history. Maybe he's playing straight with us."

"If he's not bluffing about those subliminal triggers," said Andre, "then he took an awful chance by coming in."

"It could be a bluff," admitted Lucas. "But on the other hand, put yourself in his place. If you were trapped in his universe, what would you do? Especially if you saw a chance to get back home and, at the same time, get even with an old enemy?"

"I might do the same," said Andre. "But it's an interesting coincidence that he happened to wind up in colonial Boston at the same time as Drakov did, assuming that Drakov's really here."

"Maybe it's not a coincidence," Delaney said. "You start getting into some serious temporal metaphysics when you try to figure out the Fate Factor. When Mensinger first formulated that theory, he was convinced that it was a sort of nebulous temporal principle, a Zen physics version of for every action, there is an equal and opposite reaction. But toward the end of his life, he started getting almost spiritual about it."

"You mean he thought it was God?" said Andre.

"He never actually came out and said that," Delaney replied. "He always skirted the issue, as if he was afraid of it. He probably was. But when I was studying his work in R.C.S., I became convinced that toward the end, Mensinger developed a strong belief in predestination, although he never came out and actually called it that. He kept speaking of 'an order to the universe,' that sort of thing. The closest he ever came to admitting the possibility of a guiding intelligence was when he once quoted Einstein as saying that God didn't play dice with the universe, that there was order to all things. Everyone always assumed that he was speaking metaphorically, but what if he was being literal?"

"It would make the Fundamentalists ecstatic," Andre said.

"Maybe that's why he never came out and said it," Delaney replied. "He didn't want what he was saying to be reduced to some simplistic dogma for the reassurance of the ignorant. When Einstein made that statement, newspaper headlines all over the world blared 'Einstein believes in God!' Nobody ever really understood Einstein, either. It's a funny thing. Every now and then, someone comes along who gets a brilliant insight into what might be the Ultimate Truth and people either misinterpret them or try to shut them up. Giordano Bruno was burned at the stake. Galileo was made to recant. By the time Einstein came around, they'd grown more clever. They simply made him into some sort of amiable genius, too complicated for anyone to understand, and stuck him in a university where he could do no harm. Mensinger made it simple for them. He committed suicide."

"Tea's on," said Hunter, coming in from the kitchen. "You guys find the warp grenade I hid inside the chamberpot?"

"Very funny," said Lucas.

"You know, the Lucas Priest I remember had a sense of humor," Hunter said.

"Maybe that was in my first life," Lucas said.

"Better," Hunter said. "But still not up to your old standard. Look, you guys have all my weapons, you've got my warp disc, I'm stuck here if I don't play ball with you. And don't forget, trust is a two-way street. I've also got to trust you to live up to your end of the deal when this is over."

"And do you?" Andre said.

Hunter shrugged. "What have I got to lose?"

"Quite a lot, if we decide to call your bluff and put you through interrogation," Lucas said. "You could wind up a vegetable."

"Maybe," Hunter said, nodding. "And if it was up to your friend Steiger, perhaps that's exactly what would happen. But it's not his call, it's Forrester's. And I think I can trust that man."

"Why?" said Delaney, curious.

"Because he looks a man right in the eyes and doesn't make him want to look away. Because he tolerates a slob like you under his command. Because he's out to break up the Network when he could just as easily go along with it and take his cut or simply sit back and do nothing, because the Network isn't really endangering the timeline. They're only out to make some dirty bucks. But mostly because I saw his face when you mentioned Drakov."

Hunter paused a moment and they were all silent.

"There was a lot of pain there," Hunter continued. "And a man who knows that kind of pain doesn't go around inflicting it."

Delaney gave him a long look. "You don't miss much, do you?"

"Just part of being a survivor, pilgrim," Hunter said. "How do you take your tea?"

Just as The Bunch of Grapes was the favorite gathering place of the Sons of Liberty, so the Peacock Tavern was a Tory bar. Boston was becoming polarized. Its citizens preferred the company of like-minded thinkers and although no one was very happy with the actions of the ministry and Parliament, there were still many who considered themselves loyal Englishmen and sought a rapprochement with Britain. Among them were men who held offices as tax commissioners and customs officials, merchants who were alarmed over the increasing talk of a boycott of British goods, and citizens who were outraged by the actions of the mobs of rioters who roamed the streets and gathered in the Common and in the taverns on the waterfront.

"They speak of liberty and property," said Thomas Brown, sarcastically. "The mob always shouts those words when they're about to tear down a house. And they are allowed to do so with impunity. You know, the governor heard that MacIntosh was the leader of the mob that wrecked Hutchinson's home, so he sent Greenleaf out to bring him in. The sheriff arrested the blackguard, but the Sons of Liberty gave him an ultimatum. They sent a group of men to tell him that unless MacIntosh was immediately released, not one man would volunteer to join the patrols the Town Meeting had voted to send out in order to prevent the rioting. I was at the council meeting when Greenleaf made his report to Hutchinson. The result? The man was released. And now he crows about it to anyone who'll listen! I ask you, of what use are the patrols if the rioters can so easily intimidate them?"

"I heard that Governor Bernard has offered a reward of three hundred pounds to any man who will identify the leader of the rioters," said Hewitt. "Needless to say, it isn't MacIntosh they're after. They realize the cobbler is nothing but a tool. Bernard and Hutchinson both know that Adams is behind it all, yet not one man can be found to come forward and give evidence against him, not even for three hundred pounds!"

"Having seen what they did to Hutchinson, not to mention Oliver, Hallowell, and Story, would you come forward to give evidence?" said Moffat. "To be sure, three hundred pounds is quite a large sum to the average man, but what good are three hundred pounds when they come to tear your house down in the middle of the night?"

"There is no law in Boston anymore," said Brown, bitterly. "The mobs grow bolder by the day."

"I must admit that appears true," said Drakov. "Why, the very day that I arrived, I saw them put a party of Royal Navy men to flight with rocks and bricks."

"A press gang," said Hewitt, sourly. "I can feel little sympathy for such as they. Nor can any here, I'll warrant."

"I will not dispute the point," said Drakov. "I was merely

commenting upon the boldness of the mob, to go up against armed men of the King's Navy. And it took but a nod from Samuel Adams."

"You mean you actually heard Adams give the order?" Hewitt said.

"Well, not in so many words," said Drakov. "I was present in the tavern when that man, Furlong, was impressed. Adams was there, too, with a group of his companions. I saw him give a nod to them and they quietly left the tavern. Moments later, a mob had been assembled upon Hancock's Wharf to rescue the man who'd been impressed. I was impressed myself, so to speak, that it could have all been done so quickly."

Brown smiled. "No surprise there, Mr. Dark," he said. "Sam Adams has many friends among those who work the docks. He plays to their sympathies and plys them with drink, no great matter for one who owns a brewery, and if a man be hard-pressed, why, a job can always be found for him on one of King Hancock's vessels or in one of Avery's warehouses. Grant them that, they take care of their own."

"What do they say in London about events here?" Hewitt asked Drakov.

"They call the colonists 'rebellious children,'" Drakov said. "All good citizens of England must pay taxes. They don't see why the colonists should be exempt."

"Yes, quite," said Brown. "But try to tell that to the Sons of Liberty!"

"Sons of Liberty, indeed!" snorted Moffat. "They respect only the liberties of those who feel the way they do! Let any man speak out against them and he will soon find out what liberties he has! He'll enjoy the liberty of having a paving stone heaved through his window. Try to tell them that you have the right to disagree with them and they will demonstrate their right to break your head for you! You cannot hope to reason with such men."

"That's true enough," said Brown. "You'll not convince the Sons of Liberty with logic."

"Perhaps they can be convinced in other ways," said Drakov.

"What do you mean?" asked Hewitt.

"I was thinking of the headless horseman," Drakov said.

"What?" said Brown. "A headless horseman, did you say?"

"Yes, haven't you heard?" said Drakov. "Moffat here was telling me about it just this morning."

"What's this about a headless horseman, Moffat?"

"Then you haven't heard?" said Moffat. "It's been the talk of all the taverns on the waterfront. A tale of a ghost rider, gentleman, a specter with no head who rides the streets of Boston after dark."

"What manner of nonsense is this?" said Brown.

"I report only what I hear, gentlemen," said Moffat. "It seems that the other night, Ebenezer MacIntosh and some of his fellow so-called Sons of Liberty received what one might call a visitation. MacIntosh, so the word goes, was raving drunkenly when a jack-o-lantern came crashing through the tavern window and knocked him from his chair."

"No, really?" Hewitt said, grinning.

"The broken window was real enough," said Moffat. "I saw them fixing it myself."

"Go on," said Brown. "What happened then?"

"Well," said Moffat, "it seems that MacIntosh and his friends ran out into the street to see who'd done it. They were ready to break heads, I gather, but instead, so the story goes, they all got the fright of their lives. The street appeared deserted, with no sign of whoever had thrown the pumpkin through the window. They looked all around, but there was simply no one there."

"The fellow ran off," said Hewitt.

"Be quiet, John," said Brown. "Let Moffat tell it."

"As I said, the street appeared deserted," Moffat continued, "when suddenly, they all heard the sound of hoofbeats and a rider came galloping at them from out of nowhere. A rider dressed all in black, on a black horse. A rider, gentlemen, *who had no head.*"

"No head, you say?" said Hewitt, frowning. "Balderdash!"

"MacIntosh does not think that it was balderdash," said Moffat.

"The man was obviously drunk," said Hewitt. "He was seeing things."

"Then all who were with him shared the same delusion," Moffat said. "They all swore that it was true."

A crowd had gathered around their table to listen as Moffat went on with the story.

"The rider came galloping straight at them, so they said, as if to run them down. They scattered and the rider galloped past, then reined in and turned his horse and came at them again. Jeb Stiles wasn't quick enough to get out of the way. He was struck solid by the rider's horse. I hear it broke his ribs."

"That's true!" said someone in the crowd. "His wife told me he couldn't finish mending my chair because his ribs were broken! She said he'd been struck down in the street by a horseman!"

"Go on, go on!" said someone else. "What happened then?"

"The headless horseman reined in once again and his black stallion reared up," said Moffat, playing to the crowd. "They heard him laugh. A wild, screeching laughter that echoed through the night! Ransome Howard drew his knife and threw it at the rider. And all who were there said they saw it pass right through him, as if he wasn't there!"

"He simply missed," said Hewitt, skeptically, though he too had become caught up in the story.

"Howard never misses!" someone in the crowd said. "He's deadly with that knife of his. I've seen him pin a squirrel right to a tree!"

Others who'd seen Howard throw his knife attested to his skill with it.

"So then what happened?" someone in the crowd said.

"Well," said Moffat, "they say the headless rider screeched like a soul being torn apart in Hell and came galloping straight at them once again. And an instant before he was upon them, both horse and rider vanished into thin air right before their eyes!"

"Vanished, did you say!"

"Disappeared like smoke," said Moffat.

"A ghost!" said someone in the crowd.

"Since when do ghosts break people's ribs?" asked Hewitt.

"No, that's true enough, they don't," said Drakov. "And I, for one, do not believe in ghosts."

"Nor I," said Hewitt. "It all sounds like some silly school-boy's tale to me."

"Perhaps," said Drakov. "But then Moffat here said they swore it was all true."

"And so they did," said Moffat. "Ben Edes said he'd swear it on the Bible."

"Then how do you account for it?" said Hewitt.

"Well, it's true enough they had been drinking," Moffat

said, with a shrug. "And think on it, would a man as proud of his knife-throwing as Ransome Howard admit it if he'd missed?"

The people in the crowd around them nodded and murmured among themselves.

"But you said they saw the horseman vanish like a ghost!" said someone in the crowd.

"So they said," admitted Moffat. "For my own part, I cannot attest to the truth or falsity of that, since I was not there myself."

"Then how do you explain it?" someone said.

"Yes," said someone else, "one drunken man can have his eyes play tricks on him, but you say they all saw the same thing."

"Well, so they *say*," said Drakov. "But then, gentlemen, consider the alternative."

"What do you mean?" asked Brown.

"You all tell me what a bold and swaggering lot the ruffians who call themselves the Sons of Liberty have become," said Drakov. "And how many of them were there that night, five, six, more? And doubtless, there were those present in the tavern who were not among their number, and who prudently chose to remain inside rather than risk being caught up in a brawl out in the street. Yet they saw that someone had thrown that pumpkin through the window, knocking MacIntosh down to the floor. And they doubtless heard the commotion in the street, and then saw Stiles being carried back inside with his ribs all busted up. What were the gallant Sons of Liberty to say, that six or more of them were bested by one man? That one man put them all to flight?"

The crowd murmured its agreement.

"Even so, Dark," said Hewitt, "why should they concoct such an outrageous story? Why not simply claim they were outnumbered?"

"Perhaps," said Drakov, "because there was a witness or two who were not among their number, not members of the Sons of Liberty, that is to say, who were outside with them and could assert that they were only up against one man. And, gentlemen, let us ask ourselves, if what they saw was not, in fact, a spirit of some sort, then what must they have seen? A man dressed all in black, on horseback, perhaps with his cloak pulled up so that they could not see his face? Is it not possible that rather than vanish, he merely galloped quickly down some convenient alleyway when they scattered before his horse, so that he only seemed to disappear?"

"That sounds much more plausible to me than the idea of some ghost," said Hewitt. "In which case, bravo to that man! Let us drink a toast to him!"

"Hear, hear!" said a few people in the crowd.

"Yes, by all means, let us applaud that man, whoever he may be," Drakov concurred. "But, gentlemen, before we drink our toast, let us consider that we might well profit from that unknown man's example."

"Indeed?" said Brown. "How so?"

"Consider the Sons of Liberty, gentlemen," said Drakov. "Who are they? What are they? Men much like ourselves, no more, no less. And yet, day by day, it appears that more and more, the city falls under their grip. And why, I ask you? Because they are better men than we?"

"No, by God!" said Brown.

"Indeed, no, they are not," said Drakov. "And yet what makes them so different from ourselves that they seem to have such power? What, precisely, *is* their power, gentlemen? That, with the exception of a very few, their members are not known."

"But we all know who they are," protested Brown.

"Do we?" Drakov asked. "How many of them can you name? Six? Eight? Ten, perhaps? Fifteen or twenty, at best? Yet when they stage their demonstrations, how many of them are there? Forty, fifty, sixty or more? When they come to threaten people in the night, are not many of them masked, or their faces blackened with burnt cork?"

"Yes, that's true enough," one of the tax commissioners said. "I can readily attest to that."

"Their power, then," said Drakov, "seems to lie in the fact that they accomplish much of what they do by stealth. By being unknown, by heaving stones through windows in the night and such. And now, it seems, a loyal subject of King George has given them a taste of their own medicine, paid them back in their own coin." He raised his eyebrows and looked around at them. "Can we not learn from his example, gentlemen?"

John Hewitt smiled. "A wise man can always profit by the good example of another," he said. "I wonder who our 'headless horseman' is. And I wonder if he will ride again soon?"

"I should not be in the least surprised," said Moffat.

"In the meantime," Drakov said, "perhaps his fellow loyal subjects of King George should discuss how best to give the horseman our support?"

"What do you propose, Nicholas?" said Brown.

"Gentlemen," said Drakov, picking up his glass of wine, "the Sons of Liberty are bent upon visiting their deviltry upon us. They give us deviltry, I say we rebel against it and pay them back with hellfire!"

"Hear, hear!"

"Well said! Well said!"

"Gentlemen," said Drakov, rising to his feet with upraised glass, "I give you the headless horseman! And all those with the courage to ride along beside him!"

"I'll drink to that!"

"And so will I, by God!"

"Me, too!"

"Your glasses, gentlemen! Raise up your glasses!"

"To the headless horseman!" Moffat said. "Hellfire to the Sons of Liberty!"

They all joined in the toast and drank.

"To the headless horseman! Hellfire to the Sons of Liberty!"

"I wonder," Moffat said, as if musing to himself, "does anyone among us stable a black stallion?"

They all started glancing at one another.

"John, don't you have a black stallion in your stable?" Moffat asked.

"What, *me*? The headless horseman?" Hewitt said, with a snort. "Not I. It's true, I have a black horse in my stable, but it is an old mare. A walking country horse. Hardly the sort of mount for clattering about the streets of Boston in the middle of the night!"

"Stoddard has a black horse!" someone cried. "And it's a stallion, too!"

"No, no, my stallion is a bay!" Stoddard protested.

"Perhaps it was a bay they saw that night!"

"No, it was black, they said, like jet."

"Gentlemen, gentlemen!" said Drakov, raising his arms to get their attention. He waited till they'd settled down. "What does it profit us to speculate upon who this man might be?"

"Do you happen to own a black stallion, Mr. Dark?" said someone in the crowd.

"As it happens, I do not own any horses whatsoever," Drakov said. "And these gentlemen can tell you, I had not yet arrived in Boston when the headless horseman first made his appearance, so I think that we can all safely assume I am not he."

"Yes, that's quite true," said Hewitt. "Nicholas has only just arrived in the colonies. He does not even have a place to call his own yet."

"Quite so, gentlemen," said Drakov. "But my point is simply this. Our mysterious horseman may be among us even now, for all we know, or he might be dining at this very moment in some other part of town, altogether unaware of our interest in him. In either event, what difference does it make? He serves all our interests best by being unknown. Remember that if we cannot discern his true identity, then neither can the Sons of Liberty."

"Your point is well taken, Dark," said Brown. "But then how may we let him know that there are those among us ready and willing to lend him our support?"

"Well, our horseman is clearly a Tory, that much we know," said Drakov. "And we all know who our fellow Tories are, do we not? I say we spread the word among all of our friends. That way, whoever he may be, the word must surely reach him. Let it be known that there are those among us who stand ready to oppose the lawlessness of Samuel Adams and his mob. And if the horseman wants our help, then surely a man of his resources must find a way to tell us."

"You think he will respond?" said Hewitt.

"We can only wait and see," said Drakov. "But if our headless horseman is the man of action he appears to be, then I think we may be hearing from him soon."

Benjamin Hallowell was not the sort of man who was easily intimidated and he had very little sympathy for the grievances of Boston's radicals, especially after the Sons of Liberty attacked his home. He did not care for Boston. He much preferred the civility of London, but the new regulations had required him to personally assume his post as a collector of customs duties in the colonies.

In the past, it had been the usual practice for men appointed to his office to remain in England and appoint people in the colonies to act in their place, as their deputies, but the ministry had put a stop to that. The colonists were all too often sympathetic to the smugglers and the colonial deputies had often looked the other way, accepting bribes from merchants and their captains to ignore the smuggled goods. Hallowell was an ambitious man and he did not intend to settle down in Massachusetts. He meant to impress his superiors in England with the efficient way that he performed his duties and to use his post in Boston as a step up the ladder to further his career in government service.

For a long time, he had been waiting for the opportunity to make an example of one man in particular, a man who was notorious for his flagrant disregard of the Acts of Trade and Navigation, and now, thanks to the recent arrival in port of the *Romney* and the *Lawrence*, it seemed the moment had arrived to teach the haughty John Hancock a lesson that was a long time overdue. Hallowell listened grim-faced as his chief collector, Joseph Harrison, made his report.

"From the moment that I saw the *Liberty* pull into the wharf," said Harrison, "I suspected that her holds were loaded full of smuggled goods. She rode low in the water, far too low to account for what was on her manifest." Harrison snorted. "When I boarded her for my inspection, the captain claimed that the ship's entire cargo consisted of twenty-five pipes of Madeira. And yet any fool could see the ship was loaded to capacity!"

"So you insisted on making a personal inspection, of course," said Hallowell.

"Yes, and no sooner had I done so than they offered me a bribe!" said Harrison. He drew himself up stiffly. "I refused, of course."

"Of course," said Hallowell. "What happened then?"

"They bullied me," said Harrison, his tone almost that of a small boy who had been picked on by his elders. "The ship's crew gathered around and threatened me, tried to make me take the bribe, but when I still refused, they seized me—actually seized me!—and dragged me down below decks, where they locked me up in one of the cabins! I pounded on the door, but they only laughed at me and said that I should cool my heels for a while and think things over. For three hours or more they left me there, heedless of my protests, until the sun went down!

And then I heard the ship being unloaded. And they unloaded far more than twenty-five pipes of wine, I can tell you that, sir! Afterward, when they were done with the unloading, they let me out and made out as if it had all been some mistake! They even had the barefaced effrontery to suggest that I had locked myself inside the cabin! The brass! The very brass of them! And now, even as we speak, they're loading up the ship again and making ready to leave port, doubtless with more contraband bound for the Indies, and of what use is it to demand to see the contents of their hold? They will do the same thing once again, or worse!"

"No, they most certainly will not," said Hallowell, grimly. "Hancock has gone too far this time. I will not have my customs collectors bullied about, no, sir! John Hancock might well be the richest man in Boston, but that does not put him above the law!"

"But what can we do?" asked Harrison.

"We can hit him where it hurts him most, Joseph. In his pocketbook. I intend to seize his ship."

"His crew will never stand for that, sir! They are a rough lot, indeed. I tell you, it would be as much as worth my life to serve seizure papers on them, sir. I have a family to think of . . ."

"Calm yourself, Joseph," Hallowell said. "I would not send you alone to risk such treatment once again. I will request Capt. Corner of the His Majesty's Ship *Romney* to provide us with an armed escort. After that incident with the press gang, I'll warrant those men are itching to get back some of their own. We will wait until the ship is fully loaded and then, my friend, we shall seize her, complete with all her cargo, and have her towed under the *Romney*'s guns, least they should try to board the ship at night and sail it away. I will teach Hancock's ruffians to harass one of my men, by God! I'll not suffer their insolence one moment longer! Here, have this message delivered to the *Romney*'s captain. And here are your seizure papers. As of this moment, the *Liberty* and all her cargo are the property of His Majesty, the King!"

The *Liberty* lay fully loaded at the dock and awaiting the next tide when the longboats from the *Romney* pulled up to the wharf. The same officer who had led the press gang was in command and this time, he moved quickly, before the crowd had time to gather. In the company of Ben Hallowell, Thomas Irving, the inspector of imports, Joseph Harrison and his eldest son, Richard, who was a customs clerk, the officer marched his men up on the *Liberty*'s deck and served the ship's captain with the seizure papers.

"Sir, you are charged with violation of the Acts of Trade and Navigation and henceforth, this ship and all her cargo are forfeit to His Majesty, the King," said Hallowell.

"The hell it is," the captain said.

At a signal from the officer, one of the *Romney*'s men knocked him to the deck with the butt end of his musket. Several of the crew started forward angrily, but stopped when they found themselves staring down the barrels of muskets loaded with grape shot.

"All right, you scurvy, smuggling lot," the officer said firmly. "Face right about and down the gangplank with you, every man jack of you! Move sharply, now! First man who hesitates, I'll have his guts for garters! Move!"

Sullenly, the *Liberty*'s crew marched down the gangplank. The word had already been spread along the docks and an angry crowd was quickly forming. The men from the *Romney* wasted no time in running lines out to the longboats for the *Liberty* to be towed out into the harbor, close beneath the *Romney*'s guns.

"Well done, sir," said Hallowell to the ship's officer. "My compliments to Capt. Corner."

"I will convey them, sir," the officer said. "And now, with your permission, we'd best get on about our business. That crowd yonder on the dock has an ugly look about it. I would not linger overlong if I were you."

"No need to worry," Hallowell said smugly. "They may stand there and jeer till dawn for all the good it does them, damn their eyes for their impudence! Come, gentlemen, we've done our duty."

No sooner had they stepped off the gangplank than the first stone came sailing out from the crowd. The *Romney*'s men made haste to pull the gangplank in and the rowers hurriedly bent to their task. Slowly, ponderously, the sloop began to move as the men in the longboats strained at their oars to tow the ship out into the harbor. The men still aboard the *Liberty* took shelter as they were pelted with a rain of rocks and bricks from the angry crowd. Ben Hallowell watched smugly as the *Liberty* was slowly towed away from the dock.

"Take that, John bloody Hancock!" he said.

"Ben," said Irving, pulling at his sleeve.

They turned and found their way blocked by the crowd. The crew of the *Liberty* were among them. Some of the men were holding clubs. Hallowell looked around nervously, but there was nowhere for them to go.

"Let us pass," said Hallowell.

Nobody moved.

Hallowell swallowed nervously.

"Let us pass, I said!"

"Get the bloody bastard!" someone shouted.

The crowd surged forward. Irving tried to draw his sword, but it was snatched from him and broken. He went down beneath a flurry of swinging fists. A club struck Hallowell's head and he crumpled to the ground, blood streaming from his forehead.

"Run, Dick!" Harrison shouted to his son.

In an instant, the mob was upon them and Harrison cried out as a club glanced off his shoulder. He lashed out wildly and felt his fist connect with someone's face. He felt hands clutching at his coat and another club struck him in the back. Someone punched him in the face and blood spurted from his nose. He heard his son cry out behind him. They had knocked him down and several men were kicking him, then they grabbed him by his hair and dragged him screaming through the street. As more blows rained down upon him, something in Harrison broke and with a keening sound, like some wild animal, he thrashed and shoved his way through the press of men as hands and clubs struck out at him. He stumbled, but regained his balance, and then, miraculously, he was in the clear and running down the street as fast as his legs could carry him.

He heard them running in pursuit and blind panic surged through him as he bolted down a narrow alleyway, tripped, fell, scrambled to his feet again and kept on running, not even knowing where he was running to, just fleeing in abject terror. He didn't stop until he was blocks away, completely out of breath. He collapsed against a pile of wooden crates stacked in an alley and cowered there, trembling, his breath rasping in his throat, tears streaming from his eyes and mingling with the blood. He drew his legs up to his chest, put his head down in his arms, and sat there, weeping in the dark.

Back at the docks, the mob hauled Ben Hallowell's pleasure skiff out of the water, tied ropes to it, and dragged it through the streets to the Common, where it was set on fire. One group broke off to go running across the open grass to Hallowell's house, where they pelted the windows with rocks and bricks. Another group stoned Harrison's windows while his wife cowered inside, hysterical with fear. Eventually, the mob broke up, to proceed in small groups to the taverns on the waterfront, where they toasted one another's courage and patriotic ardor before stumbling to their homes.

Boston had no street lamps yet, so at night, the streets were as dark as country roads. Zeke Chilton, Johnny Long, Dick Tillotsen, and Edward Crenshaw were staggering and weaving down Fish Street, their arms around one another's shoulders and their voices raised in drunken song when they were hailed by the watchman.

"Who goes there?"

"Freedom lovin' Sonsh'a Libi'ty, God damn yer eyes!" roared Chilton. He was the one whose club had felled Ben Hallowell, as he had proudly boasted no fewer than two dozen times that night to anyone who'd listen.

"You're drunk," the watchman said.

Chilton heaved a bottle at him and it shattered on the street. Mumbling curses to himself, the watchman beat a hasty retreat.

"That'll show'im," Chilton slurred, "God damn 'is eyes!"

"Liberty an' prop'ity!" shouted Johnny Long.

"God damn their eyes!" said Chilton, staggering against him.

From behind them came the sound of hoofbeats rapidly approaching.

"Liberty an' prop'ity!" yelled Tillotsen, turning around to face the rider, but he froze when he saw the horseman bearing down on them, his long black cloak billowing out behind him. "S'truth!" he said. "It's '*im*!"

The horseman's wild laughter echoed through the night.

A whip cracked. Tillotsen screamed with pain and dropped down to his knees, clutching at his face. Eyes rolling, the black horse reared up before them and the whip cracked once again. It snaked around Chilton's throat and pulled him to the ground. Crenshaw turned to run, but suddenly a dark figure was before him. A club flashed and Crenshaw fell, unconscious. Drakov swung the club again and Johnny Long crumpled to the street. A moment later, Chilton joined him, and then Tillotsen was struck down.

The next morning, all four men were discovered hanging from the stout boughs of the Liberty Tree in Boston Common. Pinned to the chest of each corpse was a placard reading, "Hellfire to the Sons of Liberty!"

4

For a change, no one interfered with the sheriff when he went to cut the latest display down off the Liberty Tree. Boston's mood was suddenly subdued. There had been riots, there had been looting and destruction, men had been beaten bloody and senseless, but this was the first time men had died.

Lucas, Finn, and Andre stood apart with Hunter on the fringes of the silent crowd that had gathered to watch Greenleaf and his men remove the corpses. Andre wore male clothing and to look at her, no one could tell she was a woman. She looked like a young boy of eighteen.

"It's started," Hunter said. "I had a feeling it would come to this."

"Hellfire to the Sons of Liberty," said Lucas. He glanced at Hunter. "That mean anything to you?"

Hunter shook his head. "I haven't been associating much with Tories. I'm one of the Sons of Liberty, you know." He reached inside his shirt and pulled out a small silver medal on a chain. It was stamped with an image of the Liberty Tree. "They all wear these," he said. "They were contributed by the silversmith, Paul Revere."

Ben Edes spotted Hunter and approached them. "A grim sight for a spring morning," he said tensely.

"Aye, that it is," said Hunter. "You know anything about this?"

Ben Edes shook his head. "A few of the people in the crowd are saying that the horseman did it."

"The horseman?" said Delaney.

Edes glanced at them. "It seems that Boston has a ghost, sir. One who rides a black horse and has no head. Forgive me, but I haven't had the pleasure of making your acquaintance."

"Oh, my apologies," Hunter said. "These are old friends of mine, Ben. Allow me to present Mr. Finn Delaney, Mr. Lucas Priest, and young squire Andrew Cross, Mr. Delaney's ward. This is my good friend, Benjamin Edes, editor and publisher of the *Boston Gazette*."

They shook hands. "Would that we could have met under more fortunate circumstances," Edes said. "You're new to Boston?"

"We only arrived yesterday," said Lucas, "from New York."

"I hear that there are many Tories in New York," said Edes, watching them closely for their reactions.

"Yes, but we have had our share of demonstrations, too," said Finn. "Of course, General Gage and his troops are quartered there, and they have largely kept events under control."

"Yes, so I have heard," said Edes. "I understand that Governor Bernard has requested aid from General Gage. He thinks that Boston should have troops. Would they have prevented this? I wonder. They say the horseman rode the streets last night and that this is his grisly handiwork."

"No one saw anything?" asked Hunter.

Edes shook his head. "A watchman saw Chilton and the others in the street last night," he said. "He said they were all drunk as lords. You heard about the *Liberty* affair? Hallowell seized Hancock's ship for smuggling. The *Romney*'s crew towed it out into the harbor, where it is protected by the *Romney*'s guns. A crowd gathered, but they were too late to prevent the ship being seized, so they turned their anger against Hallowell and his agents. Hallowell was beaten senseless. Harrison also, though he managed to escape. His son, Dick, was badly beaten and dragged through the street by his hair. Thomas Irving was set upon, as well. An ugly spectacle. Yonder you see what's left of Hallowell's boat. The mob dragged it from the water and burned it on the Common. They stoned Harrison's and Hallowell's homes, as well. Chilton was one of the mob's leaders, or at least so he claimed. They say he was boasting that it was he who broke Ben Hallowell's head for him and led the riot. He claimed to be a Son of Liberty, but Sam swears he had nothing to do with what occurred last night."

He glanced uncertainly at Lucas, Finn, and Andre, as if suddenly afraid that he had said too much.

"It's all right," Hunter said. "They're with us in the cause."

Edes nodded. "Forgive me, but these are troublesome times," he said. "A man cannot be too careful. The council is meeting even as we speak. Hancock has lodged a formal protest against the seizure of his vessel and a delegation is to be sent to Governor Bernard, requesting that the *Romney* be removed from port. Meanwhile, the customs agents have left their homes and taken refuge in Castle William. Nor can I blame them. No one ever wanted it to come to this."

"What has Sam said?" Hunter asked.

"He has called a special meeting at the Long Room," Edes said. "I was just now on my way there."

"Would it be possible for my friends to come, as well?" asked Hunter. "Or would that be an imposition?"

"If they are patriots, sir, and you vouch for their discretion, then they are indeed welcome. And I am sure our friends would want to know how things are going in New York. Come, I will take you there."

They went down Treamount Street, then turned into Dock Square. From there, they took Ann Street for a block or two until it became Fish street. The same streets in Boston often had different names from block to block, the better to enable citizens to orient themselves since there was, as yet, no organized system of house numbering. Fish Street became Ship Street after a few blocks, running close by Clark's Shipyard. They passed The Castle and The Mitre taverns and turned into the Salutation, a tavern on the corner of Salutation Alley and Ship Street whose devotees were fervent Whigs. It was not a fashionable tavern, catering mostly to the North End ship-wrights, caulkers, and mast-makers, but its sign depicted two gentlemen bowing to each other, which resulted in the tavern being nicknamed "The Two Palaverers." It was not as rowdy or notorious a tavern as The Bunch of Grapes, but it was here where the North Caucus met in its private room.

Sam Adams belonged to all three of Boston's caucuses, the

North, the Middle, and the South. It was Deacon Adams who had first organized these clubs, the word having grown from "caulker's club," since the majority of the original members were all in the shipbuilding trade. Here, in the smoke-filled private chamber known as the Long Room, much of the business of the Boston Assembly was actually conducted around a bowl of punch, with a roaring fire in the hearth. There were some sixty members in the North Caucus, but today, the group that gathered here were the members of the original Loyal Nine and the leaders of the Sons of Liberty.

There was Sam Adams' young cousin John from Braintree, plump, boyish-looking, and quick to speak. Hunter pointed out Dr. Joseph Warren and Dr. Benjamin Church; William Molineaux, the hardware merchant; Bill Campbell, the owner of the tavern; John Pulling, whose fame was to be eclipsed by Paul Revere's, though it was he who would hang the lanterns in the Christ's Church steeple to give Revere the signal that the British troops were coming; the gargantuan silversmith, Benjamin Burt, who weighed almost four hundred pounds and required the room of two men at the table; James "Jemmy" Otis, the flamboyant orator whose reason was slowly slipping away, rendering him unpredictable and temperamental, given to frequent emotional outbursts that often made no sense at all; young Josiah Quincy; the Cooper brothers, Samuel, the pastor of the Brattle Street Church, and William, the town clerk; Thomas Dawes; John Winslow and Thomas Melville, still only in his teens and fresh from Harvard, whose grandson Herman would one day write the immortal epic *Moby Dick*. The silversmith, Paul Revere, was also in attendance, stocky, square-faced, with his brown hair unpowdered, and his simple homespun looking shabby next to the slender Hancock's tailored finery. And, of course, there was Sam Adams, portly and rumpled, looking like someone's absentminded uncle, yet the real power behind the coming revolution. He called the meeting to order.

"Gentlemen, your indulgence, please," he said, rapping on the table with his knuckles. The room grew silent. Adams looked around. "I see that most of us are here. However, I note a few unfamiliar faces."

"These are Reese Hunter's friends, recently arrived from New York," said Edes. "Mr. Lucas Priest, Mr. Finn Delaney, and young Andrew Cross. They've come to observe events in

Boston for themselves and report back to our friends in the New York colony. Reese vouches for them."

"Very well," said Adams, nodding. "In that case, welcome, gentlemen. You have arrived upon a dark day, indeed. Four of our number have been foully slain and we are met to discuss how to proceed."

He looked around to make sure he had everyone's attention.

"There have been times," he said, "when we have not acted nobly. Yet, hard times demand hard actions. And the mobs cannot always be controlled. Things have been done in the name of our cause that I regret, despite the fact that our cause has been advanced by them. Men have been set upon and beaten, and yet I cannot truly say that they did not well deserve a beating. There are those whose homes have been invaded and torn down, yet they were men who, by their actions, sought to invade our rights and to tear down our liberties. Men have been pressured to resign their offices, and yet it can be said that tyrants have no business holding office."

"Hear, hear," said someone.

"We must, of necessity," said Adams, "use whatever means are open to us in order to achieve our ends, and sometimes those means are hard, indeed . . . but, gentlemen, we have never yet committed murder."

"Not yet," said Quincy, grimly, and several of the men grumbled their assent.

"Not *ever*," Adams said. "Not ever." He looked around at all of them. His hands began to tremble, so he clasped them. "We are patriots, my friends, not murderers. And if the time should ever come when blood is to be spilled, then let it be in honorable warfare, and not foul murder in the night!"

At the mention of the word "warfare," the men began to mumble among themselves.

"Yes, gentlemen, war," said Adams. "It is the first time we have used that word among us, though I have known for some time now that war must inevitably come. It is not yet time for us to speak of war in public, but those of us present in this room must give due consideration to that eventuality. For I am certain that it must come to that. We in the colonies are not, as they call us in Parliament, 'rebellious children.' We are grown into adulthood and the time has come for us to make our own way in the world, independent of Great Britain."

"Amen to that!" said Edes, and several voices joined him in chorus.

"But must it come to war?" said Otis. "Gentlemen," he said, rising to his feet, "there is no more noble society on earth than that of Britain! Why, we are all of us Englishmen! True, I will admit, we have had our disagreements with our mother country, but surely these disagreements can be settled without resort to—"

"Oh, do sit down, Jemmy," Hancock said softly, in a weary tone.

"I have the right to speak!"

"Sit down, Jemmy," said Bill Campbell. "Sam has the floor now."

Amid a chorus of "Sit down, Jemmy! Sit down!" Otis reluctantly resumed his seat and fixed a morose gaze upon the punch bowl. He said nothing more, but his lips moved silently.

"There was a time, Jemmy," said Adams, sadly, "when your fire was the brightest flame among us. But now the time is past for speeches. And the time is long past for talk of reconciliation. English we may be, by law, but when we are denied our rights as Englishmen under England's law, then that law has ceased to serve us. Englishmen we may be, but Americans we must become!"

"Well said, well said!"

"Spoken like a patriot!"

"Enough," said Adams. "As I have said, the time is past for speeches. We must free ourselves from England, but England will never willingly let us go. It is our duty, gentlemen, to prepare the populace for what must come. We must gain their sympathy and unite them to our cause. But we cannot hope to do so if we should stoop to murder. *There must be no killing.*"

"There has already been killing," said John Winslow.

"And we must not add to it," said Adams.

"Tell that to MacIntosh and Swift," said Edes. "They are not men to turn the other cheek, Sam."

"No one asks them to turn the other cheek, Ben," Adams said. "The murderers must be found and brought to justice. Aye, let them hang, but let them be tried for murder in a court of law and be brought to their punishment by jury! We must have no lynchings by the mob! There are those in England, gentlemen, who are sympathetic to our cause. They will not long remain so if we start to murder our own citizens. Boston sets an example for all the other colonies. Their eyes are all upon us. Already, there are many who decry our methods, who condemn mob violence, as we must openly condemn it. You saw how the people of the town responded when the mob destroyed Hutchinson's house. What will they say of us if we start to murder Tories? Governor Bernard has petitioned General Gage for troops. Would you play into his hands by giving Gage a reason to dispatch them?"

"The troops may well be sent in any case," said Church, sourly.

"Then let them come as a further affront against our liberties," said Adams, "not as protection for the citizenry against roving killers in the night. How can we cry out, in indignation, that the Tories murder freedom-loving men if we respond in kind? I say again, the killers must be found and brought to justice. Our hands must remain clean in this affair."

"But how are we to find the murderers?" asked Cooper.

"Aye, where does a man look to find a ghost?" asked someone else.

"I have never heard of a ghost who was political," said Adams, wryly. "Rest assured, gentlemen, this mysterious so-called 'headless horsemen' we've all heard of is made of flesh and blood. *Tory* flesh and blood. He is someone with the wit to hide his face so that he remains unknown and, doubtless, he has Tory confederates to help him. We must find out who they are so that they may be punished for their crime."

"But how are we to find out who they are, Sam?" Hancock asked. "Of whom can we make our inquiries? I hardly think that the Tories shall share anything they know with us. The sympathies of every man who is present in this room are well known to all of them."

"Not every man," said Hunter. "They do not know my friends here."

"Nor, for that matter, do *we* know them," Paul Revere said. "No offense intended."

"None taken," said Lucas. "We know that we are strangers here and only present because our friend, Reese Hunter, vouched for us. But we are patriots, the same as you, and there are many in New York who think as we do. We've come to confer with Boston's patriot leaders, to share goodwill and seek advice, but we have also come to offer help if needed. Now as Mr. Hancock said, if most of you are known to the Tories here in Boston, then you can hardly expect them to help you find whoever killed your friends. However, we three are not known here. We arrived only yesterday, and except for Reese, you are the first citizens of Boston we have spoken to. We could just as easily be Tories recently arrived in Boston. We could go where the Tories gather and strike up friendships with them, then pass on anything we learn to you."

Adams looked thoughtful. "Your idea has merit," he said. "But you realize that you would be taking a great risk if they discovered that you were deceiving them?"

"We have already taken a great risk in coming here and meeting with known radicals," said Delaney. "That's the sort of thing that could tarnish a gentleman's reputation."

His comment provoked laughter.

"You may joke, sir," Adams said, "but spying is a very serious business."

"So is murder," said Andre.

"Yes, so it is," Adams replied gravely. "How old are you, lad?"

"Eighteen, sir," Andre said.

"Eighteen," said Adams, with a sigh. "Eighteen is very young."

"I see others here scarcely older than myself," said Andre. "And seventeen is old enough to join the militia."

"True," said Adams, "but drilling with a rifle does not make one a man."

"Nor does plotting in back rooms or smashing windows in the middle of the night," said Andre.

Hancock chuckled. "He has you there, Sam."

"A man is one who is willing to stand up for his beliefs, sir," Andre said. "I came here willing to stand up for mine."

Adams smiled. "Well said, young man. Very well then, I accept the offer of your help. We need all the help that we can get and we could do with a spy or two among the Tories of this town. I would dearly like to find out who this 'headless horseman' is and who his friends are. He could scarcely have accounted for those four men alone. But for this plan to work, you must be careful not to be seen with any of us. We must devise a way for you to secretly report your findings."

"With your permission, sir," said Lucas, "we would rather see to that ourselves. The moment we discover anything, we will send Reese to you with the information or one of us will contact you directly, at a time and place of our own choosing. In that manner, if there is to be no set time and place for us to meet, then no one can find out about it."

Adams stared at him for a moment. "You sound as if you have some experience in such matters, Mr. Priest."

"As you yourself said, Mr. Adams, these are troubled times," Lucas replied. "I have merely learned how to be cautious. And now, with your permission, if we are to begin tonight, we'd best be on our way. Good day, gentlemen. You will be hearing from us."

"Good fortune to you," Adams said. He waited till they'd left the room, then turned to Paul Revere. "Paul, I think it would be best if someone were to keep a weather eye upon those three. That new apprentice of yours you've been telling me about, young Jonathan, who came here with his uncle from the Pennsylvania frontier, you say he is a most resourceful lad?"

"Aye, made friends with the Indians, he did," Revere said. "I've seen him use his fowling piece to drop a deer at over a hundred paces. Moves through the forest like a cat, he does."

"You said that he was eager to join us," Adams said. "Let us see, then, how resourceful he can be. Follow those three and find out where they go, then send young Jonathan to keep an eye on them discreetly and inform us of their movements."

"I'm on my way," Revere said, picking up his coat and hat.

"You don't trust them?" Edes said. "But Hunter vouched for them."

"Reese Hunter seems like a good man," Adams said. "MacIntosh speaks highly of him. But then Mac speaks highly of anyone who will stand him to a drink. We have learned, most tragically, that there exists a group among the Tories who will stop at nothing to oppose us, not even murder. If we send men to spy upon them, then they can just as easily send men to spy on us. I, too, have learned how to be cautious, Ben."

They had gone about eight blocks when Delaney said, "We're being followed."

"I know," said Hunter. "It's Revere. I spotted him about two blocks ago. Adams must've sent him after us."

"Not a very trusting sort, is he?" Lucas said, smiling to himself.

"That man was born too late," said Hunter. "He would have made one hell of an intelligence chief."

"Do we shake him?" Andre asked.

"No, what for?" Delaney said. "Let him report back to Adams that we're doing exactly what we said we'd do."

"This is as far as I'd better go," said Hunter. "The Peacock Tavern is around the corner, at the end of the street. They should be serving the ordinary about now, so there'll be plenty of people there, especially after what happened this morning." He paused. "What'll you do if you run into Drakov? He knows you."

"Well, we don't know for sure he's here yet," Lucas said. "But if we should happen to run into him, we'll try to take him alive."

"Knowing Drakov, that's not going to be easy. Especially if he's got friends among the Tories," Hunter said.

"I know," said Lucas. "But we have to try to find out how many clones of himself he's made and where he's planted them. We won't take any chances, though. We can't afford having him cause a temporal disruption."

"Meaning you'll kill him if you have to," Hunter said.

"Only if we have to," Lucas said. "In which case, we may have to clock out in a hurry, so be where we can find you."

Hunter nodded. "I'll be at my place. Either way, you'll be getting back to me tonight?"

"Soon as we get a chance," said Lucas. "In the meantime, we'd better see about renting a place of our own somewhere in town. It wouldn't do for three Tories from New York to be seen associating with a Son of Liberty."

"You can probably get rooms upstairs at the tavern," said Hunter, "but it's liable to be a little noisy. If you want something more private, ask around. A lot of the merchants usually have property to rent around the waterfront. Don't be afraid to dicker price, it's expected."

"Thanks."

"Good luck. And watch yourselves, okay? You're my only ticket out of here."

The tavern was crowded, as Hunter had predicted. They had to wait a while for a table to be free, so they went up to the bar. There was no sign of Drakov, but they kept their eyes on the door, just in case. They each had a brace of loaded dueling pistols hidden underneath their coats and small lasers tucked away in well-concealed shoulder holsters underneath their shirts. Wearing them that way meant they wouldn't be able to get at them very quickly, but it was a necessary tradeoff for optimum concealment.

Ordnance Section had experimented with disguising the laser pistols as more primitive weapons, but none of those experiments had proved terribly successful in terms of being able to wear the weapons hidden. And the plasma weapons were simply too large for any such attempt to be practical. The smallest one was about the size of a 10 mm. semiautomatic with a slightly longer barrel. On covert field missions, it was generally standard practice not to carry them unless absolutely necessary. For added safety, each weapon was failsafed so that if the safety catch wasn't properly released, the weapon would self-destruct. The lasers would simply fuse and become useless lumps of molten nysteel. Anyone holding the weapon when the failsafe mechanism became activated would have a very brief instant of warning as the weapon suddenly started to become extremely hot. If that warning was not heeded and the weapon wasn't immediately dropped, the result would be excruciatingly painful and permanently disabling.

Many temporal agents simply resorted to more primitive, but in proper hands, no less effective tools, such as various martial arts weapons or lead projectile pistols. Steiger, who was a weapons collector, often went armed with a semiautomatic pistol or two. Others carried tiny, flat, plastic dart guns known as "stingers," small enough to be concealed in the palm of the hand and loaded with slim magazines that held miniature needle darts loaded with powerful tranquilizer drugs or instantaneously lethal poisons. These weapons were almost completely silent in operation, making only a brief, very high-pitched whistling noise when fired. Each of the agents were armed with one of these, snapped butt down into spring-loaded holsters strapped to their forearms and hidden underneath their sleeves. Each of them also carried a slim commando knife in a sheath strapped either to the forearm or carried down the back. None of them carried any weapons in their pockets, the better to avoid the possibility of a skilled pickpocket coming away with an unexpected prize.

Fortunately, the clothing of this period was loose and somewhat bulky, which helped to hide the weapons, but they still only planned to use them as a last resort. If there was a need for any shooting to be done, especially with witnesses about, they would first reach for the dueling pistols, which to all outward appearances, looked no different from any other flintlock pistol of the time. In fact, they had been constructed in the 27th century of superior materials and cleverly designed so that they could be loaded with powder and ball and fired like any other flintlock, or a strip of metal in front of the trigger guard could be pushed forward and a narrow, spring-loaded magazine could be inserted, turning the dueling pistol into a semiautomatic that fired specially designed, high-velocity ball ammo. The hammer for the semiautomatic function was machined into the flintlock hammer, so that there were actually two hammers, side by side, with the hammer for the semiauto designed to strike a hidden transfer bar that relayed the impact to the primer. The barrel of the dueling pistol was in reality an ingeniously camouflaged slide and extractor, with the actual barrel concealed inside. Only a close examination would reveal that the pistols were much more than they appeared to be.

While they were waiting for a table to be free, Lucas, Finn, and Andre ordered ale at the bar and took careful stock of their surroundings. Not surprisingly, most of the conversation centered around the four men who had been found hanging from the Liberty Tree.

"If you ask me, they got what they damn well deserved," one man sitting at a table close to them was saying to his friends. "It's time those Sons of Violence were treated to a taste of their own medicine!"

"I'm sorry, John, I don't agree. I say no good will come of it," said one of his companions. "Say what you will about the Sons of Liberty, they are hooligans and skulkers, to be sure, but they have never murdered anyone."

"They might just as well have killed Ben Hallowell," the man named John said. "They split his skull for him! It's only by the grace of God he was not killed! And how many people have they stoned? A thrown rock can kill as surely as a musket ball! I tell you, it is only by pure chance that they have killed no one as yet. Perhaps now they will think twice before they attack a loyal subject of the king!"

"And perhaps now that four of them were slain, they will not hesitate to take a Tory life," the second man said. "Where does it stop, John? Already it is no longer safe to walk the streets at night."

"And who is to blame for that?" asked John. "The Sons of Lawlessness, that's who! What is Boston coming to? Our officials are afraid to enforce the laws; the governor is helpless; the sheriff hides his face; the watchmen hide whenever they hear a group of men approaching, if they are not themselves part of the mob; the militia cannot be counted on, for the radicals control them; and unlike New York, we have no British troops who can keep order. Are we merely to sit idle and do nothing while Boston is reduced to anarchy? Something must be done! I, for one, am not ashamed to say that I applaud whoever was responsible for hanging those four men! They got no less than what was coming to them! Hellfire to the Sons of Liberty, I say! Hellfire and damnation to them all!"

"Hear, hear!" said several other men at nearby tables.

"Is that your answer then?" said John's friend. "That we take the law into our own hands? If we do that, then we are no better than the radical scum who call themselves the Sons of Liberty."

"So what would you have us do, Carruthers?" John said. "Give in to the rioters?"

"No, most certainly not," said Carruthers. "But I, for one, have no stomach for committing murder. Violence merely begets more violence. I think Governor Bernard has the right idea and I think we should give him our support, rather than condemn him. He has petitioned General Gage to send troops from New York. We, as private citizens, can add our voices to his. For we *are* private citizens, gentlemen, not soldiers. We have families to care for and businesses to run. Let the king's troops deal with the lawbreakers. Mark my words, you'll see no more riots and demonstrations when the troops arrive."

"On the contrary, sir," said Lucas. "You may well see even more riots and demonstrations."

They turned to look at him. "What do you mean, sir?" asked Carruthers.

"Forgive me," Lucas said, "but I could not help but overhear your remarks. And though I have no doubt but that they were well intentioned, they were just as surely wrong."

"Indeed?" Carruthers said stiffly. "And who might you be, sir, that you speak with such authority about these matters?"

"One who knows firsthand," said Lucas. "My name is Lucas Priest and these are my companions, Mr. Finn Delaney and his ward, young Andrew Cross. Until recently, we were shopkeepers in New York."

"New York, you say?"

"That's right," said Delaney. "Before you all decide to join your governor in petitioning General Gage for troops, you might want to know just what it means to have British soldiers quartered in your town. You should know what manner of men are to be found in the British army. The officers are often gentlemen, that's true, but the enlisted men are from society's dregs, often men who chose the army over prison, which would have been their destination."

"And you should know how their officers must keep these men in line," added Lucas. "Before you start clamoring for troops to keep order here in Boston, consider if you want your wives and children to see the spectacle of soldiers being whipped in public till their backs are bloody for the least offenses."

"Whipped in public, do you say?"

"Aye, and the lash laid on by their Negro drummers, no less," continued Finn. "And if such a spectacle does not offend you, then consider what ideas such displays might give your slaves. Consider also that soldiers of the Crown are permitted to seek employment among the civilian population when they are not on duty. And they will work more cheaply than your average laborer. In New York, we have seen many men lose work and have their sympathies turned to the radical cause as a result. We have had our worship and our rest disturbed by the troops drilling on the Sabbath. We have had our stores reduced by being charged to supply rum and victuals for the troops. And we have often seen our daughters, their heads turned by the sight of pretty uniforms, used poorly by the soldiers, many of whom do not hesitate to rape when they cannot have their way. Is that what you want for Boston, sir? For that is what you'll get if troops are sent here. You will see the public feeling turn against the soldiers and against those who asked for them, as well. I have no sympathy for radicals, far from it, but if General Gage sends troops to Boston, then you will see an increase in their numbers, I assure you."

"There!" said John Hewitt. "There speaks a man who knows! You see, Carruthers? Troops are not the answer. We do not require outsiders. It is for the citizens of Boston to see to their own troubles. And as we have seen this morning, there are those who do not hesitate to do so!"

"You speak of murder, John Hewitt," said Carruthers.

"Does he?" asked Lucas. "I did not know those men, but if they were indeed guilty of the things you say, then I do not think that you can call it murder."

"What else can you call it?" Carruthers asked.

"I will reply to your question with another question, sir," said Lucas. "Was it murder when we fought in the recent war against the French and Indians to protect our homes and property? And is it murder to protect yourself against a mob that would tear down your house and belabor you with clubs and stones? Is it murder to strike down men who would tar and feather you, as the radicals have done to officials in New York? Do you know what it means to be tarred and feathered or ridden on a fence rail until your groin splits? Is it murder when you are forced to kill in order to protect your life and liberty?"

"No, by God, it most certainly is not!" responded Hewitt, smashing his fist down on the table. "Those four Sons of Licentiousness were never murdered! They were brought to justice!"

"That reasonable men should call a lynching justice frightens me," Carruthers said. "Had those men been arrested? Were charges brought against them? Was there a trial and was there a jury to convict them?"

"I do not know how things are in Boston," Finn said, "having only recently arrived here, but in New York, we would be hard-pressed indeed to find a jury to convict such men. The presence of the soldiers and the way the troops comport themselves make many of the citizens inclined to sympathize with radicals. And the Sons of Liberty are diligent in placing their friends upon the juries or threatening those who might have voted to convict. Would *you* render a guilty verdict if you knew that the Sons of Liberty would pay you and your family a visit in the middle of the night?"

Carruthers sighed heavily. "I must confess that I probably would not. I have a family to think of."

"You see?" said Lucas. "Do not blame yourself, Mr. Carruthers. No one can blame a man for thinking of the welfare of his family. And it is for the sake of the welfare of our families that something must be done about these people. I don't know how others think, but as for myself, I am encouraged that there are men in Boston who are willing to take a stand on the side of justice and do what must be done. We had begun to think that there were no men of courage left in these colonies. I am glad to discover we were wrong."

"You are a man after my own heart, sir," Hewitt said. "Will you and your two friends do me the honor of having a drink with me?"

"Thank you, it would be our pleasure," Lucas said.

Carruthers pushed his chair back and got up. "Forgive me, gentlemen," he said, "but I cannot in good conscience lift my glass to toast a lynching. I may not have a ready answer to your arguments, but I cannot believe that there is not a better way to solve our problems. May God help us all if there is not. Good night to you."

Hewitt shook his head as Carruthers left. "Do not think ill of him, gentlemen," he said, as they joined him at the table. "He means well."

"I am sure he does," said Lucas. "I cannot fault him for his principles. I only regret that he has not the backbone to stand up and fight for them."

"Would you?" said Hewitt. "Be willing to fight, I mean?"

Lucas grimaced. "I *was* willing to fight, for all the good it did me," he said, improvising as he went along. "To protest the Stamp Act, I was asked to join a boycott against British goods. If you can call it asking, that is, when then give you no other choice. I sought to reason with them. I am only a simple shopkeeper, I told them. How would my refusing to sell my customers the goods they wished to purchase solve the problem of the Stamp Act? And *why* should I refuse them? If a woman wished to purchase silk imported from Great Britain, how could selling her that silk be treason to the colonies? Whom would it hurt if I chose not to sell it to her? Would it hurt the ministry? Or would it not hurt my customer and my own profit, which I have a right to? And what about the British goods I had in storage, which I had paid good money for? What was I to do with those? How could I conduct my business if I could not sell the goods that I had purchased? Would Parliament repeal the Stamp Tax simply because I was losing money?"

"And how did they respond?" said Hewitt.

"Need you ask?" Lucas replied. "They threatened me. We had words and I told them to get out. It almost came to blows, but they left, warning me that I would soon have cause to reconsider. I feared there would be trouble, so that night I slept inside my shop. My partner, Finn, and Andrew slept upstairs. Sometime past midnight, I was awakened by my windows being shattered. Finn and Andrew heard the noise and they ran down to help me, but there were just too many of them. They covered their faces, or blackened them with soot so that they could not be recognized, but I knew they were the same men who had threatened me earlier that day. We tried to fight them, but it was no use. Andrew had his nose bloodied and his head cut, Finn was knocked down, senseless, and I was seized and held with my arms pinned behind my back, forced to watch as they ransacked our wares and destroyed our shop. We lost everything."

"Damn the bastards!" Hewitt said.

"Aye, damn them, indeed," said Finn, following Priest's lead. "What they didn't break, they stole. What they didn't steal, they threw out into the street and burned. We hoped to make up some of our losses by selling the goods we had stored in the warehouse, but seeing the damage done to our shop, our customers stayed away. They were afraid to be seen buying goods from traitors! We were forced to sell what we had left in storage to other merchants, who had agreed to join the boycott and planned to keep the goods in storage until the boycott ended. We could not afford to do that, so we were forced to sell our goods in storage at a loss and leave New York."

"Shameful," Hewitt said. "Shameful, indeed."

"Things are not much better in the other colonies," said Lucas. "There are even more radicals in Rhode Island than in New York, but at least here in Boston, you seem to have men with the courage to stand up to them."

"I'd like to shake their hands, whoever they may be," said Andre.

"I only wish that I'd been there to help them" said Delaney.

"Perhaps, next time, you can," said Hewitt. He leaned toward them and lowered his voice. "Have you heard of the headless horseman?"

Lucas frowned. "The headless horseman?"

"There are those who say he is a ghost," said Hewitt. "He rides at night, on a black stallion. He appears out of nowhere, strikes out at the Sons of Liberty, and then disappears again without a trace."

"What sort of joke is this?" asked Finn.

"The four men found hanging in the Common this morning did not think it was a joke," said Hewitt.

"Who is this horseman?" Andre asked.

"No one knows," said Hewitt. "But word has it that he leads a band of men known as the Hellfire Club, loyal subjects of King George, who are not afraid to do what must be done to bring law and order back to Boston. And word has it that there is room among that band of men for those with the courage to join them."

"Where can these men be found?" asked Lucas.

"I have heard," said Hewitt, "that there is a certain country chapel where they meet. In fact, I have been curious to go myself to their next meeting. Perhaps you would like to come along?"

They exchanged glances.

"Yes," said Lucas, with a smile. "Yes, I think we'd like that very much, indeed."

5 _____

They took two rooms upstairs at the inn, one for Lucas and one for Finn and Andre, since Andre was posing as his "ward." The bed was barely large enough for Delaney alone, so no one thought it was unusual when they asked to have a cot brought in for "young Andrew."

"One of us should go and tell Hunter what's going on," said Andre.

"Yeah, I suppose you're right," said Lucas. "I can clock on over there and be back in—"

"No, I don't think that would be such a good idea," Andre said. "I was thinking maybe I should walk over there alone."

Lucas frowned. "Why?"

"For all we know, Adams is still having us watched," she said. "If that's the case, then one of us should be seen going over to Hunter's. That way, we'll appear to be doing exactly what we said we'd do."

"She's got a point," Delaney said, nodding.

"Besides," said Andre, "I'd like to find out if they're still keeping tabs on us. We've got no idea what to expect from this scenario. If I spot anyone following me, I don't want to have to wonder if it's someone Adams sent or somebody else. I can flush a tail much better on my own than with you two along and it would look less conspicuous if only one of us left to meet with Hunter. We need to convince Adams that we know what

we're doing and that we can be trusted, otherwise we're liable
to be tripping over Sons of Liberty everywhere we go."

"Okay," said Lucas. "I guess you're right. But be careful.
The streets of Boston aren't safe after dark these days."

She grinned at him. "I learned how to take care of myself
long before I met you, Lucas," she said. "But I appreciate the
thought. See you guys in a while."

She picked up her coat and hat and left the room. Delaney
went over to the window and pulled the curtain back slightly so
he could look out into the street below. A few moments later,
he saw Andre come out into the street. He continued to watch.
Several seconds later, someone came out after her and quickly
crossed the street, keeping to the shadows, heading in the same
direction.

"She was right," Delaney said. "Adams still has somebody
watching us."

"Was it Revere?" Lucas said, joining him at the window.

"I couldn't tell for sure," Delaney said, letting the curtain
fall back into position and turning around. "Could've been
someone else, I—"

He suddenly threw himself to one side, hit the floor and
rolled, coming up to a kneeling position with his pistol cocked
and ready.

"Well, that was certainly amusing," Dr. Darkness said.
"What will you do for your next trick?"

He had appeared sitting in the wooden chair across the room,
with his legs crossed casually and a heavy blackthorn walking
stick held across his lap. He was dressed in dark brown tweeds
and a long, brown Inverness wool coat, which he wore
unbuttoned. He wore a heavy gold watch chain in his tweed
vest and a paisley silk ascot loosely tied around his neck. A
brown fedora was tilted rakishly low over his right eye. They
could see the back of the chair right through him. He seemed
to flicker like a ghost on a television screen, parts of his body
appearing solid one moment and transparent the next, the result
of his atomic structure having been permanently tachyonized,
making him "the man who was faster than light."

Delaney exhaled heavily and lowered the hammer on the
gun. "Christ, Doc, I wish to hell you wouldn't *do* that!"

"What did you expect me to do, Delaney, come to the door
and knock?" said Darkness. "Somehow I don't think you'd

enjoy explaining to the locals what a ghost was doing knocking on your door in the middle of the night."

Delaney got up and put away the pistol.

"I always did rather enjoy Boston," Darkness said, pushing his hat back on his head, "but not during this particular time period. Another hundred years or so and it will be a worthwhile place to spend a weekend." He reached inside his coat and produced a bottle of wine. "I took the liberty of bringing this up from the wine cellar," he said. "Not exactly your California red, but I suppose it will do if you're not terribly particular."

He tossed the bottle to Delaney. Finn caught it one-handed and went over to the sideboard, where they had a decanter and some glasses.

"Come to check up on the old prototype, eh, Doc?" said Lucas, wryly.

"No, I just happened to be passing through this century and I thought I'd stop by for a drink," said Darkness, sarcastically.

Delaney held a glass of wine out to him and Darkness negligently reached for it. His hand passed right through it. Delaney almost dropped the glass. Darkness frowned and grunted with annoyance. He reached for the glass again, this time more deliberately, and succeeded in taking it from Delaney's hand.

"It's getting much worse, isn't it?" said Lucas.

"Well, it isn't getting any better," Darkness said. "How about you? Any problems?"

"So far, so good," said Lucas.

"Taken any unscheduled trips lately?" Darkness asked.

Lucas grimaced. "Not lately, no. I try not to allow myself to have any stray thoughts about specific times and places. I do my best to keep my mind on the here and now, wherever the here and now might be."

"Don't you find that a bit of a strain?" asked Darkness.

"It was a hell of a strain at first, but it seems to be getting easier. I guess my concentration is improving."

"What about when you go to bed at night? Don't you find your mind wandering? Do you have nightmares?"

"I meditate," said Lucas. "I try to focus my mind. Like I said, it seems to be getting easier. I haven't had any nightmares for a while. At least, none I can remember. And I keep waking up in the same place, which seems rather encouraging."

"Yes, it certainly does," said Darkness. "Perhaps you're

finally getting used to it. On the other hand, perhaps its because you're exercising greater mental discipline. One would think that would go by the boards when you fell asleep . . . unless you're conditioning yourself with some sort of auto-suggestion through your meditation." He frowned. "It would be just like you to find a way to screw up the field testing by exercising greater self-control."

"Well, excuse me all to hell," said Lucas, sourly.

"You're missing the point, Priest," Darkness said. "While it is certainly laudable that you're working to improve your already considerable powers of concentration, it is nevertheless not the object of this exercise."

"Oh, it's an exercise?" said Lucas. "Forgive me, I thought we were talking about my life here."

"Which, I will remind you, I had gone to particular trouble to preserve," said Darkness. "The point is that an infant does not learn to walk by using various objects to steady itself. At some point, it has to let go and fall down a few times."

"Yeah, well, if I should happen to 'fall down,' as you put it," Lucas said, "I'll wind up in some other time period, possibly in a highly unpleasant situation. And in case it's escaped your notice, we're on a mission here. I don't exactly have the time for any side trips."

"Your mission here is only of secondary importance," Darkness said. "The telempathic temporal transponder will revolutionize time travel, but the field testing has to be completed first. That is the primary consideration, above everything else."

"To you, maybe," Lucas said. "To me, the primary consideration is staying in control. One slip and I'm liable to pop off to some other century. You have any idea what it's like having to live with that?"

"As a matter of fact, I do," said Darkness. "I have to live with the fact that I may discorporate at any time and cease to exist . . . or exist everywhere at once. Becoming some sort of cosmic phenomenon was never my ambition, Priest, but it was the price I had to pay in order to perfect the device I've given you."

"Well, forgive me if I'm not suitably grateful," Lucas said, "but I never asked to be your guinea pig."

"I don't expect your thanks," said Darkness.

"My *thanks*? For *what*? For playing God with my life?"

Lucas snorted. "Christ, Darkness, your arrogance is simply unbelievable!"

"Arrogance?" said Darkness. "Mine is the greatest scientific mind in the history of temporal physics. That isn't arrogance, it simply happens to be the truth. And there have been many times when I've wished it were not so. It's an awesome burden. I must find a way to overcome the confluence phenomenon because, indirectly, it was my work that brought it about. In the meantime, it's imperative to prevent the occurrence of a timestream split, because that could bring about a chain reaction of temporal disasters that nothing could overcome. The telempathic transponder is a vital element to maintaining the integrity of the timeline and you're the key to its success. Your personal concerns are insignificant compared to that responsibility. I can't afford to be concerned with individual sensitivities, Priest. There's far too much at stake. The instability in the timestream is increasing because of the confluence phenomenon. We must try to buy some time . . . before we literally run out of it."

Lucas sighed. "All right. What do you want me to do?"

"Let go," said Darkness. "Stop fighting it. You won't be able to keep it up anyway. Sooner or later, you're bound to succumb to the strain. The transponder is designed to function on conscious thought. You have to become adapted to it just as an infant must learn how to walk. Eventually, you should be able to control it as easily as you control your appendages. But you have to give yourself a chance to become accustomed to it. In order to learn how to exercise proper control, you must first take the risk of losing it."

"And what happens if I lose it and translocate to some other time period right in the middle of a crisis, when my partners need me?" Lucas said.

"It's a risk you'll simply have to take," Darkness replied. "If you can keep your head about you and refrain from panic, you should be able to return just as quickly. That's the advantage of the telempathic transponder. You don't have to waste time programming transition coordinates. It's all designed into its particle-level chronicircuitry. Your thought triggers the process and the desired transition coordinates are automatically computed and selected. Don't be afraid of it, Priest. Give it a chance to serve you."

"And what if it induces molecular instability?" asked Lucas.

"Highly unlikely," Darkness said. "I believe I've solved that flaw in the process."

"You *believe*?" said Lucas. "You mean you don't know for sure?"

"I'm a scientist, Priest. I can never know anything for sure. What do you want, guarantees? There aren't any in life."

"Or in death, it seems," said Lucas.

"I would strongly suggest that you stop agonizing over the metaphysical implications of your existence," Darkness said. "Concentrate on what you know and leave eschatological questions to philosophers. Otherwise you'll only give yourself an ulcer. My regards to Miss Cross."

He disappeared.

"That man is a stone lunatic," said Lucas.

"Maybe," said Delaney. "But like it or not, he also happens to be right. He *does* have the greatest scientific mind in the history of temporal physics. If I was in his shoes, I'd probably be a bit around the bend myself."

"A bit around the bend?" said Lucas. "Hell, he *is* the bend."

"Don't think about Hell," said Delaney, with a grin. "If you do, the transponder just might send you there."

"Somehow I doubt that even Dr. Robert Darkness could have programmed *those* transition coordinates," said Lucas, with a wry smile. "Although on the other hand, I'm not all that sure I'd be surprised."

Andre had spotted her tail within four blocks. And she knew right away that it wasn't Paul Revere. Whoever he was, he was very good. Revere had been clumsy in his shadowing attempts, but this man moved with a quick and silent grace, like a cat, keeping a careful distance and taking full advantage of the darkness. Several times, she had almost thought she lost him, but he was always there, dogging her heels persistently. She was almost to Hunter's place on Long Lane when she decided to make her move.

It was time, she thought, to demonstrate to Samuel Adams that the Sons of Liberty were not the only ones adept at skulking in the night. She turned a corner into Milk Street, ducked into an alleyway, and waited. She reached behind her neck and drew her knife. The shadower was on top of her almost before she knew it. He moved through the dark streets without a sound. As he passed the mouth of the alleyway, she quickly stepped out behind him, brought her arm around his neck, yanked him close, and held the knife up to his face. He gasped.

"If you resist, I'll cut your throat from ear to ear," she said, though she had no intention of making good on the threat.

"Don't!" he said. "Please!"

She swung him around and pressed him up against a wall, holding the knife point to his throat. He stared at her with fear. She quickly patted him down and relieved him of a large hunting knife in a beaded sheath at his belt.

She was surprised to see that he was just a boy, no more than sixteen or seventeen years old, slim and slightly shorter than she was, with light brown hair, dark eyes, and smooth, regular features. He probably hadn't even started to shave yet.

"You've been following me ever since I left the inn," she said. "Who are you?" For added emphasis, she pressed the knife point against his throat, not hard enough to break the skin, but enough to frighten him.

"J-Jonathan Small," he stammered. "I—I meant no harm, I swear."

"Who sent you?"

He swallowed hard. "M-Mr. Revere. I—I am his apprentice. He—he said that I should follow you and your friends, see where you went and—and whom you met with."

"So," she said, taking away the knife. "It seems Sam Adams doesn't trust us. You're a Son of Liberty, then? Show me your medallion."

Jonathan looked down at the ground. "I—I haven't got one," he said. "Mr. Revere said that if I performed my task well, I would be accepted But it seems that I have failed. They will not want me now."

"If they will not want you, then neither should they want Revere," she said. "It took me far less time to spot him following us from The Two Palaverers than it took me to notice you, and you may tell him that I said so. Where did you learn to stalk like that?"

"I learned my woodcraft from the Indians in Pennsylvania," he said. "They taught me how to hunt with bow and arrow, how to use a knife and hatchet, and to move through the woods without making a sound. I thought that I had learned it well, yet it appears that I could not even fool a city dweller."

She smiled. "Don't be so hard on yourself, Jonathan," she

said. "You would easily fool most people, but I am not without some knowledge of woodcraft myself."

"How old are you?" he asked.

"Eighteen," she lied.

"You are scarcely older than myself," said Jonathan.

"True," she said, "but sometimes a year or two can make all the difference in the world. I have seen my share of hardship and adversity. You have nothing to be ashamed of, Jonathan. You did very well, indeed. Do your friends call you Johnny?"

"Yes."

"Well, Johnny, mine call me Andre, because my mother was a Basque. I hope we can be friends."

She gave him back his knife and held out her hand. He smiled and they shook.

"I'm on my way to see Reese Hunter and tell him that we have made contact with the Tories," she said. "With a man named John Hewitt, who promises to take us to a meeting of men who follow the horseman and oppose the Sons of Liberty. And give a message to Sam Adams that if he continues to send men to follow us, he may give us away. We are already risking much. We do not need him adding to the risk. Tell him we came to him forthrightly to offer our help. He must make up his mind whether to trust us or not."

Johnny nodded. "I will tell Mr. Revere, exactly as you said. And for whatever it is worth, I will also tell him that I trust you."

"Thank you, Johnny," Andre said. "Now perhaps you'd best be on your way before——"

The stillness of the night was suddenly shattered by the sound of rapidly approaching hoofbeats. A rider turned into the street, his handsome black stallion galloping at a breakneck pace. The rider was dressed all in black, a long black cloak with a high collar billowed out behind him like a cape. The high collar made it impossible to see his face and it appeared as if he had no head.

"The headless horseman!" Johnny said. "Run, Andre!"

He drew his hunting knife, holding it high, ready to throw, then shoved her away with a hand on her chest. He gasped and his eyes went wide. He had felt the breasts beneath her shirt.

"By God! You're a *girl*!"

"Johnny, look out!"

There was a hissing sound as the horseman's whip whistled

through the air and cracked like pistol shot. Johnny cried out in pain and clutched his wrist as the knife fell from his hand. The horseman was upon them. Andre quickly drew her pistol, cocked the hammer, and fired. The shot had no effect. The horse struck her a glancing blow and she went spinning to the ground. Her pistol clattered to the street. She grunted with pain and Johnny was suddenly beside her, helping her up.

"Get up!" he said. "Get up quickly, or we're done for!"

She looked up and saw the black rider rein in and turn his horse. A figure ran out from the shadows into the street. Andre saw him lift his arm, aiming a gun, and a bright, pencil-thin beam of light shot out and seemed to strike the horseman squarely in the chest . . . and go right through him.

And suddenly the horseman was no longer there. He had simply vanished.

"What . . ." said Johnny, stunned. "Did you see? It's true! The horseman really is a ghost! He vanished into thin air! And that light . . ."

"It was only muzzle flash," said Andre quickly. "Doubtless one of your fellow Sons of Liberty."

"But . . . where did he go?" asked Johnny.

"Took his shot and ran, most likely," Andre said.

"And who can blame him?" Johnny said, apparently accepting the explanation of the "muzzle flash." He shook his head with disbelief. "A ghost! A real ghost! You saw it, didn't you, the way he disappeared?"

There was shouting as people flung open their windows and started to run out into the street. Andre grabbed Johnny by the arm and pulled him along down an alleyway. When they had gone far enough that they were well out of sight, she stopped and turned to face him.

"I'm not certain what I saw," said Andre. "But his horse felt solid enough to me. And you felt his whip."

"Aye, that I did," he said, looking at the bloody welt on his wrist. "But . . ." He stared at her. "But . . . you're a girl! I felt your . . . that is, I—I—" He looked away, flustered and embarrassed. "Forgive me, I—I never meant to—"

"Johnny, look at me."

He met her gaze, his eyes wide.

"You said you trusted me," she said. "Did you really mean it?"

He nodded.

"Then I must trust you to keep my secret and never tell a soul," she said. "Will you?"

He nodded.

"Will you swear?"

"I swear it," he said. "I will tell no one if that is what you wish." He grimaced, ruefully. "Anyway, how would it look if they knew that I was bested by a girl? But—but *why*? Why do you pretend to be a boy?"

"Because I am as good a patriot as you are," she said, "and because I want to do my part as badly as do you. But would they let me if they knew I was a girl?"

"No, naturally not," said Johnny. "That is a man's work."

"And can you deny that I can take care of myself as well as any man?" asked Andre.

Johnny looked down at the ground again and shook his head. "No," he said. "No, in truth, I cannot. I must admit that you are powerful strong. For a girl. And you can shoot, too."

"Not well enough, apparently," said Andre. "I missed the horseman."

"At such close range?" said Johnny. "I do not think so. You had aimed straight at him. The ball must have passed clean through him. And that other man, who fired from across the street . . ."

"We both missed, Johnny," she insisted. "I was forced to rush my shot. There was no time to take a careful aim. And a fast-moving target is difficult to hit. I do not believe that there is such a thing as ghosts."

"But we both saw him disappear!" said Johnny.

"We only thought we saw him disappear," said Andre. "Sometimes the eyes play tricks. Have you never been hunting in the woods and seen something move out of the corner of your eye, then turned to see that there was nothing there?"

"Yes, truly," Johnny said, "but this was different. We were both looking right at him!"

"And the street was dark," she said. "And there were people shouting from their windows and flinging open their doors. The horseman could have turned quickly into a narrow alleyway and in all the noise, we'd not have heard the stallion's hoofbeats. Now admit it, does that not sound much more likely than the existance of a ghost rider and a ghost horse, who seem to be solid flesh and blood one moment and disappear the next?"

Johnny sighed. "I suppose so," he said. He grimaced. "You make me feel like a fool."

"It seems this horseman has fooled a lot of people," she said. "He clearly knows the streets of Boston well, knows all of the back alleys, knows of places to hide. He rides only when the streets are dark and the shadows can conceal him. He is a very clever man, but he is no ghost. And you are no fool, Johnny Small."

"I have never in my life met a girl like you," he said.

"Nor I a boy like you," said Andre. She smiled and touched his cheek.

Suddenly he darted forward and kissed her quickly on the lips. He seemed as taken aback by his own action as she was. Before she could respond, he turned and quickly ran down the alley and into the next street.

For a moment, Andre was too surprised to move. She slowly brought her fingertips up to her lips.

"Bit young for you, isn't he?"

She spun around and saw Steiger, leaning with his arms folded against the wall.

"Damn it, Creed! Don't go sneaking up on me like that!" She was grateful that in the darkness, he couldn't see her blush. "What the hell are you doing here?"

"Officially, I suppose I'm A.W.O.L.," said Steiger. "Unofficially, I've assigned myself to keep an eye on Hunter. Frankly, I don't trust him."

"That was you back there, firing the laser," she said. "That was stupid. The boy saw you."

"Yes, but I think he accepted your explanation about the muzzle flash," said Steiger. "And the ghost rider made a much more lasting impression. As, no doubt, did you." He grinned. "I think that's called contributing to the delinquency of a minor, Lieutenant."

"Forget the wisecracks," she said. "What did you make of the horseman?"

"Well, he wasn't any ghost, that's for sure," said Steiger. "Somebody equipped with a warp disc, programmed for a fugue clocking sequence, so that he keeps clocking in and out faster than the eye can follow. What you see was only there a fraction of a second earlier. It's risky as all hell, a good way to wind up in the dead zone if you're not very careful, but it's certainly effective."

"That's what I figured, too," said Andre. "It's the only possible explanation. You think maybe it was Drakov?"

"Maybe, but I'd guess not," said Steiger. "He's too smart to take those kind of chances. It might well have been a hominoid. Which means that Hunter was right. Drakov is unquestionably here."

Andre nodded. "Or one of his clones is," she said. "Either way, it amounts to the same thing. Big trouble. And thanks to your using a laser, now he'll know we're here, as well."

"That ought to make things interesting," said Steiger.

"That really wasn't very smart, Creed."

"You'd rather I'd have let him run you down? You're lucky I was there. I had Hunter's place staked out from a room across the way. When I saw what was going down, I had to move fast. There wasn't a lot of time for planning something smart."

"We'd better go see Hunter," she said.

"No, you go see him," Steiger said. "I don't want him to know I'm here."

"But his information has panned out," she said. "Drakov *is* here. A temporal disruption is in progress."

"All the more reason not to alert Hunter to my presence," Steiger said. "That way I can keep an eye on him, just in case he decides to take advantage of the situation. Or have you forgotten that he's on the other side?"

"I haven't forgotten," she said. "But he's been dealing straight with us so far."

"And I intend to make sure he keeps it that way," Steiger said. "What do you figure Drakov's planning?"

She shook her head. "We don't know, yet. A disruption, obviously, but there's no way of telling exactly what he has in mind. If we're lucky, we may get to find out soon. We're supposed to be infiltrating a secret Tory group that's working against the Sons of Liberty. Sounds as if Drakov might be behind it, because there's no record of any such group in colonial history. The horseman is apparently their leader or at least their symbol. They've all been talking about him. Last night, four Sons of Liberty were hanged from the Liberty Tree."

"A temporal anomaly," said Steiger.

"Yeah," said Andre. "The Sons of Liberty were essentially unopposed during this time period. Sam Adams led them in agitating the colonies against the British. There are Sons of

Liberty groups forming in other colonies and Adams will soon be running them all, through dispatch riders like Paul Revere, who will eventually become the core of the Committees of Correspondence between the colonies. The governor of Boston has sent to New York for British troops, but they're not due to arrive for a while yet. If the Sons of Liberty are stopped here, before things really get rolling, it could change the course of history. Drakov might actually be trying to prevent the American Revolution."

"Interesting," said Steiger.

"What do you mean?"

"In the congruent universe, the American Revolution was won by the British."

"What are you saying?"

"I just find it interesting that Hunter put us onto this in the first place and that the disruption appears to be intended to alter our timeline in a way that would match the timeline of the congruent universe. Don't you find that interesting?"

She stood silent for a moment. "You think there's a C.I.S. team here that's behind all this and Hunter's trying to lure us into a trap? But if the horseman's one of Drakov's hominoids, then how does that fit with—"

"We don't really know he *is* a hominoid," said Steiger. "And if he is, we don't know if he's one of Drakov's hominoids, do we? The hominoids were originally developed in the congruent universe by Dr. Moreau as part of Project Infiltrator, before Drakov hijacked the entire project. The C.I.S. could still have some hominoids left. And there's also another possibility. For all we know, Hunter could be working with Drakov."

"I don't buy it," Andre said. "Drakov almost had Hunter killed. Hunter wants revenge."

"Or so he says," said Steiger. "Maybe they buried the hatchet. Maybe Drakov promised Hunter a trip back home in exchange for trapping us. Maybe Hunter isn't even Hunter."

"What do you mean?"

"Maybe he's a hominoid."

Andre expelled her breath. "Jesus, we never even considered that. How the hell did you manage to come up with that one?"

"You play games with the T.I.A. and the Network for as long as I did, you learn to suspect everyone and everything," said Steiger. "Don't forget, I infiltrated Drakov's old organization back when I was undercover as Sgt. Barry Martingale. I know how the man thinks. I wouldn't put it past him to play out a hand like that. Think about it."

Andre sighed. "You may be right, that's the scary thing about it," she said. "The trouble is, how would we know?"

"The early hominoids had run numbers tattooed on them somewhere, often high up on the inner thigh," said Steiger. He grinned. "I'll leave it up to you to decide how you can manage to get that close. But if Hunter's got a run number on him somewhere, then he's probably a C.I.S. hominoid left over from Project Infiltrator. If he hasn't got a run number on him anywhere, then he may be one of Drakov's more advanced models, the result of genetic engineering and implant programming. Which means he's essentially as human as you and I are, only Drakov doesn't think of them that way. Or maybe he's actually who he claims to be. Only that still doesn't tell us whose side he's really on."

Andre shook her head. "I sometimes wonder what it's like inside that mind of yours," she said. "It must get very complicated."

"Not really," Steiger said. "There's a refreshing clarity to knowing that when it gets right down to it, you can depend on one thing and one thing only. Yourself."

"I see," she said. "I wonder, if that's what it comes down to, how can you be sure that *I* am who I say I am?"

Steiger chuckled. "Go see your friend, Hunter," he said. He touched his warp disc and clocked out.

6

"So," said Drakov, leaning back in the velvet upholstered reading chair, "it appears that we have been discovered."

"It was only by chance that the fugue clocking sequence saved me," Moffat said, removing his black horseman garb. He was visibly shaken. "*How*? How could they *possibly* have known?"

"What difference does it make?" said Drakov. "There are any number of possible explanations. The man with the laser might have been a Temporal Observer stationed in this time period. Or he might have been a member of the Underground or of the Network. In their fear of temporal interference, the fools have so thoroughly infiltrated the past that they are only making our job easier. However, I think it would be best to proceed on the assumption that a commando adjustment team has been dispatched to this temporal scenario. And if that's the case, then that should make things very interesting, indeed."

"It's become too dangerous for you," said Moffat. "You must leave at once, for your own safety."

"Leave?" said Drakov, raising his eyebrows. He chuckled. "I wouldn't dream of it."

"But *why*? There is no need to take unnecessary chances. I can carry on for you here," Moffat said. "From what you've told me of the Time Commando units, they won't rest until they find you. The risk to you is far too great—"

"What is life without the spice of risk?" said Drakov, interrupting him. "Besides, the risk to me is negligible. They do not know where I am and now that I have been forewarned, I will not be so careless as to frequent public places. The advantage is still mine. I can still act anytime I choose."

"Then let's kill Adams and have done with it," said Moffat. "We can wipe out the entire leadership of the Sons of Liberty in one quick stroke and completely change the course of history. They will be helpless to do anything about it and we can all make our escape."

"No," said Drakov, firmly. "I will choose the precise moment when to strike, so that the damage will have the greatest impact. I have planned this operation down to the final minute detail and I will not cheat myself of the opportunity to settle an old score. This time, the odds are on my side. The horseman and his followers are the obvious temporal anomaly that they must deal with first and in doing so, they are certain to reveal themselves. And while they have their hands full with the horseman and our Hellfire Club, thinking that is the main focus of the disruption, I will be free to make my move at the appropriate time. Their presence here changes nothing. Let us see what happens at the meeting tomorrow night." He smiled. "Who knows, we may even have visitors. We shall have to do our best to make them welcome."

"I don't like it," Lucas said after Andre had finished giving her report. "This boy could cause us real problems if he talks."

"I don't think he will," said Andre. "I think we can trust him to keep quiet about me."

"What makes you so sure?" Lucas asked.

"He's infatuated with me," Andre said.

"I see. And you're willing to trust him on the basis of a kiss and a quick feel?" Lucas said.

Andre gave him a hard look. "I'm just going to pretend I didn't hear you say that."

Lucas shook his head. "I'm sorry. That was out of line. But the fact remains that Johnny Small has become a complication. An infatuated seventeen-year-old is completely unpredictable."

"I can handle him," said Andre.

"Can you?" Lucas said. "How much experience do you have with teenagers having a crush on you? A seventeen-year-old boy with his hormones in full roar can be one hell of a handful, especially if he's got something to hold over you. What'll you do if he decides to pursue this infatuation to its logical conclusion?"

"I don't know," said Andre, "he's a cute kid. Maybe I'll let him."

"Very funny," Lucas said. "But suppose he makes a pass. At his age, he probably won't handle rejection very well. What happens if he threatens to expose you unless you accept his advances?"

"Well, then maybe for the sake of the mission, I'll just have to make the sacrifice and go to bed with him," said Andre.

"For Christ's sake, Andre, I'm serious!"

"What do you want me to do, Lucas?" she said angrily. "You want me to take him out because he's jeopardizing the security of the mission?"

"No, of course not, but—"

"What then?"

Lucas sighed in exasperation. "Hell, I don't know. But we've got to do *something*."

"Why?" said Delaney.

"What do you mean, *why*?"

"Just that. Why?" Delaney said. "So what if he tells the Sons of Liberty that Andre is a woman? How does that jeopardize our mission? What's the worst that could happen? We might encounter some 18th-century sexism? I'm not sure it would even be a problem. The American colonies are fairly progressive for this time period. Women here own and operate their own businesses; on the frontier, they share in the work, hunt and help defend the homestead. The Sons of Liberty might raise a few eyebrows if they found out that Andre was passing as a male, but I hardly think it would cause any serious problems. Are you sure that's what's really bothering you?"

"Just what is that supposed to mean?" said Lucas.

"You tell me," Delaney said. "Are you quite certain that your apprehensions aren't based on a more personal reason?"

"Such as?"

Delaney stared at him. "We've known each other for a long time, partner," he said. "I don't really have to say it, do I?"

"Yes, I think you do," said Lucas. "Spit it out."

"Stop it, both of you!" Andre said. "This isn't getting us anywhere. Our personal problems can wait until the mission is completed. I don't want to talk about this anymore. Finn's right. If Johnny talks, it might do some damage, but it won't be very serious. Anyway, I don't think it will come to that. I said I could handle him. It's my responsibility. Let me worry about it, okay?"

"Okay by me," Delaney said.

"Lucas?"

"Yeah, yeah, all right. I just hope you know what you're doing."

"Are you questioning my judgment?" she said.

Lucas shook his head. "No, it isn't that, it's just . . . hell, forget it. It's your call. Do what you think best."

"All right, then," she said. "Now that that's settled, the question is what do we do about Hunter?"

"How much did you tell him?" asked Delaney.

"Everything, except I left out the part about Steiger, of course. In light of what Creed said, I think we have to assume that he *could* be double-dealing us. It's possible. There's still too much we don't know."

"Creed's been a spook so long, paranoia is a way of life with him," said Lucas. "But frankly, I feel better knowing that he's keeping tabs on Hunter. It'll make our job a lot easier. I think we should keep Hunter on a 'need-to-know' basis; use him as a liaison with Adams and the Sons of Liberty, but don't tell him anything that could affect the outcome of the mission. What he doesn't know can't hurt us."

"Hunter's not stupid," Andre said. "He's liable to figure out we're holding out on him and he isn't going to like it."

"That's his problem," Lucas said. "He doesn't have to like it. But if he's being on the level with us, he'll have to do things our way or he doesn't get to go back home."

"*Does* he get to go back home?" said Andre.

"Forrester gave his word," said Lucas.

"I know," she said, "but Steiger didn't like it."

"Creed's not stupid enough to go against Forrester's orders," said Delaney.

"Maybe not," said Andre, "but I've been thinking about it and knowing Creed, I wouldn't put it past him to find a loophole. Such as the fact that Forrester didn't say *when* Hunter would get to go back home. Creed just might decide to put him through interrogation first and find out if he was bluffing about those subliminal triggers."

"Are you saying we should try to stop him if he does?" said Lucas.

"Are you saying that we shouldn't?"

"Hunter *is* the opposition, Andre," Delaney said.

"That's not the point," said Andre. "If Hunter doesn't play straight with us, okay, all bets are off, but if he lives up to his end of the bargain, I think we ought to live up to ours."

"Steiger might not see it that way," Lucas said.

"That's exactly what I'm talking about," she said. "I just want to know what we're going to do about it if it comes to that."

"Let's just make sure we understand each other here," said Finn. "If Creed decides to take Hunter back when this is over and put him through the wringer before sending him back home, are you saying we should try to stop him? Lose the chance of gaining valuable intelligence and take the enemy's side against one of our own people?"

"We made a deal," Andre said.

"Things aren't always that simple, Andre," Lucas said.

"They're simple enough for me," she said. "I'm sorry if I'm not sufficiently modern to compromise my integrity for political expediency, but when I give my word, I keep it. We made a deal with that man and we all shook hands on it. That may not mean a lot to Steiger, but it means a lot to me and I've always believed it meant a lot to you. Or was I wrong?"

"No, you weren't wrong," said Lucas. "But I don't think Creed will understand."

"What about it, Finn?" she said, looking at him anxiously.

"Well, I guess we'll just have to make him understand, won't we?" said Delaney.

There was a soft knock at the door.

They exchanged quick glances. Delaney reached for his laser and held it out of sight. Lucas and Andre both took out their dueling pistols.

"Who is it?" Lucas said.

"A friend," came a soft voice from beyond the door.

Lucas glanced at Andre. "Let him in, but stand clear the moment you open the door."

Andre went to the door and slipped the bolt, then quickly opened it and stepped out of the way. The man who came in with his hands held out to his sides and slightly raised was Carruthers, the Tory who'd been sitting with John Hewitt.

"Easy," he said. "I'm unarmed."

Andre closed the door behind him, then quickly patted him down.

"He's clean."

"Lt. Paul Carruthers. Col. Priest, I presume?" Carruthers said, looking at Lucas.

"Who sent you?" Lucas said, still covering him with the pistol.

"Col. Steiger," he said. "It is all right if I put my hands down?"

Lucas nodded. "Steiger sent you from H.Q.?" he said.

Carruthers frowned. "No, this is my permanent post. Col. Steiger's here in Boston. You didn't know?"

Lucas lowered his gun. "Yeah, I knew. But you can't be too careful."

"I understand. I reported a temporal anomaly and was told that a team had already been dispatched. Steiger briefed me about Hunter. Unusual situation."

"Yes, it certainly is," said Lucas.

"I'm sorry to come so late, but I just got my orders," Carruthers said. "Col. Steiger told me to report to you."

"Why did Steiger know there was an Observer stationed here and we didn't?" said Delaney.

"Because my commission's not in the Observer Corps," Carruthers said. "I'm Temporal Intelligence, section chief in this sector."

"Section chief?" said Lucas. "That implies you have a fully staffed field office here."

"That's right," Carruthers said, sitting down in one of the chairs. "I'm in charge of thirty field agents spread throughout the thirteen colonies."

"How come we didn't know about it?" Lucas said. "There was nothing in the briefing tapes about a field office here."

"That's because we're deep cover," said Carruthers. "The C.I.S. has already raided our data banks once, so the I.S.D. established undocumented, deep-cover units in a number of high risk temporal scenarios. Besides, there's also another reason. We've discovered that the Network has a very active branch here."

"Terrific," said Delaney. "Steiger sets up his own deep-cover operation and doesn't even tell Forrester about it.

Anyone else involved in this scenario that we don't know about? The Girl Scouts, maybe?"

"What about the Network?" Lucas said. "What've you got on them?"

"Not very much," Carruthers admitted. "We know they've infiltrated the East India Company and we have good reason to believe they have some influence in the British Parliament, as well. They're involved in the colonial smuggling trade, but we haven't been able to establish exactly how or with whom. There are so many smugglers in the colonies that it's been difficult to get a line on their activities. But we know they're here."

"And so is Drakov," Delaney said. "Or maybe the C.I.S. Or maybe both Drakov *and* the C.I.S. And we've got a temporal disruption going down in the middle of the whole damn thing. Jesus, what a mess."

"Yes, it could get a little sloppy," Carruthers agreed. "That's why Col. Steiger ordered me to put my entire section at your complete disposal. We can't predict what the Network's going to do, but by now, they probably know that an anomaly is taking place in Boston. The question is, how will they respond? A temporal disruption threatens them as much as it threatens us. The trouble is, they're not very likely to offer us their help, for obvious reasons."

"In other words, we could easily wind up working at cross purposes," said Lucas. "That's just wonderful. If Drakov is behind this, he couldn't have picked a more ideal situation."

"What are your plans?" Carruthers asked.

"We're supposed to be patriots from New York, working undercover as Tories for the Sons of Liberty," said Andre. "Your friend, John Hewitt, promised to take us to a meeting of some kind of secret Tory organization that's behind this headless horseman."

"The Hellfire Club," Carruthers said. "I know about it."

"I seem to recall something about the Hellfire Club," Delaney said. "Wasn't that—"

"A society of sexual libertines in England, headed by Sir Francis Dashwood and John Wilkes," Carruthers finished for him. "This isn't quite the same thing, though it's apparently modeled on that group. I've managed to get a few people on the inside, but it hasn't helped much."

"What do you mean?" said Andre.

"Nobody seems to know who started it or who's behind it," Carruthers said. "It's almost as if it all sprang up spontaneously, practically overnight. Ask too many questions and you get frozen out, suspected of being a radical. They meet at a small abandoned church outside of Boston. The property belongs to a local Tory. They all know one another and the times of meeting are passed informally by word of mouth. It's impossible to track down the source. They put on black robes and masks and have themselves an orgy with booze and naked women, also wearing masks. It's a nice touch. You know who's there, but because everyone is masked, you can't tell just who is doing what to whom. I suppose it keeps their Puritan sensibilities from being offended. And at some point during the festivities, they receive their orders from the horseman."

"You mean he actually shows up?" said Finn.

Carruthers shook his head. "No, only his voice is heard. With the dim candlelight and the weird acoustics in that place, there's no way of telling where it comes from. We've searched that chapel after they all left, but we didn't find anything unusual. Whoever he is, he's probably among the crowd, wearing a robe and mask, and he leaves with them."

"What about the women?" Lucas said.

"It's widely assumed that they're all prostitutes," said Carruthers, "but we've found out that a good number of them are young local girls from good families and even a few prominent Boston wives. Makes things rather interesting. In that dim light and with all those robes and masks, they could be doing it with their neighbors' wives or their own daughters and not even know it. Swinging Boston, eh? And it gives them all something in common. Booze, politics, and sex. Half the Sons of Liberty are liable to defect just to join the party."

"Well, so much for *my* attending the meeting," Andre said.

"Yeah, I guess that leaves you out," said Lucas.

"But you and Finn are still going, I suppose," she said dryly.

"I'm afraid we'll have to," Lucas said.

"But you'll try to bear up under the strain," she said sarcastically.

"Very funny," Lucas said.

"I wonder if Johnny Small is busy tomorrow night," she said.

Lucas gave her a wry look, but said nothing.

"Exactly how many of your people are in Boston at the moment?" asked Delaney.

"An even dozen, myself included," said Carruthers. "Six are stationed in New York, three in Virginia, three in Rhode Island, three in Pennsylvania, and three in Carolina. I can mobilize the entire section at any time. Want me to bring them all here?"

"Not yet," Delaney said. "For all we know, the opposition could have disruptions planned in the other colonies, as well. Leave your men where they are for the time being. Don't take this the wrong way, Carruthers, but how certain are you of your men?"

"I picked them all myself and every one of them has been cleared," Carruthers said. "Col. Steiger has personally taken charge of the section. He's assigned two of my men to keep Hunter under surveillance so he could have maximum mobility. He just left to brief the rest of my people. He said to tell you he'll be difficult to get in touch with, so my orders are to coordinate things at this end. I'm to report directly to you. I've already established my cover as a Tory sympathizer, so under the circumstances, our being seen together shouldn't raise any suspicions."

"Where can we get in touch with you?" asked Lucas.

"It'll be easier for me to get in touch with you," Carruthers said. "You can leave word with the bartender downstairs, a man named Horace Stedwell. He's not one of my men, he's a local, but I pay him under the table to carry messages for me. I've been infiltrating the smuggling trade here in Boston, trying to get a line on the Network. But if an emergency comes up and you need me in a hurry, you can get in touch with my men in that apartment Steiger rented to keep an eye on Hunter. Just don't go clocking over there. We've established security procedures so that nobody makes transition directly to the surveillance post, just in case the Network gets a line on the place and attempts to drop some people in on top of us. If anybody clocks in over there, my people are under orders to shoot first and ask questions later. Use the back stairs, instead. The password is 'counterstrike,' okay?"

"Counterstrike," said Lucas. "Got it. Who are your people on the inside in the Hellfire Club?"

"That's not going to help you," said Carruthers. "Everyone'll be disguised, so you won't be able to spot them in any case and they won't be able to spot you. However, just in case anything goes wrong and you have to shoot your way out of there or something, they'll use the same password to identify themselves. Just remember that if you're going to the meeting, you'll be badly outnumbered and on their home ground. They also keep guards posted outside. Their number varies and they move around. It's not a good place to start anything."

"We'll keep that in mind, thanks," Delaney said. "Just to keep the record straight, what orders do you have concerning Hunter?"

"We're to keep him under close surveillance," said Carruthers. "If he makes contact with anybody and we can't absolutely verify who it is, we're to take him into immediate custody and await further instructions from Col. Steiger. He doesn't want to take any chances that Hunter might be contacting a C.I.S. team if there's one in the vicinity."

"All right," said Lucas, "but you are not to clock out anywhere with Hunter unless you've had specific instructions from me, is that clear? Regardless of what Col. Steiger says."

Carruthers gave him an appraising look. "You mind explaining that?"

"Col. Steiger is not in charge of this mission, I am," Lucas said. "I just don't want anybody doing anything unless I know about it. Any questions?"

Carruthers shook his head. "No, sir, but suppose the situation should come up and Col. Steiger decides to take custody of the prisoner personally. I have no authority to prevent him, and with all due respect, I'm not going to put my ass in a wringer just because two senior officers might disagree on how to conduct a mission. I just want to make sure you understand that. I don't want to get caught in the middle of anything."

"Noted," said Lucas. "In that case, you are to report directly to me and inform me immediately of Col. Steiger's action."

"Yes, sir," Carruthers said. "Is there anything else?"

"Just make sure your people understand that I don't want anyone taking any direct action whatsoever unless they've been cleared by one of us to do so," Lucas said. "And if Col. Steiger issues any orders to the contrary, I am to be informed of it at once. Understood?"

"Understood," Carruthers said. "Colonel, you mind telling

me what this is all about? Is something going on between you two that I should know about?"

"Like you said, Carruthers, you don't want to get caught in the middle," Lucas said. "If you've got a problem with any of my orders, I want to know about it now."

"No, sir, no problem," said Carruthers.

"Good. That's all, then."

Carruthers came to attention and saluted. "Yes, sir," he said, a touch stiffly. "I'll be in touch."

"He didn't seem very happy about that," Andre said when he had left.

"Well, I'm not either," Lucas replied. He sighed. "We've got enough to worry about without having Steiger running his own operation in the middle of all this. We're all supposed to be on the same team, for God's sake."

"Steiger's never been much of a team player," Andre said. "Maybe we'd better have a talk with him."

"Won't do much good," Delaney said. "For one thing, we don't know where the hell he is right now and for another, if he feels strongly enough about it, he'll just go ahead and do it his way. You're not going to convince him that he's wrong."

"We could have Forrester order him off the mission," Andre said.

"No, that's not the way to handle it," said Lucas. "There's already too much friction between the I.S.D. and the regular personnel. I'm not going to exacerbate the situation just because of Hunter. We'll handle Creed ourselves."

"Can I make a suggestion?" Delaney said. "Why not just clock Hunter out of here right now? Let's take him to the confluence point we brought him through and send him home ourselves before he becomes a problem."

"We've been over that already," Andre said. "You know how he's going to respond to that suggestion."

"I don't think we can afford the luxury of giving him a choice, Andre," said Finn. "The situation's changed. There are simply too many ways it could go wrong. Carruthers is Steiger's man. I'd rather risk annoying Steiger now then get into it with him when it's already hit the fan. Frankly, Hunter simply isn't worth it."

"I agree," said Lucas. "We don't really need him anymore and if we allow him to remain here, he's gong to be a liability.

We've given him more than a fair shake already. I say we send him back."

Andre nodded. "Okay, I guess he's got no right to expect any more than that."

"Right," said Lucas. "Let's get it over with."

"Right now?" said Andre.

"Right now. Let's clock over there and do it before Carruthers decides he doesn't like his orders."

Moments later, they materialized inside Hunter's house on Long Lane. Moving silently, they made their way up to his bedroom and woke him up. He came awake instantly.

"What the . . . oh, it's you! Christ, you scared the hell outta me! What's up?"

"Get dressed," said Lucas. "Quickly."

Hunter wasted no time in getting out of bed. Andre stepped out into the hall while he got dressed.

"What's going on?" he asked, quickly tucking his shirt into his breeches and sitting on the bed to pull on his stockings and his shoes.

"You're going home," said Lucas.

Hunter glanced up at him. "What are you talking about?"

"Just what I said. Go on, finish getting dressed. We're taking you back through the confluence."

Hunter remained sitting on the bed. He glanced from Lucas to Delaney. "What is this? I thought we had a deal."

"That's right," said Lucas, "and now we're living up to our end of it. Come on."

"Hold on a minute, pilgrim," Hunter said. "This wasn't our agreement. I thought we'd been through this already. You promised me a crack at Drakov. What's happened to make you change your mind?"

"Not that it's any of your business," said Delaney, "but something's come up and we have good reason to believe that some of our people might decide to put you through interrogation and see if you were on the level about that conditioning of yours. They figure it's worth taking a chance to get some information out of you and if you happen to fall into a coma in the process, then it's your hard luck."

"It's Steiger, isn't it?" said Hunter.

"Look, you want to get home in one piece or don't you?" Lucas said. "We're trying to be fair about this. We'll take you back ourselves and send you through, from there you're on your own. It's the best we can do. Take it or leave it, but stop wasting our time. You're being watched."

Hunter grimaced tightly. "Damn it to hell," he said. "All right, I appreciate what you're doing. I'll—"

"Hold it right there," said a voice from behind them. "Don't anybody move."

"Shit," said Hunter, looking past them.

Finn and Lucas froze.

"Slowly now, put your hands on top of your heads and clasp them," the voice said.

All three of them complied, being careful not to make any quick movements.

"Now turn around, very slowly."

They turned. There were two men standing behind them in the darkened bedroom. They were both holding laser pistols aimed straight at them.

"It's a good thing we had a mike aimed at this place, in case our boy talks in his sleep," one of them said.

"Are you guys crazy?" Lucas said. "Put those weapons down. That's an order. The password's counterstrike."

"Sorry, I'm afraid we don't take orders from you, Colonel," one of the men said.

"I think you'd better do as he says," Andre said, standing in the doorway behind them. "I've got a gun aimed right at your backs, gentlemen. Drop your weapons on the floor. *Now.*"

The two men hesitated, then dropped their pistols at their feet.

"That's just fine," said Andre. "Now kick them over—"

She stopped suddenly as she felt the barrel of a laser pistol press against the back of her head.

"Hold the gun out to your side, Lieutenant," Carruthers said, standing in the hall behind her. "Two fingers, please."

Andre tensed.

"Don't do anything stupid," said Carruthers. "I don't want to kill you."

Her shoulders slumped. She held the laser out from her side where Carruthers could reach around and take it from her.

"Carruthers, what the hell do you think you're doing?" Lucas said. "Put the gun down!"

"Sorry, Colonel," he said. "I can't do that." He pushed Andre ahead of him into the room. "You should have left well enough alone. We were going to try to work with you on this, but you had to go and blow it, didn't you?"

"You're not I.S.D.," Delaney said, with sudden realization. "You're with the Network."

"That's right," Carruthers said. "And I'm afraid that knowledge is going to cost you." He glanced at his men. "Don't just stand there, you idiots. Pick up your weapons."

As the men bent down to retrieve their pistols, Hunter lunged across the bed and reached under his pillow. Carruthers quickly shifted his aim and fired, but Hunter was already on the floor and rolling. As Carruthers aimed again, Lucas disappeared. He reappeared instantly, standing beside Carruthers, and knocked his arm up. The shot went wild. Hunter's silenced 9 mm. semiautomatic coughed twice. The two Network men went down with slugs through their foreheads. Lucas drove his fist into Carruthers' solar plexus, threw him back against the wall, and punched him again. Carruthers slumped down to the floor, the wind knocked out of him.

Delaney reached for his gun.

"Don't do it!" Hunter said sharply.

Delaney froze.

"Come on, Hunter, take it easy."

"Hands back on your head," said Hunter, leveling the automatic at him. "All of you, right now!"

"Reese, listen—" Lucas said.

"Shut up! I've got to *think*, damn it!"

Carruthers sat on the floor, clutching his middle and gasping for breath.

Hunter moved back against the wall, his gun moving back and forth, keeping them all covered. He centered his aim on Andre. "Don't try anything, Priest, or I'll put one right through her, so help me."

"All right, Hunter, take it easy . . ."

"There could be more of them," he said.

"Carruthers said he had only two men in that apartment . . ." Delaney's voice trailed off as he realized what that meant. "Damn it! They've got Steiger!"

Ignoring Hunter, he bent down over Carruthers and dragged him to his feet. "Where's Steiger, you son of a bitch? *Where is he?* What've you done with him?"

Carruthers couldn't talk. He was still struggling to get his breath back. Delaney slammed him hard against the wall.

"Talk, you bastard!"

"Hold off, Finn," said Lucas. "Give him time to get his breath back."

"Get his warp disc," Hunter said.

Delaney grabbed his arm and pulled the warp disc off his wrist.

"Toss it here," said Hunter.

Delaney glanced at him. "Like hell I will."

Hunter fired. The pistol coughed and Andre cried out, grabbing at her shoulder where the bullet had just grazed her flesh.

"Do as he says, Finn," Lucas said quickly.

"Toss it on the bed," said Hunter.

Scowling, Delaney threw the warp disc on the bed.

"Stay right where you are, Priest," Hunter said, keeping his gun steady on Andre. "Please. Don't force me to do something I don't want to do."

"All right, Reese," said Lucas. "Stay cool. You're calling the shots for now. We had a deal, remember?"

"Yeah, I remember," Hunter said, edging over carefully and picking up the warp disc without taking his eyes off them. "I just want some insurance."

He fastened the warp disc around his wrist.

"When you deliver me safely to that confluence point, you'll get this back," he said. "Meanwhile, I'm not going anywhere until I'm good and ready. Now I believe you wanted to ask that man some questions. Go ahead. I'll wait."

Delaney and Lucas exchanged glances. Lucas nodded.

"All right, Carruthers," Delaney said, holding the man up by his shirtfront. "Talk. Where's Steiger?"

"You go to hell," Carruthers gasped.

Delaney brought his knee up sharply into the man's groin. Carruthers made a brief, high-pitched keening sound and sagged in his grasp. Delaney lifted him up effortlessly and slammed him against the wall again.

"You tell me what you've done with Steiger or I'll break every bone in your body," he said.

Carruthers shook his head. Delaney brought his fist back and smashed it into his face. Blood spattered on the wall behind Carruthers as his head snapped around with the force of the blow. His nose was broken.

"Your ribs are next," Delaney said. "And then your knee-caps. *Where is he?*"

Carruthers coughed and drew a ragged breath. "If I tell you, I'm dead."

"You're dead if you don't tell me," said Delaney. "Did you kill him?"

Carruthers shook his head. "No . . . we've got him . . ."

"Where?"

Carruthers shook his head again.

Delaney drew his fist back once more and drove it with piledriver force into the man's chest. Something cracked.

Carruthers made a grunting, wheezing sound and sagged down once again. Delaney let him fall. He knelt over him, his knee over the man's leg, his hand grasping the back of his calf.

"Okay, hard guy, your knee goes next. I can keep this up all night."

"Do your worst, damn you," Carruthers said in a croaking voice. "But if you kill me, Steiger's had it."

Delaney was about to yank up on the man's leg when Lucas stopped him. "Finn, wait! Forget it. Let him go."

Delaney stood up. "I'll make the bastard talk," he said.

"No. It's no use. We're not going to get anything out of him this way," Lucas said. "Let's clock him back to headquarters and let the I.S.D peel back his mind and take a look inside."

Carruthers suddenly lunged toward the bodies of his two men. His fingers closed around one of the pistols they'd dropped. Hunter shouted a warning and fired. Carruthers collapsed to the floor, a bullet through his shoulder. Before any of them could respond, he pulled the pistol toward him, put the barrel in his mouth, and squeezed the trigger. His cheeks seemed to light up and a thin beam of light came up through his skull. He fell down, dead.

"God *damn* it!" Delaney swore.

"I'm sorry," Hunter said. "I couldn't get a clear shot at the gun . . ."

"It wasn't your fault," said Lucas.

Hunter shook his head. "Yes, it was. It's my fault all this happened in the first place. I wanted a crack at Drakov and now I've got you in a real mess." He sighed. "I'm sorry about the shoulder, Andre. You all right?"

She nodded. "It's just a minor flesh wound. But I'm glad you're a good shot."

Hunter grimaced. "What happens now?"

Lucas gave him a long look. "I guess that's up to you," he said. "You're the one who's got the gun."

Hunter glanced down at the gun, then tossed it on the bed with disgust. "What the hell are we doing?" he said, a note of genuine confusion in his voice. He shook his head. "You're supposed to be the enemy and here I'm trying to help you. You don't trust me and meanwhile your own people are trying to kill you. This whole thing is a fucking joke."

"Nobody's laughing," Lucas said. "Except maybe Drakov."

"Look," said Hunter, "you're up against both Drakov *and* the Network now. They've already got Steiger. Frankly, far as I'm concerned, they can keep him, but if we don't work together on this, Drakov's going to win and then everybody loses. We can't afford not to trust each other. The bottom line is you're going to need my help, whether you like it or not."

"He's right, Lucas," said Delaney. "We've got no choice now. We have to find Steiger, fight the Network, *and* stop Drakov. We're spread too thin. We're going to need all the help we can get."

"Yeah," said Lucas, nodding. "It's time to send for some reinforcements. Andre, you clock back to headquarters and tell Forrester what's going down. Get him to send as many teams as he can spare. We don't know for a fact how many Network people there are back here, and they know about this place and our rooms back in the Peacock Tavern. Hunter, we need a secure location for a transition point. You got any suggestions?"

"Yeah," Hunter said, "I took the precaution of arranging a safehouse for myself, just in case you people tried to double-cross me. It's where I had the gun stashed and a few other things, besides. I always clocked directly there from this place, so I don't think that Steiger or anybody else watching me could've known about it. It should be fairly safe."

"All right, where is it?"

"I'll give you the coordinates. It's a small house near Hudson's Point, on Lime Street, by the cemetery and the foundries. And speaking of coordinates . . ." He took off the warp disc and tossed it to Lucas. "Call it a gesture of good faith." He picked his gun up off the bed and tucked it in his breeches. "Now I strongly suggest we dispose of those bodies and get the hell out of here before the Network finds out that three of their people have been wasted."

7

Johnny Small was feeling an exhilaration unlike anything he'd ever known. Consciously, he put it down to finally being included among the members of the Sons of Liberty, but subconsciously, it was much more than that. At the age of seventeen, he was beginning to experience sexual awakening and he had fallen in love. He could not get Andre out of his mind.

Paul Revere had several apprentices, so he could easily afford to excuse Johnny from his duties at the silversmith shop, so that he could devote most of his energies to his assignment for the Sons of Liberty. Johnny regarded this vote of confidence almost with reverence. He was one of them now, a patriot, and they were no longer treating him like a boy. Revere had been impressed with his report and he had taken him straight to Samuel Adams himself, in the middle of the night, so that he could tell their leader what he'd learned.

Adams, dressed in his nightclothes, had listened impassively in the drawing room of his house on Purchase Street while Johnny told him about following Andre to the street where Hunter lived and then described how the headless horseman had appeared out of nowhere and attacked them. He had not told either Revere or Adams what he had discovered about Andre, but her explanation of the night's events had colored his report, so that he described an unknown man who had stepped out of the shadows and fired a pistol at the horseman, missed, and how the horseman had taken advantage of the confusion and the noise in the street to escape down some convenient alleyway. He told Adams that the three New Yorkers had made contact with some Tories in the Peacock Tavern and had taken rooms there, the better to pursue their inquiries. When he had finished, Adams nodded and clapped him on the shoulder.

"You've done well, lad," he said. "Very well, indeed."

Johnny felt flushed with pride at the praise.

"Perhaps we can trust these New Yorkers, after all," said Revere.

"If they can help us find out who this horseman is, then they will indeed have proved their worth," said Adams. "However, I believe it would be prudent to keep watch on them, just the same. There is much at stake. Can we count on your help in this matter?"

"I will do anything you ask," said Johnny, proudly.

"Good. We still do not know these people well enough. It would be wise to remain cautious." He stroked his chin thoughtfully. "Part of our problem, Paul, is that there are many patriots like us throughout the colonies that we do not know well enough. We are united in our aims, but not in fact. There is too little contact between us. I have been giving much thought to this."

"What do you have in mind?" Revere asked.

"Our strength here in Boston is in our unity," said Adams. "We must unite ourselves with patriots in the other colonies, as well. It is not enough to merely express our views in the *Gazette* and urge all good citizens to join our cause. We need more direct action. A means of keeping in touch with other patriotic groups. These new commissioners that Townshend has sent to the colonies have been incorruptible because they are all wealthy men. There is little we can offer them in the way of inducements that they do not already have, but unfortunately, there is much that they can offer to our friends.

"I have been hearing most disturbing news," he continued. "We have driven our own commissioners to seek refuge in Castle William, but in the other colonies, it is said that these new commissioners draw sympathy from people by entertaining lavishly, inviting merchants and influential citizens to balls and dinners, turning their heads with their fine clothes and splendid carriages and sumptuous repasts. I have heard that in

Philadelphia, good Whig wives and Tory gentlemen drink rum punch together and dance the minuet. Such gaiety and idleness are destructive to our cause. We must give people a reason to unite against such frivolous displays."

"What do you propose to do?" Revere said.

"The new strict enforcement of the customs duties has resulted in a growing shortage of hard currency," said Adams. "My father had sought to bring stability to our paper currency, but when the Land Bank was outlawed by those mountebanks in Parliament, the people took to hording British silver, as you well know. They hide silver coins in mattresses and jars until they accumulate enough to bring them to a silversmith such as yourself and have them melted down, to cast into such things as cups and punch bowls. We all trade and barter with one another, but the customs commissioners accept only British silver, as do the British merchants, and the supply of hard money is dwindling more and more. Imported goods from England are becoming ever dearer and fewer people can afford them and they feel poorly for it, embarrassed when they cannot afford the luxuries their neighbors have. If we can turn that to our advantage by making a virtue of their insufficiency, we can give people a reason to unite behind our cause."

"How can we do that?" Revere asked, while Johnny listened with fascination, immensely flattered that these two men would discuss their plans in front of him.

"By uniting *all* the colonies in a concerted boycott of all imported British goods," said Adams. "We can give those plagued with debt a virtuous excuse for cutting back on their expenses if they can say they do it for the common good, rather than for lack of money. We can help them to look upon it not as insufficiency, but as self-sacrifice, an act of pride and patriotism. A wife who cannot afford to make a dress of silk can then take pride in wearing homespun and be able to look with disdain upon her neighbor, who can afford a finer dress, because she does not choose to sacrifice her comfort and her luxury for a common good, you see? If we can make an act of pride out of their need to tighten up their purse strings, we will give them a reason to support us in our cause."

"Aye, and save husbands' money in the bargain, which will help them to look kindly on our methods," said Revere. "It is an excellent idea, Sam. But how shall we implement it?"

"I have drafted a circular letter, which I intend to send

around to all the colonies and have printed in the newspapers,"
said Adams. "We will ask all in the colonies to sign the letter
as a form of personal committment. We will ask them to agree
to give constant preference to those merchants who do not
import from London. We will ask for a boycott of all ships that
continue to bring in British goods. We will ask them to
consider all traders who do not sign as traitors to our cause. We
will sway the common people to our cause first. A dock porter
or a washerwoman could never afford to purchase silks or
velvets, much less imported furniture and ready-made apparel,
but if they sign an agreement to not purchase them, then they
can say that they *refuse*, not that they are unable. Thus, we
elevate their station."

"But there is no way that we can force everyone to join the
boycott," said Revere. "And there are many merchants who
will undoubtedly find a way around it."

"Then we shall see to it that those merchants will have their
names published in the newspapers," said Adams, "and it will
hurt their trade. And meanwhile, those merchants who are less
well off will see that trade improve by agreeing to join us in the
boycott. If we appeal to their pocketbooks, Paul, then we shall
win their hearts."

"It is a sound plan," said Revere. "When do you intend to
start?"

"As soon as possible," said Adams. "Bernard daily sends
requests to Gage for troops and petitions Parliament for help.
The commissioners who have taken shelter in Castle William
add their pleas to his. The troops are certain to arrive before too
long. There can be no doubt of it. We must take steps to sway
popular opinion to our side so that when they do arrive, they
will be widely perceived as an intrusion on our liberties."

He turned to Johnny. "Your role in this is especially
important, Jonathan," he said.

"It is?" said Johnny, his eyes wide.

"It is absolutely vital," Adams said. "We must find out who
this mysterious horseman is and who his followers are, so that
we may take the proper steps to stop them. We cannot work
against them if we do not know who they are. I have heard
rumors of the foul things that they do at their secret meetings,
depraved practices that I shall not enumerate for your young
ears. It is clear to me that the leaders of this 'Hellfire Club'
seek to draw men to their cause by appealing to their basest

instincts. And we have already seen that once aroused, these instincts will make them stop at nothing, not even murder. It is a very dangerous assignment you've been given, Jonathan. Whatever happens, you must steer clear of these men. If you can, try to discover who they are, but you must avoid contact with them at all costs. Let us see what information the New Yorkers bring us. Your task is to keep watch on them, but no matter what occurs, do not involve yourself. Do you understand?"

"Yes, sir," Johnny said breathlessly, wondering what sort of "foul practices" these terrible men indulged in and feeling suddenly afraid for Andre.

"Good," said Adams. "Take this, then." He pressed something into Johnny's hand. "You've earned it."

Johnny felt a lump in his throat as he gazed down on the silver Liberty medallion in his palm. Given to him by Sam Adams, himself!

"You're one of us now," said Revere, squeezing the boy's shoulder. "Go and do us proud."

Johnny left the house on Purchase Street in a daze. He could hardly wait to show Andre the medallion. He felt a slight, momentary twinge of guilt at not having told Adams and Revere what he had leaned about her, but he was certain that they wouldn't understand. Each time he thought of her, he remembered how she had realized that he was trailing her despite all the precautions that he took, how she had outwitted him, how she had bravely stood up to the horseman, whom even grown men feared!

She reminded him of the Indian girls that he had seen when he lived on the frontier and sometimes accompanied his uncle on his trading trips to their village. He would often lay awake at night and think about those Indian girls, about how different they were from all the white girls he had known, the simple and yet somehow beautiful way they dressed in their buckskins, the delicate way their feet looked in their leather moccasins, their pretty ankles and the way they walked, with a purposeful, slightly pigeon-toed stride, never flouncing or primping or flirting. The way they'd look at him and then shyly avert their eyes when he looked back. He would dream about them sometimes and wonder what it would be like to talk with them, to walk through the woods and perhaps even to hold their hands, but of course he didn't dare.

And he kept thinking about how it had felt when he kissed
Andre. He did not know what had come over him. He did not
know how she could possibly forgive such insufferable boldness, and yet she had not reacted angrily. She had been just as
surprised as he was, but she had not looked angry. He felt like
a fool for running away. And he kept thinking about that brief
instant when his hand had come in contact with her breast.
More than anything, he wanted to see her once again. There
was a bond between them now, he told himself. They shared an
adventure and a secret. For the first time since he had come to
Boston, he felt happy and alive. He felt a sense of purpose.
And, somehow, he knew that something wonderful was going
to happen. For a long time, he had felt that he had a destiny that
he had discovered. He believed that now, at last, he knew what
it was.

The house on Lime Street had been rented from a merchant
who owned several similar properties along the waterfront. It
was a boxy, wood frame structure with heavy wooden doors
and mullioned windows with wood shutters. The brick chim-
neys rose about three feet above the shingled roof and the
exterior was weathered from exposure to the salt sea winds.
The house was located on a bend in the road where Lime Street
curved around and met with Lynn Street. There was a foundry
across the street and from the windows of the upper story they
could see the docks near Hudson's Point. Not far away was the
ferry to Charles Town near the old windmill and within several
blocks of them was Christ Church, on Salem Street.

Hunter had rented the place with some of his ill-gotten gains
from the riots and he paid the landlord extra to insure his
privacy. The landlord did not inquire into this special need for
privacy. He was simply grateful to have the property rented and
to receive the added bonus. He understood about men who did
not want anyone inquiring into their affairs. After all, he was
himself a smuggler. Perhaps Mr. Hunter was using the house as
a place of assignation where he kept a mistress on the side, as
many of his own friends did. Perhaps he was engaged in the
smuggling trade himself and was using it as a place of storage
for his goods. Perhaps he was a radical and holding clandestine
meetings there in the middle of the night. The landlord didn't
really care. If anyone had told him that Hunter was a soldier
from another universe and that the house on Lime Street was

being used as a temporal transition point and field headquarters for a strike force of elite commandos from the 27th century, the landlord might merely have nodded absently and said, "No skin off my nose, so long as the rent is paid on time."

Corporal Linda Craven stood at the window, looking out discreetly from behind the curtains, watching a merchant sloop sail past on a parallel course with the shore. She was twenty-two years old and this was her third mission. She had received her baptism of fire during her first assignment, in 19th-century London, when she was just a rookie, part of a support unit attached to the team of Delaney, Cross, and Steiger. When it was all over, only two of that support unit had been left alive. She had learned fast and she had learned the hard way.

Since then, she and the other surviving member of that unit, Corporal Scott Neilson, had completed one other temporal adjustment mission, during the Second World War. On that occasion, they had been teamed with Lt. Wendell Jones, but the logistics of this assignment had required a new partner for them this time. Jones was black and there were certain historical scenarios where a black man simply couldn't function very well. In colonial Boston, there was a fairly large population of blacks, but most of them were slaves, and even though many of the Boston colonists—such as Sam Adams, who objected to slavery in principle—had freed their slaves, they still did not possess the same rights as white men did and would not for many years to come. Because of this, Craven and Neilson had been teamed with Master Sergeant Rico Chavez, a veteran of Anglo-Chicano ancestry, whose physical characteristics could easily allow him to pose as anything from a Spaniard to an Italian to a Balkan or what was known as a "black Irishman," descended from mixed Irish and Spanish stock. In addition to them, Forrester had dispatched another team, two being all that he could spare, consisting of Capt. Michael Seavers, one of the original members of the First Division, Sgt. Ivan Federoff, a veteran of over two dozen missions, and Lt. Geoffrey Stone, a former field agent for the T.I.A.

As Linda Craven was getting her first look at colonial Boston, Stone, Federoff, and Seavers were in the other bedroom, taking advantage of the time to grab some sleep. Chavez was behind her, relaxing on the bed and reading, but Nielson, as usual, was too keyed up to rest. A trick-shooting enthusiast and collector of antique firearms, he was eagerly examining the small arsenal of handguns Hunter had obtained in the 20th century.

"A CZ-75," he said admiringly, picking up a black 9 mm. Czech-made semiautomatic. "This one's a collector's item. And a .45 Colt Combat Commander; a couple of Berettas, a Model 84 .380 and a 9 mm. 92F; a snub-nosed Colt King Cobra .357 Magnum; a couple of small double-action Walther .22s; a 10 mm. Springfield with convertible barrels and magazines; and Christ, look at this thing!" He picked up a huge cannon with a dull black steel frame. "An Israeli Desert Eagle .44 Automag with a ten-shot clip! He's even got a reloading press complete with dies! You'd think he was expecting an assault team!"

"He was," said Chavez, without looking up from his book. "Us."

"Us?" said Nielson, puzzled.

"Well, not us specifically," Chavez said, "but he didn't trust Priest and the others any more than they trusted him. Not that I can blame him. If I were in his shoes, I'd have done the same thing. Prepared a safehouse and laid in some weapons, just in case. Looks like he picked some good ones, too."

"Why only lead projectile weapons?" Linda asked. "If he thought he might have to go up against the agency, we'd have him easily outgunned."

"I wouldn't bet on that," said Chavez. "Never underestimate *any* sort of firearm," he said. "I'd sooner go up against a street punk armed with a laser than a good shooter armed with a .22 rimfire. In the hands of somebody who knows what they're doing, it would kill you just as dead. In the 20th century, where Hunter picked these up, a semiauto .22 rimfire was frequently the chosen weapon of professional assassins. It's a very high-velocity round, and soft, so you get good expansion with practically no recoil. Light and very accurate."

"No stopping power, though," said Neilson.

Chavez chuckled. He made a "gun" with his thumb and index finger and pointed it at Neilson. "I know what you're thinking," he said in a slightly breathy, menacing voice. "This here's only a .22 rimfire, a piddly little round with no stopping power to speak of. So I'm just going to have to shoot you six times in the head."

Neilson grinned. "I see your point."

"Actually," said Chavez, "what the pros used to do with those things is a technique they called 'the zipper.' They'd start at your midsection and work up in a straight line, rapid fire—bang, bang, bang, bang, bang," he demonstrated with his finger gun, moving up an imaginary line along Neilson's body. "That way, even if none of the individual shots proved fatal, the cumulative effect of the trauma would be. All this talk about stopping power you antique collectors get into is just a lot of nonsense. Shot placement is what counts. Of course, you don't have that problem with lasers, plasma pistols, or disruptors. You don't need to be as accurate, but then it would have been difficult for Hunter to get his hands on those without some connections. Hell, even the regular troops don't get issued disruptors, they're so paranoid of letting those get loose. And they're not easily concealable. Let me see that automag," he said to Neilson.

Neilson picked up the Desert Eagle, made sure the safety was on, and handed it to him.

"Jeez, heavy sucker, isn't it?" said Chavez, hefting it experimentally. "Never fired one of these myself. Must have one hell of a kick."

"About the same as a compensated .45," said Neilson. "I have a .44 Magnum in my collection, but it's a revolver. Kicks about twice as much as that thing. But the nice thing about that round is that it gives you a lot of versatility if you load your own cartridges, which is what that press is for. See, depending on what kind of bullet you use and how much powder, you can pretty much tailor-make your ammunition to suit your purpose. You can load a soft-point bullet that'll spend most of its energy on impact and hit like a sledgehammer or you can load for penetration. Use a copper-jacketed hollow-point bullet, stoke the casing with enough powder, and you can shoot through walls or vehicles."

"Primitive, but nasty," Chavez said. "I wouldn't underrate them."

He gave the pistol back to Neilson.

"With weapons like that, I'm surprised they didn't have stricter firearms regulations in the 20th century," said Linda.

"The laws varied, but they had the same basic problems we've got," Nielson said. "The law of supply and demand. Hell, look at Boston. Right now, the British are enforcing the customs regulations more stringently than ever, with the Royal

Navy backing them up, yet at least half the merchants here are into smuggling. If people really want something, somebody will provide it. You could ban weapons manufacture, but someone would simply set up a machine shop and start turning them out illegally."

"I remember an assignment I had in L.A. back in the 20th century," said Chavez. "We had to bust up a Network drug-running operation. The kids in the barrio could get just about anything they wanted, but even if they couldn't buy a gun, they sometimes made their own by breaking a radio antenna off a car, taping it to a wooden handle, and using a piece of metal and a rubber band for a firing mechanism. Stick a .22 shell in the damn thing and you've got yourself a single-shot zip gun, as they called them. Liable to blow up in your face, but it could be surprisingly effective if it didn't."

"They tried gun control laws," said Neilson, "but they only wound up taking weapons out of the hands of honest people who deserved the right to protect themselves. If a person takes it in his head to kill somebody, he'll manage to find a way. You can control weapons to some degree, but you can't really control people."

"So what are you saying, Scott?" Linda said. "Let anyone who wants to buy a plasma gun or a laser? The streets would be a war zone."

"In case you haven't noticed, the streets *are* a war zone," Neilson said. "Okay, I understand what you're saying and I'm really not unsympathetic, but consider where we are now. In a few years, these people are going to fight their war for independence and the incident that's going to kick the whole thing off is when the British troops march on Lexington and Concord. They'll fail because the farmers of this time have access to muskets and powder and they'll fight to protect their rights."

"The old argument about the constitutional right to keep and bear arms," said Linda. "The founding fathers weren't talking about the right to own and carry guns, you know. They were talking about a militia."

"Really? Then why wasn't everyone disarmed when Cornwallis surrendered?" Neilson said. "What did they mean by a militia, after all? It's when you gather armed citizens together for defense, like they did at Lexington and Concord. The exact wording in the Constitution is, 'A well-regulated militia, being necessary to the security of a free state, the right of the people to keep and bear arms shall not be infringed.' It doesn't say that the right of the people to bear arms *in a militia* shall not be infringed, it says that the right of the people to keep and bear arms shall not be infringed because there may be a need to raise a militia. The Minutemen didn't turn their guns in when they stopped drilling. They took them home with them because they were their own personal property."

"It would be interesting if we could speak with some of the founding fathers and find out exactly what they had in mind when they framed the Constitution," Linda said. "Unfortunately, the timing isn't right, let alone the fact it would be dangerous."

"I wonder what they'd say if we asked them what they meant when they wrote 'the right to life, liberty, and the pursuit of happiness'?" said Chavez. "Did they mean the right to live free or did they mean no abortions? And that phrase appeared in the Declaration of Independence, not in the Constitution. In the Constitution, it merely says that no person shall be deprived of life, liberty, or property without due process of law. It certainly never occurred to them that it might become necessary to define exactly what constitutes a person. They also guaranteed freedom of religion, but contrary to popular belief, nowhere in the Constitution does the word 'God' even appear. 'One nation, under God' is only in the pledge of allegiance, which technically has no constitutional authority behind it. Let's face it, they never realized that things would get so complicated."

"But you have to admit one thing," said Neilson, "if it wasn't for the fact that the colonists were able to keep and bear arms, the British would have rolled right over them."

"Well, maybe so," said Linda, "but I'd hate to think what would happen if any citizen in the 27th century could walk into a store and buy a plasma weapon. I somehow doubt the founding fathers would have approved of that."

"Oh, I don't know," said Neilson, with a grin. "Just think what the Minutemen could have done with a few plasma guns and laser rifles. And it's interesting that when you take relative population figures into account, the incidence of violent crime with firearms was far less in times when weapons were not regulated than when they were."

"Maybe, but you gotta watch that," Chavez said. "Statistics are always misleading. It depends on what you use for your data. It doesn't make much sense to compare 19th-century Dodge City, for example, with 21st-century New York. You can take relative population figures into account, just as you said, but that still doesn't make for a complete picture. You're forgetting about the psychological factor of stress given increased population density and things like pollution and noise, which had demonstrable adverse effects upon the central nervous system, making people more aggressive. It's inevitable that with increased population density and industrialization, you'll get increased violence. Besides, come to think of it, Dodge City would be a bad example anyway. One of the first things Wyatt Earp and other frontier marshalls did was to institute a very basic form of gun control at shotgun point. Surrender your gunbelt within city limits or get out of town. Or take your chances with a load of 'double-ought.' They had to run the towns and they understood real well that a gun only gives you power when no one else has got one."

"You know, right now in Boston, there are no laws of any kind restricting firearms," said Nielson." In fact, there were no such laws at all in America until the middle of the 19th century, when carpetbaggers started passing them to disarm former Confederates. Up until that time, the courts upheld the right of citizens to carry arms, openly *or* concealed, in order to defend themselves. At this time in Boston, it's very common for men to carry swords or pistols. There's been rioting in the streets, but interestingly, not one citizen of Boston has been run-through or shot."

"Not yet, but they will," said Linda.

"Only after the British troops arrive," said Neilson. "Remember, the first fatalities didn't occur until the Boston Massacre. The Sons of Liberty were a rowdy bunch of streetfighters with easy access to firearms, but though they busted a few heads and tarred and feathered a few Tories, they never actually killed anybody until the British sent armed troops against them. To seize their arms and ammunition."

"Yeah, like you've seized mine," said Hunter, coming into the room and seeing his cache of weapons spread out on the table along with the commandos' gear. "I suppose you found the hand grenades and the plastique, as well?"

"What?" said Linda.

Hunter grinned. "Just kidding, Corporal. You've got it all, scout's honor."

"Cross your heart and hope to die?" said Linda, wryly.

"Hey, not me," said Hunter. "I'd like to get out of this thing in one piece, if you don't mind." He smiled. "You know, I couldn't help overhearing some of your conversation. It's funny, in a way."

"Funny?" Neilson said.

"Yeah. We have the same sort of conversations over on our side," Hunter said. He grinned. "Get a bunch of C.I.S. agents together and they start sounding like a faculty meeting of some university history department."

"Not so unusual," said Chavez, pulling out a pack of cigarettes. "What we all have in common is that our lives often depend on our knowledge and understanding of historical events." He lit one and tossed the pack to Hunter.

"Thanks," said Hunter. He glanced at the label. "Noncarcinogenic, huh?"

"The benefits of genetic engineering," Chavez said. "Taste better, too."

"We banned 'em," Hunter said, lighting up. "Our tobacco companies started selling dope instead."

"Seriously?" said Linda.

"Seriously," said Hunter. "We instituted a system of addict registration. Cut the market out from under organized crime and still managed to turn a tidy profit and generate some tax revenue. You guys ought to try it. 'Course, now the crime families push cigarettes . . ."

Craven and Neilson exchanged glances, not certain if he was serious or not.

"No, it's a funny thing about soldiers," Hunter continued, inhaling deeply and blowing out a long stream of smoke. "Not just modern temporal soldiers, but even soldiers in the past, wherever you're dealing with a culture that's got a decent rate of literacy. You've always got a substantial number of military personnel with academic or philosophical inclinations. They read like crazy. Take graduate degrees. Write books. Learn languages. Study everything from psychology to engineering, but especially history. History's always been big with soldiers. I wonder why."

"Maybe it's because soldiers never get to see the big picture," Chavez said. "It's what we're always told, isn't it? Some poor grunt in the middle of an Asian jungle, thousands of miles away from home, just can't understand why he's been asked to take the same fucking hill six times, only to pull back each time and let the enemy have it once again. He's told it's all part of the big picture, which is something he never gets to see because only the high command sees the big picture. So if he's lucky, he survives the action and when he gets back home, he picks up a book and reads about some old battle, hoping he might be able to see the big picture there and relate it somehow to the big picture that he had been a part of. Try to figure it all out. Only that doesn't make sense, either, because he reads about how the high command screwed up in that old battle and got all these people killed for nothing.

"So he reads some more about the history of that period where the old battle took place, to see if there was some reason for it, only he can't find one, so he continues reading, still trying to figure it all out. And meanwhile, while he's doing all this reading on the side, he gets promoted and eventually he winds up a general, part of the high command, and now suddenly he's supposed to be in a position to see the big picture for himself. Only he still can't see it, because some politician is telling him to do something that makes absolutely no sense to him at all and when he says he doesn't understand it, he's told it's because he can't see the big picture. Only the politicians get to see the big picture."

Neilson chuckled.

"So he studies up on politics," Chavez continued, "serves his time, retires with a pension, and runs for office. Gets himself elected to the Senate. So there he is in the Senate, being asked to vote for some ridiculous appropriation that makes no sense to him at all, but he's told it's all part of the big picture. Only he *still* can't see it, because only the President and his advisors get to see the big picture."

Hunter was grinning.

"So he runs for President," Chavez went on, in a slow drawl. "Wins in a landslide because he was a war hero and a great American. Now, finally, the big picture! But no. The corporation heads who contributed to his campaign tell him that they're the only ones who *really* get to see the big picture, so he does what they tell him to and after he completes his term of office, they reward him with a seat on the executive board and now he's really excited. He's finally made it, he's going to get to see the big picture at last . . ."

"And?" said Neilson.

"And they all gather together in the boardroom, and they light up their cigars, and they go over their reports, and they examine all their charts, and they go over all their profit statements, and they have someone come in and explain it all to them so they can understand it, and they pour brandy into their snifters and loosen up their ties and congratulate one another and talk about how things will be even better during the next quarter, and they schedule their next meeting, which will take place in the Bahamas at a corporate resort complete with hookers, and they get ready to leave, and our guy suddenly jumps up and says, 'But wait! What about the big picture?' And they all look at him like he's crazy. 'The big picture!' he says again. *'What about the big picture?'* And the chairman of the board looks at him with absolute amazement and says, 'Man, you mean to tell me you were on that fucking hill, *too*?' "

Hunter burst out laughing.

"Give me that gun," said Linda. "I'm gonna shoot him."

"Got a permit?" Neilson asked.

"You go to hell."

Delaney walked in the door. "Dinner's on," he said. He glanced around at them. "What's the joke?"

"You ever hear the one about the big picture?" Neilson asked.

Delaney grimaced. "Yeah. I was the idiot on that fucking hill. Now come on, we'll have the briefing during dinner."

8

The small, secluded country chapel stood in the middle of a grove of trees, well hidden from the road. The estate on whose property it stood was out of sight over the next hill. It belonged to a wealthy Boston Tory who only made use of it on weekends, except on those nights when the Hellfire Club met. On those nights, he would saddle up his horse and ride over to the chapel, tie the horse up outside in the grove, take the hooded black robe out of his saddlebag and tie it around him with a monk's cord, then put on the black mask that covered his entire upper face and join the "congregation." He always felt a profound thrill of anticipation at such times, like a small boy about to do something that he knew was wrong. His young wife, with whom he had sexual relations perhaps once a month, would have been surprised at the vigor with which he participated in the night's events.

It was late and the moon was full as John Hewitt rode up to the chapel in his carriage with Lucas Priest and Finn Delaney. When told that "young Andrew" would not be joining them, Hewitt had merely shrugged and said, "As you think best." Then he grinned and added, "But it would have been a good education for the lad."

The grove was already full of horses and several carriages, being attended to by servants. Finn and Lucas both noticed several men moving about, armed with muskets, pistols, and swords. A wooden table stood not far away, beneath the trees, with several men seated around it, drinking wine, smoking their pipes, and playing cards by lamplight. Several more men were gathered around a crackling fire. Except for the carriages, the scene resembled the camp of a band of forest brigands.

"It seems that most everyone's arrived," said Hewitt. He reached beneath the seat of the carriage and pulled out two black parcels tied with cords. "Put these on," he said.

They were the robes and masks.

"Now remember the rules," said Hewitt in a somber tone. "You are not to ask anybody's name, under any circumstances. This is a secret brotherhood."

"How can it be secret when you all seem to know one another?" Delaney asked.

Hewitt looked irritated at the question. "That is another matter. Once the vestments have been donned, each man is without a name. We are all merely secret brothers of the Hellfire Club. Keep your vestments on at all times, and especially you must not remove your masks nor ask anyone else to remove theirs. You may not leave until the meeting is concluded. The doors to the chapel shall be bolted. If you need to relieve yourself at any time, use the side door of the chapel and follow the path to the outhouse. Remember that wandering about outside is not permitted. There are guards on duty. We must protect ourselves against unwanted intruders. Afterward, we shall meet back here at the carriage. Any questions?"

Delaney glanced at Lucas. "No, no questions," he said. "Shall we 'don our vestments,' brother?"

Lucas gave him a warning glance and Delaney rolled his eyes. They put on their robes and masks and stepped out of the carriage, allowing Hewitt to proceed ahead of them.

"I feel like Zorro disguised as a monk," whispered Delaney.

"Keep a handle on it, Finn," Lucas whispered back.

"Shouldn't we be chanting something?" said Delaney.

They joined a group of silent, hooded figures moving through the chapel doors. Spread out and hidden in the woods around them, dressed in black and with their faces camouflaged, were the other two commando teams, ready to move in quickly if anything went wrong or if Nikolai Drakov put in an appearance, though it was doubtful if they'd recognize him among all the hooded figures. They had no idea what they could expect, so they were prepared for anything. The armed guards moving around outside presented no real problem. The commandos could easily stay out of their sight, and if, by chance, one of them were spotted, the guard would be quickly rendered unconscious before an alarm could be given.

Inside the chapel, the glow of candlelight provided a dim, shadowy illumination. The pews had been removed and in their stead were wooden tables, chairs, and benches with cushions, giving the interior of the chapel the aspect of some bizarre religious coffeehouse. There was no altar, merely a tall wooden pulpit looking down upon the congregation. The robed figures were seated at the tables, many of them smoking, while masked women, dressed in white robes, moved among the tables, serving drinks. The soft undertone of conversation was broken only by the rustling of robes, the sound of pewter mugs being put down on wooden tables, some coughing and the tapping out of pipes.

"You believe this?" whispered Delaney, standing close to Lucas. They had lost sight of Hewitt, who had vanished among the hooded figures.

"I figure at least forty, fifty men," said Lucas, glancing around.

They found a table and sat down. A white-robed woman, hooded and with a white mask tied around her face, leaving only her eyes, mouth, and chin visible, wordlessly set down two mugs of wine before them. She gave them a knowing smile and proceeded on to the next table.

Suddenly the silence was broken by the sound of the chapel organ playing a dirgelike, somber melody and the white-robed figures all retreated to the back room. Everybody stood. A man robed and masked in black like all the others mounted the pulpit and stood with this hands braced on the sides, surveying the room. The organ stopped and there was silence.

"Hellfire to the Sons of Liberty!" the man at the pulpit said, in a loud voice that echoed through the chapel.

"Hellfire to the Sons of Liberty!" the congregation responded in chorus.

"Be seated, brothers."

They sat with a rustling of robes.

"You recognize the voice?" Delaney whispered.

Lucas shook his head.

"The horseman is among us," said the figure at the pulpit and an excited ripple ran through the crowd. "He is pleased to see so many loyal subjects of the king gathered here together. Long live His Majesty, King George!"

"Long live His Majesty, King George!" the congregation responded.

"We live in perilous times, my brothers," said the man at the pulpit. "We have seen the Sons of Violence attack our fellow loyal citizens of Boston. We have seen them burn and pillage. We have seen them loot and plunder. We have seen them stone our houses and smash out our windows while our families huddled terrified within and we ourselves shook with rage and indignation, helpless in the face of their superior numbers. We have been forced to stand by and watch while they tarred and feathered our officials and belabored them with clubs. And then we have all read how they justify their actions in their lying newspapers, accusing *us* of treason, accusing *us* of disloyalty, accusing *us* of being the oppressors!"

An angry undertone ran through the crowd.

"They want the freedom to speak out, but only for those who would agree with them! They want the freedom to assemble, but only so that they can fire up the common mob and break into our homes and make off with our possessions! They demand freedom of the press, but only so that they can fill their newspapers with their seditious lies! They demand freedom from taxation, but only so that they can continue smuggling with impunity! We, who import our fabrics and our wines from England, our carriages, our furniture, our tea and other necessaries, must pay our legal duties to the Crown as loyal subjects, yet they, a bunch of upstart common laborers and rabble, feel that they must be exempt! They cry out that Parliament oppresses all Americans, yet who among us has not felt oppressed by them? *Ours* are the families who have founded these thirteen English colonies. *Ours* are the families who have built the cities, who have fought the Indians and the French, who have built the ships and founded trade and established our colonial assemblies! *Ours* was the toil, *ours* the sweat and blood! And now these dock porters and simple cordwainers, these rope makers and illiterate apprentices descended from indentured servants would bite the hand that feeds them and dictate terms to *us*! Well, we shall suffer these indignities no longer! We say to them, *no more*!"

"No more! No more!"

"It's like a revival meeting," whispered Delaney.

"There is one among us who has set us all an excellent example," said the speaker. "One who has spoken to the Sons of Violence in the only language that they can understand. Until now, the rabble has been unopposed, free to strike at night and to terrorize anyone they pleased. My friends, that time has ended! The choice is ours, my brothers! We can unite and end this reign of terror, or we can huddle, quaking in our homes, waiting fearfully and helplessly to see whom the Sons of Violence will choose for their next victim." He suddenly pointed at one of the robed figures below him. "Will it be you?"

The man shifted uncomfortably. The finger moved on.

"Or will it be you? Or you? Or *you*?" He pointed at another man. "Will *yours* be the next home that they tear down?" He pointed again. "Will *you* be the next one to be seized and dragged into the Common, stripped naked for all to see, and basted with a coat of steaming tar and feathers?"

He pulled his hand back and clenched it into a fist.

"And can we believe that the outlaws will stop there?" he said. "With no one to oppose them, will they not grow bolder still? In the middle of the night, they will come and visit *you*," he said, pointing suddenly at another member of the congregation, "and in their frenzy of destruction, while they hold you helpless, they will look upon your daughter and they will find her pleasing. Two of them will hold her while she struggles, yet a third will tear her nightdress from her innocent young body; they will run their filthy, rough, and callused common hands over her sweet virgin flesh; they will bear her down and have their way with her while she weeps and screams in terror and you are forced to watch! And afterward, when you walk the streets together, which one of the carters who pass by you will smirk with secret knowledge? Which one of the drunken dock workers will call out her name after you pass?"

He looked around at the entire congregation.

"It could happen to any one of you," he said, "And it *will* happen, unless we stop it *now*!"

The sense of outrage and indignation surged throughout the crowd.

"These common criminals must be taught a lesson!" he shouted. "Who will be the next to learn?"

"Ebenezer MacIntosh!" a deep and resonant voice cried out.

"Drakov!" said Delaney, looking all around, as did many of

the others, but there was no way to tell where the voice had come from. The speaker waited until the undertone died down.

"Our friend has chosen well," he said. "The horseman has named Ebenezer MacIntosh. A drunken cobbler. A common brawler, the leader of the South End Gang. It was he who led the mob against the home of our good friend Thomas Hutchinson, thereby reducing our proudest citizen to penury. And was he punished for this crime? No sooner was he thrown into jail by our sheriff than he was released as a result of threats from the very rioters he led! And today, he swaggers through the streets and boasts of his invulnerability! *Is* he invulnerable?"

No!" the crowd yelled.

"Is he beyond the law?"

"No!"

"Is he going to pay for what he's done?"

"Yes!" voices called out. "Yes, hang him, make him pay! Hang him!"

"The jury has reached its verdict," said the speaker. "The accused, Ebenezer MacIntosh, stands guilty, as charged. So say you all?"

"Aye! Aye!"

"Then, Ebenezer MacIntosh, for your crimes against the loyal citizens of Boston, we hereby sentence you to hang!"

"Jesus, now what do we do?" Delaney said.

"We'll have to stop them," Lucas said. "We'll have to get to him before they do and warn him."

"In ancient times," the speaker continued, "warriors united in a common, sacred cause would gather on the eve of a great battle to celebrate their courage and to fortify their manhood. Thus do we revive this ancient custom. Thus do we celebrate our unity and fortify our cause! Hellfire to the Sons of Liberty, my brothers!"

"Hellfire to the Sons of Liberty!"

The organist began to play as the speaker descended from the pulpit and the white-robed women came filing out with trays of wine, ale, rum, and food. The women moved along the tables, setting down their trays and being pulled into the laps of the robed men. At the table next to theirs, a man pulled the cord holding a woman's robe fastened around her waist and it fell open, revealing her to be completely naked underneath. He started fondling and kissing her. None of the men undressed. They merely pulled open their robes and loosened their clothing underneath, pulling the laughing women down into their laps, dragging them to the floor, laying them out on top of tables and benches. One of the women came and sat down on Delaney's knee, smiling and reaching for the cord that tied his robe.

"Not now," he said. "A moment. Nature calls."

She shrugged and moved on to another man.

"Let's get the hell out of here," he said to Lucas.

They rose and moved to the side door. All around them, the orgy was in progress as masked men and women fumbled inside one another's robes, laughing and indulging in the license of anonymous sex. Finn and Lucas left by the side door and stepped out into the cool night breeze.

"Stand where you are!" said a voice out of the darkness. "Raise your hands above your heads!"

They froze and did as they were told. Several men stepped out of the shadows, holding muskets and pistols aimed directly at them.

"What *is* this?" Lucas said, in an angry tone. "Can't a man even relieve himself in peace? Put down those guns!"

Another man, this one dressed in a black robe and a mask, unlike the guards, stepped forward.

"Hold your arms out straight, away from your sides," he said. They both recognized the voice of the speaker in the pulpit. They did as they were told. "Pull back their hoods and remove those masks. If one of them so much as blinks, shoot them both at once."

They stood absolutely motionless as one of the men stepped forward, yanked back their hoods, and removed their masks.

"Do any of you know these men?" the speaker asked.

The guards all shook their heads.

"Neither do I," the speaker said. "It appears that we have caught ourselves some spys. Search them."

The man who had removed their masks suddenly jerked, then with a surprised expression, he collapsed to the ground. There were several rapid hissing noises and the remaining guards all fell, dropping their weapons. The robed man glanced around him with alarm, and then he jerked and fell as well. Chavez, Seavers, and Federoff stepped out of the shadows, holding their stinger pistols.

"Nice work," said Lucas.

"What do you want us to do with them?" asked Seavers.

"Pull them back into the trees. They'll come around. But I want that one," he said, pointing to the robed man.

Chavez bent down and removed his mask. It was Moffat.

"Know him?" he asked.

Lucas shook his head. "No. But he seemed to be the one in charge. He's working with Drakov."

"So Hunter was right, he *is* here," Seavers said.

"Yeah, he was inside," said Finn.

"You want us to take the place?" asked Federoff.

"Are you kidding? There's seventy or eighty people in there and about half of them are women. There's no way I want to risk that. Besides, Drakov could easily clock out in all the confusion, if he hasn't already. No, have everyone pull back to the safehouse. We're taking this man with us for interrogation. I want him alone in one of the bedrooms, restrained, with the windows and drapes closed, so he won't know where he is. We don't know who he is, so let's not take any chances. He sees nobody who's not in colonial dress, understood?"

"Got it," Seavers said.

"Good. Move out."

Within moments, they were all back in the safehouse, where Hunter was waiting for them with Linda and Andre. They had not risked leaving him alone. Hunter raised his eyebrows when he saw Federoff and Seavers carrying the unconscious robed man into the back bedroom on the upper floor.

"What the hell did you do, kidnap a monk?" he said.

"One of the leaders of the Hellfire Club," said Lucas. "You were right, Hunter. Drakov is here."

"You *saw* him?"

"No, but we heard his voice. I'd know that voice anywhere. It seems we owe you an apology. You were right all along."

"Don't mention it," Hunter said.

"How well do you know Ebenezer MacIntosh?" asked Lucas.

"Mac? We're old drinkin' buddies, him and I. Why, what's up?"

"They've targeted him for assassination," said Delaney. "They're going to hang him. We've got to get to him first and warn him."

"I'm on my way," said Hunter.

"Neilson, you go with him," Lucas said.

"Still don't trust me, huh?" said Hunter.

"No, I just don't want to lose you," Lucas said. "You're the only one of us Macintosh knows, so you'll have to be the one to warn him, but by now, the Network's got to know something's gone wrong. They won't find any trace of Carruthers or the other two and you've dropped out of sight, so they'll be looking for you. I want you covered and Neilson's lightning with a gun and a crack shot. Scott, take a stinger with you, but I'd rather you carried something with a bit more authority, as well. I see Hunter's got silencers for some of those pieces and I'd rather not risk using a laser or a plasma weapon on the streets of Boston."

"Help yourself, kid," Hunter said to Neilson.

Neilson walked over to the table and unhesitantly chose the .45 Colt Combat Commander. He started to attach the silencer.

"Wouldn't you like a bit more firepower?" Hunter said. "That only holds a seven-shot clip with room for one more in the chamber."

"If I can't get the job done with eight rounds, I probably won't get it done at all," said Neilson. "But I'll take some spare clips, just in case."

"Go ahead and make your choice," Lucas said to Hunter.

Hunter glanced at him.

"Be my guest," said Lucas. He smiled. "Call it a gesture of good faith."

Hunter chose the Beretta 9 mm. He screwed a silencer onto the weapon and pocketed several spare clips. He slapped in a magazine, racked the slide and jacked a round into the chamber, and stuck it in his waistband, cocked and locked, in the "Mexican carry" mode. He picked up several spare magazines and slipped them in his pockets.

"What do you think they'll do with Steiger?" he asked.

"I'm hoping they'll keep him alive so they've got something to deal with if they're backed into a corner," Lucas said tensely, "but I can't afford to worry about him now. The mission comes first. He'd have done the same in my place. But if you run into any Network people, try to take at least one of them alive."

"You mind if they're wounded just a little?" Neilson asked.

"Not in the least," said Lucas.

"Good," said Neilson. "What about if we run into these Hellfire characters?"

"Try not to," Lucas said. "But if you do . . ." He took a

deep breath. "If they get to MacIntosh before you do, don't interfere if it means shooting anybody."

"You mean let them hang him."

"Yeah. That's what I mean."

The room was silent for a moment."

"Okay," said Neilson, after a pause. "If that's the way you want it."

"It's not the way I want it, but it's the way it's got to be," said Lucas. "We're here to stop a temporal disruption, not create one." He hesitated. "Hunter, I know that as a C.I.S. agent—"

"You don't have to say it, pilgrim," Hunter said, "We've got a deal."

"Yeah. I hope so."

"What do you want us to do once we've warned MacIntosh?" asked Neilson.

"Warn MacIntosh and tell him what the Hellfire Club is planning," Lucas said. "It looks like they're going after individual leaders of the Sons of Liberty, in which case Adams is the most logical target. We'll have to keep an eye on him, but we can't keep track of all of them. If we can get the Sons of Liberty to do part of our job for us, so much the better. Tell MacIntosh to assign some of his South End boys to watch the leaders. Have several people on each of them if possible, Hancock, Otis, Edes, Revere, all of them. Then get right back here. We're going to have to play this by ear and I don't want to have to worry about where anybody is. Drakov knows we're here and that may force his hand. If our friend in the other room can't help us, we could be in a world of trouble."

Not long after Neilson left with Hunter, Moffat started to come around. They had all changed into colonial clothing by then, but their attempt at deception didn't last long. At first, Moffat was confused and disoriented. He awoke to find himself tied to a chair in a strange room with all the curtains drawn. As his eyes gradually focused and he realized that he'd been taken captive, his lips drew tight into a stubborn line and a defiant look came into his eyes.

"You have been captured by the Sons of Liberty," said Lucas. "We have some questions to put to you. If you cooperate, then you will not be harmed. But if you refuse to answer, it will not go well with you."

Moffat's gaze traveled around the room, taking in his surroundings, sizing up his captors.

"You don't fool me, "he said. "I know who you are." He gazed pointedly at Andre. "I should have killed you when I had the chance."

Andre stared at him. "You're the headless horseman," she said.

"That's right," Moffat said proudly. "But killing me won't do you a bit of good. You're too late. You're much too late to stop it. I don't really matter anymore, so do your worst. I'm not afraid."

"Our worst could be much worse than merely killing you," said Lucas. "But there's no reason it should come to that. I don't think you know what you're really involved in. If you help us, perhaps we could help you."

Moffat gave a short bark of derisive laughter. "The way you helped my master, I suppose?"

"Your master?" Lucas said.

"Lucas . . ." Finn said. "He's a hominoid."

"Of course," said Andre. "It would make perfect sense. Whom else could Drakov trust to carry out his plans?"

"I may have failed," said Moffat, bitterly, "but my master will succeed. There is nothing you can do to stop him. You've lost and in that, I'll take my satisfaction."

"Why?" said Lucas. "Why should you take satisfaction in a temporal disaster, in all the untold damage it could cause, in all the loss of life? What possible satisfaction could you find in that?"

"Forget it, Lucas," said Delaney. "Drakov has him thoroughly programmed and conditioned. You'll never get through to him."

"Maybe not," Lucas said, "but it's got to be worth a try. He can still think. He can still feel. He's still as human as the rest of us."

Moffat stared at him. "What did you say?"

"I said that no matter what Drakov may have done to you, you're still a human being, with a mind and will of your own. Think for yourself, man. At least listen to what we have to say."

Moffat glanced around at them in bewilderment. "What sort of trick is this?" he said. "Why do you tell me that I'm human?"

Lucas looked at him with surprise. "Because you are, of course," he said. "You mean to tell me that Drakov told you you're not human? What did he say you were?"

Moffat's defiance started to slip away in his bafflement. He had expected brutal interrogation, but not this. "You're trying to confuse me," he said. "I know what I am. I am one of my master's hominoids. He created me."

"That's right," said Lucas, "but that doesn't make you a machine or some sort of subhuman creature. You're serious, aren't you? You really believe that's what you are?"

Moffat had been programmed and trained to resist interrogation, but this was something he had not expected. He swallowed nervously, and deep within his subconscious, a flicker of impossible hope appeared. "You admit that my master has created me, and yet you still say that I'm human? How can that be?"

Lucas pulled up a chair and sat down in front of him, seeing a slim chance to get through to him, perhaps to circumvent his programming. No amount of psychological conditioning could be absolutely foolproof. The mind was a versatile, resilient thing. There *was* a chance. There had to be.

"What is your name?" he asked.

Moffat did not reply.

"Surely you can tell us what you're called," said Lucas. "That will give us no advantage over Drakov."

"My name is Jared Moffat."

"What do you know of your creation, Jared?" Lucas asked.

Moffat swallowed nervously again, but said nothing.

"All right, let me tell you what *I* know of your creation," Lucas said, "and you decide for yourself if it rings true or not. You know about the parallel universe?"

Moffat hesitated, then nodded.

"All right, then," Lucas said. "Hear me out. The story of your creation began in the parallel universe. It started with a man, a scientist, called Dr. Phillipe Moreau. He was a brilliant genetic engineer, a genius. He was the head of an experiment called Project Infiltrator, funded and established by the Special Operations Group, our counterparts in the parallel timeline. The scientists there believe that the way to overcome the confluence phenomenon is to try and create temporal disruptions in our universe, leading to a timestream split. They are convinced that this will result in our two timelines being forced apart, and quite honestly, they may even be right. But it might also make the situation worse. There simply is no way of telling.

"The point is," Lucas continued, "in order to accomplish their aims, they have to send soldiers through into our universe by way of confluence points, where our two timelines intersect. If those soldiers succeed in disrupting our timeline and bringing about a timestream split, then they will never be able to get back home again and the Special Operations Group had a plan to insure that these troops would be unquestioningly obedient . . . and totally expendable. Moreau was part of that plan. He had originally intended to use genetic engineering to create humans who could be designed to perform specific tasks that ordinary humans couldn't do, to be stronger, more adaptable, able to survive environmental conditions that would be hostile to normal humans. He honestly believed that he would be introducing a stronger, more versatile strain into the human race that would eventually result in an improvement in the breed. But as often happens, his obsession gave him tunnel vision. He didn't foresee all the staggering implications of what he planned to do.

"The Special Operations Group established a top secret military lab for him to carry on his work," said Lucas, "and Moreau believed he had their full support, that they shared his aims, but in fact, what the Special Operations Group had in mind was something altogether different. What they wanted were genetically tailored, cannon-fodder soldiers, intellectually inhibited and emotionally stunted, with their pain centers blocked and their minds programmed so they could fight like automatons. Moreau wanted no part of it and his frustration and sense of betrayal made him vulnerable to Drakov, who was working with the Special Operations Group at the time. Working with them entirely for his own ends, I might add. Drakov abducted Moreau from Project Infiltrator, along with all his notes and experiments in progress, and he brought him to a hidden laboratory he had set up especially for him. He convinced Moreau that he had the same goals as he did and that he shared in Moreau's sense of betrayal. What Moreau didn't know was that Drakov, himself, was already an accomplished genetic engineer, as well as a lot of other things, and a genius in his own right. He watched Moreau and worked with him and learned from him and then he took Moreau's work and carried on from there.

"A hominoid is nothing more or less than a human clone, developed from human genetic material. The only difference is that hominoids are mules, incapable of reproduction, and their genetic material can be altered or augmented to suit a specific purpose. Drakov took those purposes much further than Moreau ever intended. He created a wide variety of hominoids, some from ordinary human genetic material carefully selected for specific traits, some with human and animal genetic material combined, and he sent them back through time, so that they could mature and he could clock back and make checks on them at various points of their development."

Lucas saw a reaction in Moffat and realized that he had struck a chord.

"The result was that years would pass for the hominoids while they matured, but only days or even minutes would pass for Drakov. With some of those hominoids, at various points in their development, Drakov would bring them back to his laboratory for conditioning or biological augmentation brought about by complex surgery. At the end, some of them looked perfectly normal, but some of them were monsters. He created genetically engineered giants, harpies, werewolves, vampires, even a centaur. Because, you see, Drakov may be a genius, but he is hopelessly insane."

"No," said Moffat, shaking his head, his voice barely above a whisper. "No, it cannot be."

"What do you know about Nikolai Drakov?" Lucas asked him. "What do you know about his past?"

Moffat moistened his lips and shook his head. "Nothing," he said. "It was not my place to ask such things. It was—"

"I'll tell you about his past," said Lucas. "I'll tell you who he is. Have you ever heard him mention General Moses Forrester?"

"Yes," said Moffat. "Often. I know that he is your commander. The director of the T.I.A. My creator's greatest enemy."

"And also his father," Lucas said.

Moffat stared at him with astonishment.

"He never told you that, did he?" said Lucas. "Nevertheless, it's true. If you could see Moses Forrester, if you could look at his face and eyes, you'd have no doubt that he is

Drakov's father. When Forrester was a young temporal soldier, out on his first mission, he became stranded in time. Trapped in 19th-century Russia. He was badly injured, crippled, and he believed he'd never get back home again. A young Russian gypsy girl nursed him back to health and they fell in love. She became pregnant with his child. Forrester planned to spend the rest of his life with her, but our people finally found him and he had to go back to the future. He did not belong in that time. Only Vanna, Drakov's mother, could not go with him. Forrester knew that if he told his superiors that Vanna was pregnant with his child, they would abort the fetus. He simply couldn't do it, so he never told them she was pregnant. He said good-bye to her and tried to explain why he had to leave, and though their hearts were broken, they each understood it had to be.

"But in the brief time that he had with her," Lucas went on, "he couldn't fully explain all about time travel and the antiagathic drugs that extend our lifespans and make us immune to disease, and she would never have understood all that anyway. What she did understand, she told her son, but what she didn't understand, she filled in with her own superstitious beliefs and imagination. The result was that a young, impressionable boy came to believe that he was somehow the result of a supernatural union between his mother and some sort of a demon from the future. That, and the hardship that they suffered, and her subsequent death, and his failure to understand why he never became sick and why he aged so much slower than everyone else around him resulted in a raging hatred for his 'demonic' father and a deep self-loathing. Over the years, it drove him utterly insane.

"What Drakov wants," said Lucas, "is to strike out against Moses Forrester, against time travel, against the very world that brought him into existence. And you are an unwitting part of that insane plan of vengeance. And there's something else you may not know. The real Nikolai Drakov is dead."

Moffat stared at him with incomprehension.

"At least, we think the original Nikolai Drakov is dead," said Lucas, "but we really can't be sure. Because, you see, one of the things that Drakov did with the process he stole from Phillipe Moreau was to use his own genetic material to replicate himself. We don't know how many times. The man you know may be the original Nikolai Drakov, but for all we know, he might be a hominoid just like yourself."

"No," said Moffat, his lower lip trembling. "No, that isn't possible."

"It's not only possible," said Lucas, "it's very probable. Chances are he doesn't even know himself. But one thing is for sure. Nobody can create life out of nothing. You may not have been born in the conventional manner and you may not be able to have children, but you are the result of genetic engineering. You may have been cloned in a Petri dish and gestated in an artificial womb, you may have been programmed and conditioned with certain psychological imperatives, but you're as human as the rest of us. You think. You bleed. You feel. No matter what you've been conditioned to believe. Your own independent thoughts may have been subverted in some ways, but what do your *feelings* tell you?"

"Oh, God," said Moffat, very softly. "Sally . . ." A tear rolled down his cheek.

Lucas stood. "Leave him alone now," he said softly. He shook his head sadly. "Poor bastard."

They left the room and softly closed the door.

9 _____

Johnny Small was frantic. He couldn't find Andre and the others anywhere. The innkeeper at the Peacock Tavern said he hadn't seen them and there was no one home at Hunter's house on Long Lane, either. It was as if they'd all simply disappeared without a trace. It was his job to watch them and now he had no idea where they were. He fingered the Liberty medallion Sam Adams had given him. Adams had expressed confidence in him and now he'd failed him. He had no idea what to do.

As he walked through the dark streets of Boston, he tried to think where they might have gone. They wouldn't have gone to one of the radical taverns, surely, because except for Hunter, they were all posing as Tories. The last time he had seen them, Andre had been on her way to meet with Hunter, so perhaps they were with him, but where? He tried to think where Hunter might have gone, who his close associates were. Perhaps one of them could tell him where Hunter could be found. He tried to think and then it came to him.

Hunter had been sponsored into the Sons of Liberty by Ben Edes and Ebenezer MacIntosh. The hour was late and Edes was known to retire early, but MacIntosh was a notorious carouser. He hurried to The Bunch of Grapes, but was told that he'd missed MacIntosh by only twenty minutes. He had gone staggering home, full of rum, as usual. Johnny showed his Liberty medallion and said he had an urgent message for

MacIntosh from Samuel Adams and the lie produced MacIntosh's address. He ran all the way there, desperately hoping that MacIntosh was not so drunk that he would be passed out by the time he arrived. As he ran, he had no idea that he was being followed.

"Mac, wake up," said Hunter.

"Whhuh? Who izzit?"

"Mac! Come on, Mac, wake up, God damn it!"

Hunter grabbed MacIntosh by his shirtfront and slapped him several times across the face. He had fallen into bed completely dressed, without even bothering to take his shoes off. MacIntosh came awake with a drunken roar, sat up in bed, and took a wild swing at Hunter. Hunter easily avoided it and threw him out of bed onto the floor. MacIntosh rose to his hands and knees and shook himself. He looked up and saw Hunter.

"Reese! Damn your eyes! What in God's name are ya doin' here?" he said, his voice thick with drink. "How'd ya get in here, anyway?"

"You left the door open, you drunken idiot. Come on, get up. We've got to get you out of here."

MacIntosh remained sitting on the floor, squinting at Hunter.

"Man can't even sleep in peace . . . what the devil do y'want? Breakin' inta a man's home at this ungodly hour . . ."

"Mac, get up!" said Hunter. "If you want to live, move yourself!"

"What kinda way is that ta talk? Go 'way. Lemme alone."

"Damn it, Mac . . ." Hunter went over to the washstand and picked up the basin. He threw the water into MacIntosh's face.

"Aaarrgh!"

MacIntosh lunged up off the floor and came lumbering at Hunter like an angry bear. Hunter ducked his swing and gave him a sharp jab in the solar plexus. MacIntosh wheezed and doubled over. Hunter threw him up against the wall and slapped him twice across the face.

"Snap out of it, Mac, damn you!"

MacIntosh made a small grunting, squealing sort of noise. "Gonna be sick . . ."

"Oh, for Christ's sake . . ."

Hunter stepped away as MacIntosh doubled over and threw up on the floor.

"Mac, you're a fucking mess," said Hunter.

MacIntosh wiped his mouth with his sleeve. "Now look what ya gone an' done," he said. "I'm gonna break yer bloody neck . . ."

"It's your own neck I'm trying to save, you fool," said Hunter. "They're going to hang you!"

MacIntosh blinked. "What? *Who?* What the devil are ya talkin' about?"

"The Tories! The Hellfire Club, you idiot! The followers of the headless horseman! They could be on there way here right now to lynch you, just like they did to those four friends of yours!"

MacIntosh paled. "The horseman's men? They're gonna *hang* me?"

"That's right, you fool. Sober up if you don't want to die! You've got to get out of here right now!"

"Sweet Mother o'God," said MacIntosh. "And ya come ta warn me. God bless ya, Reese, you're a real friend. I'm sorry I took a poke at ya—"

"Never mind that now," said Hunter, impatiently. "You've got to get out of here. Are you sober enough to remember what I tell you?"

"Aye, if comes to my own neck, that I am," said MacIntosh, rubbing his face. "They're not gonna hang Ebenezer MacIntosh, by God!"

"Listen to me carefully," said Hunter. "We haven't got much time and lives depend on it. The horseman's men are going to try to kill off the leaders of the Sons of Liberty, one by one. Get to your South End boys. Tell them that they've got to place a constant watch on Adams and the others or they'll wind up dangling from the Liberty Tree. Have several men watch each of them at all times, especially at night. And you stay out of sight, yourself. You got that?"

MacIntosh took a deep breath and nodded. "The horseman's men are gonna try ta kill Adams an' the others. Have my boys watch 'em, day an' night."

"Good man. Now come on, we've got to get you out of here. Have you got a place to go where you can hide out?"

"Aye, I'll go an' see my boys. They'll take care o' me. They'll know what ta do."

"All right, get moving. Quickly, now!"

MacIntosh grabbed his coat and hat and lumbered down the stairs, Hunter right behind him.

"God bless ya, Reese," he said as they stepped outside. "You're a good friend. I won't forget this—"

"Yeah, yeah, I'm a saint, I know. Get moving. And for God's sake, keep to the alleys. Don't let anybody see you. And don't forget what I told you."

"I won't forget. I'm on my way."

He shambled off into the darkness and turned into an alleyway. Hunter sighed with relief. And then he heard the sound of running footsteps. His fingers closed around the butt of his Beretta, but he relaxed when he saw Johnny Small come running up to him.

"Mr. Hunter! Mr. Hunter! Thank God I've found you!"

The boy was out of breath. Hunter grabbed him by his shoulders.

"Steady on, lad. What is it? What's wrong?"

"Its'—it's your friends, Mr. Hunter." Johnny gasped for breath. "Andre and the others. I—I can't find them anywhere! I—have to—"

"Easy, lad, easy, get your breath back first," said Hunter.

"Hold it right there, Hunter!" said a voice from the darkness. "Don't move or the boy gets it!"

Two men with drawn weapons came walking out of the darkness. They both looked a little out of breath. As they came closer, Hunter saw that they were dressed in colonial clothing, but holding laser pistols. Network men. They must have picked the kid up at his old place and followed him. Johnny glanced up at him with fear and uncertainty.

"All right, hands out from your sides, very slowly, and clasp them on top of your head," one of them said.

Hunter did as he was told. Looking at him fearfully, Johnny did the same.

"Get lost, kid," the other Network man said.

Johnny didn't move.

"Didn't you hear me?" the man repeated. "I said get lost! Run! Get out of here!"

"No," said Johnny. "No, I—I will not run. I have my duty!"

"Stupid kid. You want to die? I said, get *out* of here!"

"Do as he says," Hunter said.

"No. No, I will not leave you like a coward."

"Damn it, Johnny," Hunter said, "don't be a fool. Get out of here! Run!"

"No, I won't run away!"

"Have it your way, kid," the Network man said, aiming his pistol at Johnny.

"Drop your weapons, *now*!"

The Network men spun around and Neilson's pistol coughed rapidly, four times. The first shot from the Colt took one of the men right between the eyes. The second shot struck the other man's gun hand and he cried out as he dropped the laser, then the third and fourth shots struck each of his kneecaps dead center, knocking his legs out from under him as if someone had yanked the street out from beneath his feet. He fell to the ground, moaning with pain. Hunter hadn't even had the time to draw his gun.

Neilson ran up and quickly stuffed a handkerchief into the wounded man's mouth, jamming it in deeply. The man started to gag. He was already in shock. Neilson picked up the laser pistol the second man had dropped and tucked the Colt into his waistband.

"Jesus Christ," said Hunter, flabbergasted. "Priest said you were lightning with a gun, but . . . *Jesus!* Where the hell did you learn to shoot like that?"

Johnny stood, speechless, staring at Neilson with astonishment.

"Practice," Neilson said. "Lots and lots of practice."

He pulled a disruptor out from underneath his coat. He aimed it at the dead man and fired a stream of neutrons. The corpse was briefly wreathed in the blue glow of Cherenkov radiation, then it disappeared.

"Let's get out of here," he said, nervously glancing up at the surrounding windows. It had all taken merely seconds, and fortunately, there hadn't been much noise. "Come on. We'll have to take him with us," he said, nodding toward Johnny as he adjusted his warp disc to a wider pattern.

Johnny didn't understand what had happened. The stranger had fired his peculiar pistol four times, with astonishing accuracy and impossible speed, all without reloading, and it had barely made a sound. And then he had somehow made the dead man's body disappear without a trace in that strange blue glow that came from that even stranger, second weapon. He was still trying to take it all in when Hunter brought him up to stand close beside Neilson and the wounded man and the next thing Johnny knew, he was no longer standing in the middle of the street outside Ebenezer MacIntosh's house, but in the center of a room somewhere, in a completely different place, and he was feeling nauseous and dizzy. He gasped and looked around him wildly, and then his eyes rolled up and he fainted. Hunter just barely managed to catch him before he hit the floor.

Moffat was missing. Drakov didn't have to wonder where he was. He would never have had the nerve to take off somewhere on his own without first asking permission and saying precisely where he was going and when he would return. Both he and the female were like servile dogs in that respect, thought Drakov, falling all over themselves to attend him. Moffat's disappearance could only mean one thing. The Time Commandos had him, which meant there was no question of returning to the house on Newbury Street. It was no longer secure.

Moffat would hold out against interrogation for a while, but they were sure to break him, as Drakov had intended that they should. He knew that people always valued something a great deal more when they had to work for it and they would have to work to break down Moffat, but break him down they would, and then they would believe him when he talked—as Moffat would, of course, believe himself—when the fact was that neither of the hoiminoids knew what the real mission was. They believed the plan was merely to kill Samuel Adams, the revolution's Grand Incendiary, as Thomas Hutchinson had christened him, but if the Hellfire Club succeeded in assassinating Adams, which was entirely possible, it would only be an added bonus. But though it was part of what Drakov intended to accomplish, he did not need Adams dead to achieve what he had planned.

The hominoids had served their purpose. Moffat would distract the Time Commandos and by the time they realized their mistake, it would be too late for them to do a thing about it.

Steiger heard the door open and slowly raised his head, staring at the newcomer through swollen eyes. He was dressed in well-tailored, elegant colonial clothing with a silk brocade waistcoat and lace at the throat and cuffs. He heard the man expel his breath sharply as he saw him.

"Jesus Christ," he said, staring at Steiger. "What the hell is going on here? What did you *do* to him?"

"Softened him up a little," said the other man, still wearing the black leather gloves he'd donned to administer the beating.

"What for?" said the man who'd just come through the door.

"What *for*? What are you, crazy? Don't you know what's going on? Don't you know who this guy *is*?"

"Do you?"

"You'd damn well better believe I do," the gloved man said. "He's Col. Creed Steiger, head of the goddamned I.S.D."

"You didn't have to do this," said the newcomer, his mouth tight. "There was no call for this."

"No call for it? Are you nuts? The son of a bitch is lucky he's alive! There's a contract out on him, in case you didn't know. You know what he's worth dead?"

"Is that what it's come to, Stevens?" said the newcomer. "We're taking contracts now? We're hitting our own people?"

"Shut up, you stupid bastard! Don't use my name in front of him!"

"What difference does it make? Do you intend to let him live?"

"Only as long as necessary," Stevens said grimly. "They got Carruthers. They took out Stiers and Aaronson, as well. Left no trace of them, not even a wet spot on the floor. This bastard's our security. They come after us, we got a hostage."

"How much is he worth dead?" asked the newcomer.

"A smooth five mil," said Stevens. "Five million fucking dollars."

"And you'd kill one of our own people for it," said the newcomer.

"He's not one of *our* people, you damn fool! He's I.S.D.!"

"And what the hell is the I.S.D.?" the newcomer snapped. "It's the internal security division of the goddamn *agency*, you moron!"

"Don't talk to me that way!"

"Do you even realize what you're *doing*?" the newcomer said. "It's one thing to run a few illegal operations to make some money, but what you're talking about now is murder!"

"They took out Carruthers and the others," Stevens said harshly. "What do you call that?"

"Carruthers must've forced their hand. He went too far. When I heard what he was planning, I thought he had gone crazy. We're supposed to be *helping* these people, for God's sake! There's a temporal disruption going down! We're supposed to be on the same damn side!"

"Is that so?" said Stevens. He jerked his head toward Steiger. "Is that why this son of a bitch is trying to nail us? Because we're on the same side? Don't make me laugh. He sold out, the bastard. He was a field agent, just like us, and he sold out!"

"To *whom*?"

"To the goddamned bureaucrats and politicians, that's to whom! Jesus, will you wake the hell *up*? This isn't some game we're playing here! This isn't the goddamned Boy Scouts! Forrester sent this guy to take us out. He's out to bust the whole damn Network! We've gotta take them out before they get us first!"

"Them?" said the newcomer. "Wait a minute, let me get this straight. Are we talking about assassinating the director of the T.I.A.?"

"You're damn straight!" said Stevens. "And the bounty on the old man's been set at ten million! Where the hell you been? Me, I'm not crazy enough to try for Forrester, but Steiger here fell right into our laps. You don't want a share, just say so. You can go back to Virginia and plant tobacco for all I fucking care. Go anywhere the hell you want, but I'm telling you right now, you get in my way, I'm gonna roll right over you."

"That's the way it is, huh?"

"That's the way it is."

"And what about the disruption?"

"Who gives a fuck about the damn disruption? We send this jerk to the cell commander in a bag and we can all retire. Especially now that Carruthers and the others have been taken out. We don't have to cut the pie as thin."

"I see. I guess that does make for an incentive."

"You better believe it," Stevens said.

The newcomer walked over to where Steiger sat, firmly tied down to a stout chair. He took him by the hair and pulled his head back so that he could look down into his eyes. Steiger squinted up at him. The man's face was expressionless.

"He'd really take us out, wouldn't he?" the man said.

"In a minute."

"I suppose that would make it self-defense, then."

Stevens grinned. "Yeah, I guess it would."

"Five million dollars *is* a lot of money," said the man in front of Steiger. "And I suppose if a temporal disruption *did* go down, we could always clock back further, where we wouldn't have to worry about it. Go underground, kick back and take it easy . . ."

"Now you're talkin'," Stevens said.

"I mean, between the rest of us in this section, we've already got a tidy sum salted away. Then there're the goods in the warehouses in Boston, Philadelphia, and Charleston, we could easily liquidate those at a fat profit, wouldn't have to cut *that* pie as thin, either . . ."

"Now you're getting the idea," Stevens said.

"You know, when you look at it that way, I suppose it does make a lot of sense," the man said, still looking down at Steiger with no expression on his face. He let his head drop and turned around to face Stevens. "Personally, I never cared much for Carruthers anyway."

"Well, you don't have to worry about Carruthers now," said Stevens.

"So tell me, what are we still doing here? We've got Steiger, why don't we just blow? Why take chances?"

"Because we don't know if Carruthers talked. Cash wants to make sure. He thinks they're onto us and he wants to cover our tracks before we risk moving the stuff. And there's still that shipment coming in."

"That's stupid. Why worry about that? If Steiger's worth five million dead . . ."

"Cash said—"

"Yeah, well, I never cared much for Cash, either." The man turned around and walked over to the window. He pulled open the drapes and looked out. "If you ask me, Cash is too damn greedy. So what if Carruthers talked? Who cares about the shipment? The way things are, hanging around here's way too risky."

"We stand to lose a lot if we leave now," said Stevens. "Cash says long as we've got Steiger—"

"Long as we've got Steiger, who needs Cash?" the other man said, still looking out the window. "Who needs any of them? We've got five million sitting right there in that chair. Split two ways . . . I mean, we could always tell the cell commander that the commandos got Cash and the others, couldn't we?"

"Yeah . . ." said Stevens, slowly. "Yeah, I suppose we could at that."

The man at the window turned around. There was a small stinger pistol in his hand. He fired and the needle dart struck Stevens in the chest. Stevens stared at him with astonishment, then collapsed to the floor.

"You stupid asshole," the man said, looking down at Stevens with contempt. "You'd kill your own mother for a buck."

He walked over to where Steiger sat.

"So you're worth five million dollars, huh?" he said, still holding the pistol.

Steiger said nothing.

He put away the pistol. "I just saved your life, Colonel. I sure hope you're the grateful sort."

He walked around behind the chair, took out a knife, and sliced through Steiger's bonds. He came around in front of him again.

"Can you stand?"

Steiger stared up at him uncertainly. "I'll manage," he said thickly. His lips were cut and swollen and several teeth had been loosened. He lurched to his feet unsteadily. "I don't get it. How come you're doing this?"

" 'Cause I want out," the man said. "I've had it. I draw the line at murder."

"What do you call that?" said Steiger, nodding toward the man on the floor.

"That wasn't a lethal dart, he'll only be out for about an hour. Name's Murphy, by the way. Tom Murphy."

"Thanks, Murphy."

"Save your thanks. Just remember me at my court martial. Now come on, lean on me. We'd better get you out of here before the others get back."

They laid Johnny out on the couch downstairs. He was still unconscious. Andre knelt down beside him.

"What happened?" she said. "Is he all right?"

"He's okay, he only fainted," Hunter said. "The shock plus the effects of transistion. Always takes a lot out of you the first time."

"You shouldn't have brought him here," said Lucas.

"He saw too much," said Neilson. "It couldn't be helped."

"Who would have believed him?" Lucas said. "You should have left him, Scott. Bringing him here was stupid."

"I'm sorry, but I thought—"

"That's just the trouble, you *didn't* think."

"Hey, lighten up, Priest," said Hunter. "He saved my bacon and brought you a prisoner to interrogate. The kid did all right."

Lucas sighed. "You're right. I'm sorry, Scott. I didn't mean to come down on you so hard. I guess it's just the strain, that's all. But the boy can't stay here. We've got enough to worry about as it is. We've got to get him out of here while he's still unconscious. Anybody know where the kid lives?"

"He's Revere's apprentice," Hunter said. "Stays in the back of his silversmith shop over by North Square."

"Andre, maybe you should take him there," said Lucas. "Since you seem to have established a . . . uh, rapport with the kid, convince him he was seeing things or something. But get him out of our hair. We have to interrogate the prisoners and I don't want him around for that."

"Okay, I'll take care of him," said Andre. She started to adjust her warp disc.

Linda Craven came downstairs.

"How is he?" Lucas asked her, referring to the wounded Network man.

"He's coming out of shock," she said. "I gave him something for the pain and I took care of his hand, but I can't do anything about his knees. Both kneecaps were shattered by the bullets. It's going to require major reconstructive surgery and prosthetics."

"Can he talk?"

"Yeah, he can talk, but he's still hurting. If I give him any more, he'll be too doped up to be coherent."

"All right, let's go have a word with him," said Lucas. "Finn, Hunter, come with me. Mike, take Rico and Ivan and check on the leaders of the Sons of Liberty, see if MacIntosh has anybody keeping an eye on them yet. Scott, I want you and Geoff on Adams, just in case the Hellfire Club pays him a call. If they do, I want you to get him out of there and I don't care how you do it. We can't let anything happen to him."

"Right, we're on our way," said Neilson.

"Okay, let's go see what our Network man can tell us,"

Lucas said. "And then we'll have another talk with our friend Moffat."

"He's been very quiet in there," Linda said.

"Yeah. He's had a lot to think about," said Lucas.

They went up the stairs. The Network man was lying on a bed, clearly in great pain, despite the narcotic analgesic Craven had injected him with, an opiate analog that dulled much of his agony. His breeches had been removed and his knees were bandaged and splinted, but mainly to stop the bleeding and prevent his moving them. There was little more that they could do for him under such primitive conditions except give him another injection that would put him out and Lucas planned to use that as a carrot on a stick.

The man was breathing raggedly, in short, gaspy little bursts, and clutching at the bedclothes spasmodically. Lucas pulled a chair up beside the bed.

"My name is Col. Lucas Priest," he said. "Can you hear me?"

The man nodded jerkily.

"What's your name?"

"Di-Dicenzo," he said, through clenched teeth. "Ro-Robert Dicenzo. God . . . it hurts . . . Gi-Gimme another shot . . ."

"We'll give you another shot and clock you out to a military hospital as soon as you answer a few questions," Lucas said.

"Shot first. God . . . the pain . . ."

"No shot," said Lucas. "Talk first, then we'll give you another shot. Knock you out and make the nasty pain go away. But I want some answers first and they'd better be the right ones, otherwise I'll get my shooter back in here and have him put a couple bullets through your ankles."

"You bastard . . ." Dicenzo gasped.

"Hey, you called it," Lucas said. "You got what you deserve. Now I don't have much time and I'm not a patient man, so what's it going to be?"

"Okay! Okay, damn you!"

"What have you done with Steiger?" Lucas asked. "Is he still alive?"

"Yeah . . . place on Short Street . . . fourth house on—on the left from Pond. S-second floor . . . end of hall."

"How many men are watching him?"

"One . . . maybe two . . . Stevens . . . maybe Cash . . ."

"You're doing fine," said Lucas. "How many of you are there?"

"Eight . . . no, you got Carruthers . . . Aaronsen and Stiers . . . your shooter got Morton, too, didn't he? Oh, *Christ . . .*"

"You mean there were only eight of you in this Network cell to begin with?"

"Y-yeah. Not—not counting cell commander . . . Randall . . . he's not here . . . another—another time . . ."

"Okay, so the only Network men left in this scenario are yourself, Stevens, and this guy Cash, right? That's only seven."

"M-Murphy," said Dicenzo, his teeth chattering. "S-supposed to . . . come up from . . . Virginia . . ."

"When?"

"Tonight."

"Carruthers said you had thirty men here," Lucas said. "You're saying only eight."

"Bluff . . ." Dicenzo said. "Not—not thirty. Only eight . . . Swear to God . . . Carruthers thought you were . . . onto to us. Wanted . . . to sidetrack you . . . keep you busy till—till we could clear the stuff . . ."

"What stuff?"

"Merchandise . . . in warehouses . . . Boston . . . Philadelphia . . . Ch-Charleston . . . another shipment coming in . . ."

"What sort of merchandise?"

"Wine . . . silks . . . s-spices . . ."

"Commodities," Delaney said, with scorn. He snorted with derision. "Do you believe it? This whole thing was about commodities. They were willing to let a disruption go down just to protect a small-time smuggling operation."

"N-not small . . . time," Dicenzo said. "Cheap here . . . big profits . . . sell further up timeline . . ."

"And for *that* you were going to let a temporal disruption occur?" said Lucas, with disbelief.

"We were gonna help . . ." Dicenzo said, twisting the bedclothes in his hands, "but—but Steiger . . ."

"What about Steiger?"

"Damn . . . oh, damn . . . he—he got onto us . . . we—we got word . . ."

"You got word? You're saying someone informed on him?"

"Yeah—yeah . . ."

"Who?"

"Don't know . . . Honest. I swear, I'd tell ya . . ."

"All right, go on."

"Carruthers and Cash said—said Steiger was worth five million dead."

"Five million dollars?"

"Yeah . . ." said Dicenzo, gritting his teeth. "Network's got a contract on him . . . the old man, too. Ten million for him . . ."

"What a bunch of sweethearts," said Hunter.

"So you decided to stall us and try to move your goods, and then collect on Steiger," Lucas said. "Just a little business enterprise, isn't that right?"

"Wasn't—wasn't my idea . . ." said Dicenzo. "About Steiger, I mean. I swear . . ."

"But you were more than willing to go along with it for a share of the money," said Delaney. "We ought to just dump you out into the street and leave you."

"No! No, please . . . you gotta get me to a hospital! I'll talk . . . I'll tell you everything I know . . . please—please . . ."

"I want you to give Cpl. Craven full details on the warehouses," Lucas said. "Where they are, what's in them, where your other safehouses are, everything you've got set up in this scenario. Then and only then will she give you another shot and clock you to a hospital. But if I find out you've held anything back, I'll personally pay a visit to your hospital room, you understand?"

"I've told the truth, I swear . . ."

"You better have," said Lucas. "And you'd better hope that Steiger's still alive. Linda, take his statement."

They left the room.

"I'm going after Steiger," said Delaney.

"All right," said Lucas. "Take Hunter with you. I'll stay here and hold the fort. I still need to have another talk with our friend Moffat."

"What do you want us to do with those Network men?" asked Hunter.

"Personally, I don't much care," said Lucas. "Try to take them alive if you can, so they can be put through interrogation, but we've already got Dicenzo, so don't take any chances. The mission has to come first. If they put up any resistance, take them out."

"You got it, pilgrim," Hunter said.

"And one more thing," Lucas said. "Stop calling me pilgrim."

Hunter grinned. "Sure thing, pilgrim. Anything you say. Come on, Delaney. We gotta go rescue the guy that wants to squeeze my brain out like a sponge. Think maybe he'll be grateful?"

He chuckled and started down the stairs.

"Watch him, Finn," said Lucas. "I could still be wrong about him. I don't want any accidents, okay?"

"Sure," said Delaney. "You're taking a chance, you know."

"You mean, sending Hunter with you? I've got no choice. We're spread too thin."

"That's not what I mean," Delaney said. "There's something likable about that guy, isn't there? Reminds us of the Hunter that we knew. You're figuring on making Steiger feel obligated to him, aren't you? That many not play, partner. Steiger's awful cold."

"You may be right," said Lucas. "But what the hell, it's worth a shot."

"You getting soft on me?" said Delaney, with a grin.

"Go on," said Lucas. "Get out of here."

He watched Delaney leave, then sighed and went down the hall to Moffat's room. He opened the door and froze. The chair in which Moffat had been tied down was empty. The ropes holding him had been snapped with incredible strength and the window was open.

"Jesus Christ . . ." said Lucas. He ran back out into the hall. *"Finn!"*

But he was too late. They had already left. Linda Craven came running out into the hall.

"What is it?" she said. "What's wrong?"

"It's Moffat," Lucas said grimly. "He's escaped."

10 _____

Andre clocked with Johnny to the street outside Ebenezer MacIntosh's house. It was a calculated risk, one she certainly would not have taken during the daytime, when the traffic on the streets of Boston would have made such a transition highly dangerous. Clocking into a set of temporal coordinates that already happened to be occupied at that particular instant by some passing citizen or cart or horseman would have proved extremely messy and extremely fatal. However, at this hour of the night, the streets of Boston were practically deserted and the lack of street lighting served to mask the transition, thereby decreasing the likelihood that anyone looking out a window would see two people suddenly appearing out of nowhere in the middle of the street. No sooner had she pulled him over close to MacIntosh's door than he began to come around. He came to lying on his back, with Andre looking down at him anxiously.

"What . . . Andre! Where am I?"

"In the street outside Ebenezer MacIntosh's house," she said. "Are you all right?"

He looked around, confused. "I—I don't understand. What happened? I was in a room somewhere . . ."

"You fell and struck your head," she said. "I was afraid you might be seriously hurt."

"I fell?" he said. "I don't remember. I was with Mr. Hunter . . . that man!"

"What man?"

"I don't know! I don't know who he was! He shot the other two!"

"The other two?" she said.

"Yes, the other two men! They had guns! They were going to kill us! And that man shot them both with that strange pistol . . . he fired several times without reloading! So fast! How could he have done that?"

"But, Johnny, there's no one here," she said.

"But I saw them, Andre! He shot them, I tell you! And then he made the body disappear—"

"*What* body? Johnny, what are you talking about?"

He stared at her. "You don't believe me!"

"You must have been dreaming," she said. "You struck your head."

"A dream?" said Johnny. "No, it could not have been a dream. I saw it, I tell you! I came running here, I was looking for Mr. MacIntosh, I thought he could tell me where Mr. Hunter was and I could ask him where I could find you and then those men came and they were going to kill him and they were going to kill me, too, and—"

"But, Johnny, I just *saw* Reese Hunter," she said. "And he didn't say anything about two men trying to kill him."

"He—he didn't?"

"No." She shook her head. "He said he spoke to you about us and then you started to run off, but you slipped and fell and struck your head. I helped him carry you over here, out of the middle of the street, and he said you would be fine in a few moments and asked me to watch over you until you came around. He had to hurry to meet with someone."

Johnny shook his head slowly. "But—but it seemed so *real*! You mean it was all a dream?"

"What else could it have been?" she said. "How can someone fire a pistol several times without reloading and then make a dead body disappear?"

Johnny grimaced and rubbed his head. "I—I must admit it does sound foolish," he said. "I don't remember falling. But—but how did you come to be here?"

"I came looking for Ebenezer MacIntosh," she said. "I came to warn him. We've discovered that the horseman's men, the ones who call themselves the Hellfire Club, are planning to kill him. It seems that they intend to kill the leaders of the Sons of Liberty, one at a time, striking in the middle of the night."

Johnny gazed at her wide-eyed. "We must warn Mr. MacIntosh!"

"He already knows. He's gone to seek protection from his friends in the South End Gang."

"We have to tell Mr. Adams!"

"That is already being taken care of," she said. "The important thing for you to do right now is rest. You've had a nasty blow. After such a fall, rest is just the thing. Come on, I'll help you to get home."

She helped him up.

"I—I feel a little dizzy," he said.

"That often happens when one's had a nasty fall," she said. "Can you walk?"

"Yes, I believe so."

"Come on, then. I'll walk with you."

"I feel so strange," said Johnny. "Nothing like that has ever happened to me before. I was only trying to find you and Mr. Priest and Mr. Delaney . . . where *were* you? Where did you go? I looked for you everywhere!"

"We had a great deal to do," said Andre. "We were with the Tories, discovering their plot against the Sons of Liberty."

"I was afraid that something may have happened to you," Johnny said. "I feared perhaps the Tories had discovered your deception. I—I don't know what I would have done if they had hurt you."

She smiled. "I'm touched by your concern."

He stopped. "It is much more than mere concern," he said. "Andre . . . I—I have never said this to a girl before . . ."

She quickly put her fingertips up against his lips. "Don't say it, Johnny," she said softly. "I know. And I am flattered more than I could say. But please try to understand. I am not free."

"You—you are promised to another?" he said.

"Yes, Johnny, I am."

He looked down at the ground. "I see. I—I suppose I dared not hope that you would—"

"There is much about you that a girl could love, Johnny," she said. "Someday, you will meet the one who's right for you and then I'm sure that you will make her very proud and very happy. But I . . ." she stopped, listening. "Did you hear that?"

"What?"

"Sssh! *Listen!*"

The sound came to them on the stillness of the cool night breeze.

"Men shouting," Johnny said. "It sounds as if it's coming from the Common."

"Something's happening. Come on, Johnny, run!" she said.

They sprinted toward the Common, Andre leading the way, Johnny running hard to keep up with her. They crossed Marlborough Street and ran toward the granary, on the corner of Common Street. The sound grew louder as they approached. They pulled up short as they reached the tree-lined Mall at the edge of the Common. A large group of black-robed figures were heading toward the Liberty Tree. Several of them were dragging along a fiercely struggling man, whose hands had been bound and whose mouth was gagged.

"They've got Mr. MacIntosh!" said Johnny. He looked at Andre with alarm. "My God, they're going to hang him, like the others! What are we to do?"

Andre thought fast. There was nothing she could do, not with Johnny there. They had already reached the Liberty Tree and were throwing a rope over one of its stout branches.

"Run, Johnny!" she said. "Get help!"

"But they will never come in time!"

She took out her dueling pistol. "I'll fire a shot in the air," she said, "then reload quickly and fire again. They may think the Sons of Liberty have come to rescue him."

"They will not be fooled!" said Johnny.

"I have to try!" she said.

"They will kill you!"

"Johnny, you're wasting time!"

"It's too late! I will not leave you! We have to run before they see us!"

They were putting the noose around MacIntosh's neck.

"*Johnny . . .*" In desperation, Andre hit him with a hard right cross. He crumpled to the ground, unconscious. "I'm sorry, Johnny."

She'd run out of time. They were already hoisting MacIntosh up off the ground. He was jerking on the rope like a fish. Andre slid the metal plate in front of the pistol's trigger guard forward, exposing the hidden magazine well, then she quickly reached into her coat pocket and removed a plastic magazine holding fifteen staggered rounds of specially designed ball ammo. She slapped the magazine into the pistol and racked the slide. She fired the pistol into the air and started running, heading around the circle of hooded figures gathered beneath the Liberty Tree, firing as she ran, trying to make it seem as if there were a number of men shooting from different directions.

At the sound of the first shot, the hooded men glanced around, startled, and with the second and the third shot, they started looking all around them in confusion. They began shouting and several of them started running. Andre kept on shooting into the air as she ran. The hooded figures bolted, thinking that a group of armed men was upon them. The men hoisting MacIntosh up off the ground released the rope and ran. MacIntosh dropped down to the ground and lay there, jerking, the noose still tight around his neck.

Andre reversed direction and ran back the other way, still firing. She had no idea how many rounds she had left, but she kept going, firing as she ran, and her deception worked. Since they were completely unfamiliar with the concept of a semi-automatic pistol, the members of the Hellfire Club naturally assumed that they were facing a force of armed men and they took off in all directions, running across the Common, some of them heading toward Frog Lane and Treamount Street, others going in the opposite direction, toward Beacon Hill, where Hancock's mansion stood. In moments, they had all scattered in panic and the grassy Common was deserted.

She ran over to the fallen MacIntosh and kneeled beside him, loosening the noose around his neck. She pulled the noose over his head and then removed his gag. He sucked in air and started coughing and retching.

"Easy, man, easy," she said, working at his bonds. "Try to breathe slowly."

He gasped and there was a rattle in his throat as he made a series of horrible rasping sounds, trying to draw air into his lungs. Andre freed his hands and propped him up, steadying him with an arm around his shoulders. He was breathing like a patient in a cancer ward and clutching at his throat.

"Slowly," Andre said. "Try to breathe slowly. Take deep, steady breaths."

She helped him to his feet and propped him up with his back against the tree trunk.

"Thought I was done for," he croaked.

"Don't try to talk," said Andre.

"Where—where are the others?" he rasped.

"I said don't try to talk! They're all chasing the men who tried to hang you."

"Who—who are . . ."

"I'm a friend of Hunter's," she said. "Stop trying to talk, for God's sake. Just breathe, slowly and steadily, in—out—in—out . . ."

His chest rose and fell as he tried to take slow, deep, steady breaths.

"You're going to be all right," said Andre. "Thank God we got to you in time."

"I—I am most grateful to you," MacIntosh said, his voice still coming out in a wheezing croak. "You—you saved my life. What is your name?"

"Never mind that," she said. "You were just lucky my friends and I were passing by."

He nodded. "Must warn Adams . . . bastards could try for him . . ."

"Can you walk? You need my help?"

"Thanks, friend, you've done enough. I'll manage. Must hurry . . ."

He clapped her on the back and shambled off across the Common, his hand still holding his throat. Andre leaned back against the tree trunk for a moment and sighed with relief, then she started heading back toward the spot where she had knocked out Johnny. She got no more than ten paces when she was struck hard across the back of her head. She grunted and collapsed to the moist grass.

Lucas felt like a sitting duck. The first thing he'd done was to have Linda Craven clock to headquarters with their prisoner. She clocked back in only minutes later, though she'd actually spent hours in the future, getting Dicenzo admitted and briefing the hospital M.P. detachment and the T.I.A. interrogation unit that would question him. They had all gone without sleep and they were tired, but the razor edge of tension kept them keenly alert. It would have been pointless to try going after Moffat, by now he could be anywhere.

Lucas cursed himself for not having kept a closer watch on him. He had underestimated the hominoid's strength, something he never should have done. They had to assume he had gone back to Drakov and now their base of operations was blown. If he didn't already know about the house on Lime Street, Drakov would know about it very soon, which meant there was a possibility they could be hit at any time.

The trouble was, they couldn't move the base. Their people were spread out all over the place and until they reported in, there was no way of letting them know what had occurred. Lucas had considered having Craven try to clock around the city, looking for them, but that would be too dangerous and he had no way of knowing exactly where the others would be at any given time. They had discussed it briefly, and when she had insisted upon staying because it would be too risky to leave him alone and vulnerable, he was forced to agree. He was not afraid for himself, but he could not risk being taken out and leaving the people under his command vulnerable when they returned to the field base, not knowing it was blown. They armed themselves and settled down to a tense wait.

"How about some coffee?" Linda said.

"You've got coffee?" Lucas said.

"What's a field base without coffee?" she said, with a smile. "Or should we go native and drink tea?"

"No, I could sure use a cup of strong black coffee," Lucas said.

"Make that two," said Darkness. "I'll take mine with sugar."

Linda gasped and spun around, instinctively going for her weapon.

"All right, if it's that much trouble, forget the sugar," Darkness said.

She expelled her breath and put away her pistol. "Dr. Darkness! You almost gave me a heart attack," she said.

Darkness had appeared sitting on the couch beside Lucas, his legs casually crossed, his right hand resting on a silver-headed, ebony walking stick, which he held upright, its tip resting on the floor. He was dressed in his habitual Inverness coat and tweeds, a faintly bored expression on his gaunt features.

"Doc, am I ever glad to see you!" said Lucas.

"Ah, well, such an enthusiastic greeting can only mean that

you're in it up to your hips," said Darkness. "What have you done now, boxed yourself into your usual corner or are you experiencing difficulties with the transponder?"

While Linda went to make the coffee, Lucas quickly filled him in.

"Hmm, it does seem as if you've bitten off a bit more than you can chew this time," the scientist said. "Drakov *and* the Network. And this Hellfire Club, as well. Drakov really is becoming a considerable annoyance, isn't he?"

"Doc, you have a positive genius for understatement," Lucas said.

"I have a positive genius for everything," Darkness said, "but that is quite beside the point. The question is, what are we going to do about this situation of yours?"

He reached into his jacket pocket for a pack of cigarettes. It was a perfectly ordinary, casual motion, but his right arm left a blurred series of afterimages as he moved, giving the effect of rapid, stop-motion photography. He removed a cigarette and lit it, inhaling deeply.

"It really is most inconvenient that your people can't carry communicators all the time," Darkness said. "That would have solved this entire problem, but I suppose it wouldn't do to have voices suddenly coming out of little boxes in colonial Boston. It could tend to upset people. And miniature receivers might still have been spotted, but under the circumstances, it would have been worth taking the risk."

"All right, so maybe I was being too cautious, but it's too late to do anything about that now. Talking about how I screwed up isn't going to help us. You got any ideas?"

"Well, part of your immediate problem can be easily solved. I can locate Steiger, Cross, and Delaney through their symbiotracers and inform them of the situation—"

"Hold it! Wait a minute!" Lucas said. "You told me their symbiotracers were malfunctioning!"

"Oh, no, I solved that little problem. It turned out to be merely a minor glitch in my receiving equipment. Simply a matter of fine-tuning. I can locate them anytime I want."

"And you didn't tell me?"

Darkness raised his eyebrows. "Well, you didn't ask."

Lucas leaned back against the couch and put his hands up to his head. *"Sweet God All Mighty!"* he said. "I don't *believe* it! Didn't you hear what I've just *said*? The Network's got Steiger! And all the time, you could have told me where he was!"

"As I recall," said Darkness, "the last time we spoke, they didn't have him or if they did, you neglected to apprise me of the situation. Frankly, I'm not really surprised. Steiger's knack for getting in over his head is rivaled only by your own. I suppose you'd like me to get him back for you?"

"*Yes*, if it wouldn't be too much trouble," Lucas said in an exasperated tone.

"No trouble at all," said Darkness. "It's not as if I haven't got several dozen more important things to do. I really do wonder, Priest, how you ever managed before I came along. Every time I see you, you're in some sort of difficulty. All things considered, it's a miracle we haven't got at least a dozen temporal disruptions to contend with—"

"*Doc!* For cryin' out loud!"

"Oh. I suppose you want me to leave *now*?"

"If you don't mind!"

"What about my coffee?"

"Jesus, give me strength! We'll keep the pot warm, okay?"

"Well, all right, you don't need to shout. You realize that I have no way of getting any sort of fix on your other people, since they're not equipped with symbiotracers."

"Just get Creed, Andre, and Delaney back here," Lucas said. "Hunter's with Delaney. Andre should be on her way back here by now. In fact, I don't know what's keeping her, unless . . ."

"Unless what?"

"No. No, that's crazy, she wouldn't."

"Can two participate in this conversation or is it a soliloquy?" said Darkness.

"Never mind," said Lucas. "It's not important. Just get them back here right away. Please?"

"Certainly. Don't go away."

He disappeared.

Linda came back into the room. "Coffee'll be ready in a min . . . where did he go? What's the matter?"

Lucas was sitting hunched over, with his head in his hands. "Just once," he said, "Just *once*, I'd like to catch him when he's solid . . ."

Steiger groaned as he tried to stand. Murphy helped him up out of the chair and pulled his arm around his shoulder. Steiger sagged.

"Come on, Steiger, you can make it," Murphy said.

"Son of a bitch really gave me a working over," Steiger said, through swollen and cut lips.

"I know," said Murphy. "I'm really sorry about this, Steiger. I never signed on for anything like this, believe me. It all seemed so harmless in the beginning. Moving goods from one time period to another, supplementing the section allocation with a little temporal smuggling on the side, just a simple business enterprise where no one would get hurt. It's practically impossible to operate a field section on our budget and they keep cutting our appropriations. I told myself the money was being raised for a good cause. And then, since we were doing so well, it seemed perfectly reasonable to divert a small portion of the profits, set a little aside for our retirement . . . ah, hell, the whole thing thing just snowballed. I never dreamed it would come to anything like this."

"Nobody ever does, Murphy," Steiger said, leaning against him for support. "Shit. My goddamn legs are cramped from being tied down to that chair." He shuffled one step forward, then another.

"Give me the coordinates for your base of operations," Murphy said. "I'll clock us out."

Steiger turned and stared at him for a long moment.

"You don't trust me," Murphy said. "You think I may still be working with the others." He nodded. "Hell, I don't blame you. But look, I gotta take you somewhere."

"You're not taking him anywhere," said a voice from the door.

They looked up to see a man in colonial dress standing in the doorway, a plasma pistol in his hand.

"Cash!" said Murphy.

"Going somewhere, Murphy?"

"Put down the gun, Cash," Murphy said. "Don't be a fool."

"Going into business for yourself, eh?" Cash said. "I thought we all had an agreement."

"It isn't what you think, Cash," Murphy said. "I was taking him out of here."

"Were you?"

"He needs medical attention. Stevens went crazy, he beat him half to death. Damn it, Cash, this has gone too far. I don't give a damn about the Network anymore. I went along with the enterprise, but I'm not going to be a party to murder. You can keep my share of the profits, I don't care, but let us go. I've had enough."

"You always were a bit too soft, Murphy," said Cash. "Too much of a guilty conscience. But like you said, you went along with it. You're in as deeply as the rest of us."

"I don't care!" said Murphy. "When we start taking contracts on our own people, it's gone beyond the realm of sanity. It's out of control, Cash. It's got to stop! Think about what you're doing, for God's sake! We all took an oath—"

"Oh, please. Spare me." Cash glanced at Stevens, briefly. "Is he dead?"

"No," said Murphy.

Cash shifted his aim quickly and fired. The low intensity plasma charge struck Stevens in the chest, incinerating most of his upper body. "He is now," said Cash.

"You crazy son of a bitch!" said Murphy.

"Morton and Dicenzo never made it back," said Cash. "The commandos must've got 'em. I figured it was time to cut our losses and settle for what we've got. But now that it's you and me and the five-million-dollar bounty on our friend, frankly, Murphy, I don't feel like sharing."

He raised his pistol.

"So long, Murphy," he said.

The plasma pistol was suddenly plucked out of his hand by an unseen force.

"What the—"

There was a loud, dull crack and Cash fell to the floor, blood streaming from the fracture in his skull. Darkness appeared out of thin air, standing over him and wiping off the heavy silver head of his walking stick with a white handkerchief.

"Who in their right mind would pay five million dollars for the likes of you?" he said to Steiger.

Murphy goggled at him. "I must be dreamin'," he said. "I can see right through that guy!"

"Friend of yours?" said Darkness.

Steiger glanced at Murphy. "Yeah. I guess he is at that."

"You look like hell," said Darkness.

"Thanks."

"Don't mention it. Priest sent me. There seems to be some trouble at the field base. They've moved it, by the way. It's in a house on a bend in the road where Lime and Lynn streets meet." He gave them the coordinates. "And here, you might need this," he added, tossing him the plasma pistol. "I'd love to stay and chat, but I've a few more errands to run. Do try to get there in one piece, won't you? Priest is having some sort of an anxiety attack."

He vanished.

Murphy blinked several times. "Who in the hell was *that*?"

"It's a long story," said Steiger. "I'll explain later. We'd better get moving. Oh, and by the way, you're under arrest."

"Yeah, right," said Murphy, with a grimace. He entered the transition coordinates Darkness gave them into his warp disc and they clocked out.

Hunter and Delaney materialized at the corner of Pond and Short streets and started moving quickly toward the house where Dicenzo said Steiger was being held. They turned the corner and hadn't gone more than twenty yards when a loud voice hailed them.

"*Halt!* Who goes there? Stand where you are and identify yourselves!"

"Damn, it's the watch!" said Hunter.

"We don't have time for this," said Delaney.

"Take it easy. I'll take care of them," said Hunter.

Three men with muskets approached them.

"Identify yourselves," one of the men said.

"I'm Reese Hunter and this is Finn Delaney," Hunter said.

"I don't know you. What are you doing abroad this time of night?"

"We're on our way to see a sick friend," said Hunter. "He's badly ill. I'm bringing Dr. Delaney to him."

"A doctor, eh?" the watchman said suspiciously. "There was some sort of a disturbance in the Common tonight. We've had reports of shooting. I don't suppose you'd know anything about that?"

"Shooting in the Common?" Delaney glanced uneasily at Hunter. "No, we've heard nothing."

"How do I know you're telling the truth?" the watchman said.

"They could be the Tories that we've heard about," one of the others said.

"No, wait," said Hunter, reaching down into his shirt. He pulled out his Liberty medallion and showed it to them. "Look."

"Excuse me," said Darkness, suddenly appearing at their side. "I'd like a word with these gentlemen, if you don't mind."

The watchman leapt back with a startled cry.

"A ghost!" shouted one of the others. He threw down his musket and took to his heels. With cries of terror, the others followed him.

"And men like these managed to win the War for Independence," Darkness said, shaking his head.

"Doc, we need your help," Delaney said. "The Network has got Steiger. They're holding him in—"

"Yes, yes, I know, I'm way ahead of you," said Darkness. "I've already taken care of it. Steiger will meet you back at the field base on Lime Street. Priest wants you to get back there right away. Apparently, one of your prisoners has managed to escape."

"Moffat!" said Delaney.

"Yes, I believe that was his name."

"And he'll go straight to Drakov," said Delaney. "Come on, Hunter. We've got no time to lose." He quickly punched up the coordinates on his warp disc and they clocked out.

"Thank you, Dr. Darkness," Darkness said, with a wry grimace. "You're welcome. Don't mention it. Aaah, I don't know why I bother . . ."

He disappeared.

Andre came to lying on a comfortable couch. She groaned and felt the back of her head. There was a lump there and blood was matted in her hair. She blinked, her vision focusing on a pretty young woman holding a laser pistol aimed directly at her.

"Please remain perfectly still, Miss Cross, otherwise Sally will be forced to shoot you and she is a very accurate shot. Show her how accurate you are, Sally."

Sally fired the laser and the thin beam burned a smoking hole in the couch right next to Andre's left ear. Andre didn't move.

"Drakov," she said.

"Ah, you remember," Drakov said, coming around to where she could see him. He was dressed in flamboyant colonial finery, in black, as usual. His coat was of black velvet with jeweled buttons, his waistcoat was black brocade shot through with gold, his breeches were black satin, and his shirt and hose were of white silk. He had silver buckles on his shoes and he wore a powdered wig, but Andre would have recognized him anywhere. That scar marring his dark, Byronic features and those unsettling, emerald-green eyes were unmistakable, as was the voice, rich and deep and resonant, a voice that stage actors would have killed for.

"Which one are you?" she said. "Do you each have your own run number or do you all think you're the real thing?"

"That is a fascinating question, Miss Cross," he said, smiling down at her. "In fact, I've wondered about it myself on occasion, not that it makes any real difference. You see, we are *all* Nikolai Drakov, sharing the same genetic template, the same memories and personality. After a certain point, that is. Childhood experiences must, of necessity, vary, but at a key point in development, each replicate's subliminal programming is triggered and from that moment on, the memory engrams of the original are manifested. All previous individual experiences are totally forgotten. Each of us shares the same memories from that point on, the same personality and past. Asking which of us is the original is pointless. We are all the same. You might say I am legion."

Sally's face was registering growing confusion, but Drakov proceeded as if she wasn't even there.

"Just think of it as an exponential increase in the opportunities for our paths to cross," he said, smiling. "You see, there you are. It's happened once again. Actually, I quite look forward to our encounters, although I confess that each time I think it will be the last. Perhaps this time we will finally conclude our business. I feel rather confident on this occasion."

"You always do," she said. "But we've beaten you each time. And we'll beat you once again."

"Oh, I think not," said Drakov. "Not this time, Miss Cross. Not this time."

"We have Moffat, you know," she said.

The woman called Sally gave a little gasp and her eyes went to Drakov, but only for an instant.

"Yes, I had already surmised that," he said. He shrugged. "Unfortunate, but it is of no real consequence. He is conditioned to withstand a considerable amount of questioning, and when your friends think they have broken him, he will tell them only what he has been programmed to tell them. Moffat has served his purpose."

The stricken look on the woman's face only served to underscore what Andre had already concluded. Sally and Moffat were in love.

"Master . . ." she said in a pleading voice, but she got no further.

"Silence," Drakov said. He deigned to glance at her. "Don't be concerned, Sally. You've done your part well. My promise to you still stands. I will provide another mate for you as soon as we are finished here."

Sally said nothing and the laser in her hand wavered only slightly, but the anguish on her face spoke volumes.

"It isn't going to work, Drakov," Andre said. "Your Hellfire Club is going to fail, just like they failed tonight with MacIntosh."

"Merely a minor setback," Drakov said. "The mere existence of the Hellfire Club has already placed a strain on temporal inertia in this time period. My final touch will deliver the coup de grace and bring about a timestream split. The plan is elegant in its simplicity. I have pinpointed the three most important men in this temporal scenario. The first of them will die tonight, right under the very eyes of your compatriots, who have been keeping such a very careful watch on him. And MacIntosh will never reach his friends in time. My assassin is already on his way."

He smiled. "I only regret that I will not be able to see the expressions on their faces when it happens. It would have been much more effective if his chief pawn, Ebenezer MacIntosh, had died at the same time, but it will make no difference. Without Samuel Adams to lead the Sons of Liberty, the task will doubtless fall to Otis. Hancock is popular, but he has no real ability for leadership and he lacks the genius Adams has for influencing popular opinion. The others will fall to arguing among themselves, and though he has already proven himself to be erratic, Otis is the only one with fire enough to draw them all together. When his mind finally snaps, the blow to the patriotic cause will be irreparable. The Hellfire Club will serve to unify the Tories and the arrival of the British troops will put an end to the rebellious spirit in the Massachusetts colony.

"The second man to die will be Lord William Howe," continued Drakov. "I have already established myself socially in England and Howe knows me as a friend. It will be an easy matter for me to see to his demise. Without his foolish indecisiveness and obstinacy, the British troops would have captured the entire Continental Army at the Battle of Long Island and the war would have been over before it even started. With Howe dead, Clinton or Burgoyne will be appointed in his place and either of them will easily prevail over the undisciplined colonial troops, especially without Washington to lead them."

He chuckled at the expression on Andre's face.

"Yes, George Washington will be the third to fall. The crowning touch. The father of his country will be assassinated by a bastard. A fitting irony, I think. I trust my father will appreciate it. The deaths of any one of those three men should be sufficient to bring about a timestream split. The assassination of all three should cause a chain reaction that will spread throughout all history."

He pulled back his sleeve and entered a set of coordinates into his warp disc. "And now, Miss Cross, the time has come for us to say farewell. It has been a fascinating game, but I'm afraid it's over now." He turned to Sally. "Kill her."

Looking stunned, Sally aimed the laser at Andre's chest.

"Sally, wait!" said Andre. "Don't listen to him! Moffat is all right! Help me! I can take you to him!"

She hesitated.

"I said, kill her!" Drakov shouted.

"No, Sally, don't!"

"Jared!"

Drakov spun around to see Moffat standing in the doorway, holding a flintlock pistol in his bloody hand. Before Drakov could speak, Moffat fired. The ball struck Drakov in the chest. Sally screamed. Drakov stared at Moffat with utter disbelief, then he toppled to the floor.

For a moment, no one moved and then the laser was suddenly plucked out of Sally's hand. She cried out as Darkness materialized, holding the laser pistol. Andre ran to Drakov and turned him over. He was still alive, but only barely. He looked up at her and coughed up blood.

"I seem . . . to have . . . miscalculated," he said, struggling to get the words out. He coughed again and brought up more blood. "No matter . . . you're . . . too late. Too late. I . . . still . . . win . . ." His eyes clouded over and his labored breathing stopped.

Andre glanced up at Moffat. "What did he mean, he still wins?"

Moffat stood there with the empty pistol still held in his hand, staring at Drakov's corpse.

"Moffat! *What did he mean?*"

Moffat's lips moved, but he made no sound. Sally ran to him sobbing and threw her arms around his neck, but he was in a daze, as if entranced.

"It's no use," said Darkness. "You won't get anything out of him now. He's in a fugue state. He's suffered a breakdown."

"Adams . . ." Andre said. "Drakov said he was going to die tonight, right under our very eyes. But if we were watching Adams, then how could . . . Doc, we've got to get out of here, *right now!*"

11 ——————————

When Johnny Small came to in the middle of Boston Common, for a moment he could not recall what had happened. He seemed to remember hearing someone speak and then . . . He rolled over on the damp grass and got up to his hands and knees. His head hurt and his jaw was sore. He felt it and his hand came away wet with blood. His mouth was cut. And then he remembered. Andre had hit him. He couldn't believe it. She had actually hit him! *Why?* He had only been trying to help.

He got up slowly and looked around. The Common was deserted. It was dark and he could barely see a thing He remembered all the hooded men. The Hellfire Club! They had Ebenezer MacIntosh! They were going to hang him! He shivered, though it wasn't a cold night. He swallowed hard. It must be over by now, he thought. With a feeling of dread, he started to walk toward the Liberty Tree.

Andre had wanted to stop them. She had told him to run for help, but he had known that it was pointless. What was the use? To whom could he have run for help? By the time he could have reached any of the Sons of Liberty, any one of them, and by the time they could have roused the others, it would have been long finished. Mr. MacIntosh would have been dead before he could have run three blocks. He had tried to make her see that it was useless, that there was nothing they could do, but she simply wouldn't listen. He had tried to pull her away

176

from the scene before they could be spotted, thinking only of her safety, but she had gone crazy, she had struck him— actually struck him and knocked him senseless! He was amazed that a girl could hit so hard. And now, as he slowly walked toward the Liberty Tree, he was afraid of what he would find hanging from its branches. But he couldn't help himself. As if in a daze, he kept on moving.

Her idea had been crazy. Firing a pistol into the air to make the hooded men think that MacIntosh's friends had come running to his rescue! It might have fooled them for an instant, but he had known they would see through it. By the time she fired, and then taken the time that was needed to reload, and then fired once more, they would have realized that it wasn't a group that they were facing, but only one person. And they would have realized that there was no shouting, no sound of men approaching, no running footsteps pounding across the Common. They would have spread out and circled around her, captured her, disarmed her, and then . . .

Johnny stopped and shut his eyes. The Liberty Tree was just ahead of him. He was afraid to look. And he couldn't *not* look. He swallowed hard and took a deep breath, then forced himself to open his eyes. The old elm tree stood starkly silhouetted against the night sky. With a feeling of horrified dread, Johnny stared up into its branches, fully expecting to see two bodies hanging there.

The branches were bare of anything but leaves.

Johnny blinked and then came closer. There was no one hanging from the tree. Not Andre, not even MacIntosh. He stared into the branches, relieved, but at the same time puzzled. How could it be? Something must have happened. Andre by herself could never have stopped those men, no matter how remarkable a girl she was. What could have occurred to prevent them from hanging MacIntosh? They had already had the noose around his neck, his fate seemed sealed. His foot touched something and he looked down to see the rope lying on the ground. If someone had come to rescue them, then surely they would never have left him lying in the Common. Surely Andre would have returned for him.

Or perhaps she hadn't wanted to.

Someone must have warned the Sons of Liberty, thought Johnny. That was the only possible explanation. While he had lain unconscious, MacIntosh's friends had arrived just in the nick of time and rescued him, and Andre hadn't bothered to return for him, disgusted with him, thinking that he was a coward when he had only been thinking of protecting her. That must have been what happened. And by now, she would have told them all what happened and they would all think he was a coward, ready to run away and let a fellow patriot die rather than risk going to his aid. And there was no way he would be able to explain it to them, no way that they would ever understand. They had been outnumbered. There were only two of them. How could they have hoped to stand against all those men alone? How could he have knowingly led a girl into such danger? A girl he loved. No, they would never understand, but he had to explain it to them somehow. He had to explain to Andre. He couldn't bear having them think he was a coward. Especially Andre.

He started walking away from the Common. He felt the Liberty medallion in his pocket. They would probably take it away from him now. He wanted to cry, but he simply couldn't. There were no tears in him. He just felt empty and hollow inside. And utterly, inconsolably miserable.

He headed south down Summer Street, his shoulders hunched, his hands jammed deep into his pockets. He wasn't sure where he was going. The streets were dark and silent. Before long, it would be morning and Johnny didn't want to see the sun. He didn't want anyone to see him. He simply wanted to run away somewhere and hide. But he couldn't run away. He couldn't hide. There was something that he had to do.

He took his hands out of his pockets and pressed them up against his temples as he walked. His head hurt. He couldn't think straight. He passed Bishop's Avenue and kept on walking straight, unconsciously picking up his pace. The pain in his head was getting worse. All he ever wanted to do was help and he had only made things worse. Mr. Revere had trusted him and he had let him down. Andre would never forgive him. And as for Mr. Adams, who had paid him the highest compliment by personally giving him the Liberty medallion, saying, "Your role in this is especially important, Jonathan. It is absolutely vital."

Absolutely vital. There was something he had to do that was absolutely vital. Johnny was running now, still clutching at his head. He ran past Cow Lane, still heading south on Summer

Street, past South Street, toward the docks. He turned left on Purchase Street and kept on running . . . then he suddenly stopped. He waited to catch his breath. The pain in his head was gone now. The breeze coming in off the sea felt fresh and cool on his face. He was standing in front of Samuel Adams' house. He went up to the door and tried it. It was locked.

Still staring at the door, he reached inside his coat and took out a laser pistol. He aimed it at the door . . .

"Stop where you are!" someone called out. *"Don't move!"*

Slowly, Johnny turned around. Several men stood spread out in the street behind him, pointing weapons at him.

"Drop the gun!"

Johnny continued to hold onto the laser. He stared at the armed men with confusion.

"Johnny, put down the gun."

He squinted at the dark, shadowy forms. "Andre?"

"Yes, Johnny, it's me. Put the gun down, Johnny. Please."

His mouth felt dry. He moistened his lips. His head had started to hurt again.

"There is—there is something that I have to do . . ." he said.

Andre came toward him. "Please, Johnny. Put the gun down. You don't want to hurt me, do you?"

"Hurt you? N-No, I—I would never . . ." He started to breathe heavily. The pain in his head grew worse. "I must do . . . something . . ."

Lucas suddenly appeared standing close behind him. Andre shook her head slightly and Lucas hesitated. The boy's finger was right on the firing stud. If he didn't grab it quickly enough . . .

"I'll help you, Johnny," she said, slowly moving closer and keeping her voice very steady. "We'll do it together, okay? But you must give me the gun."

"You—you hit me . . ."

"Yes, Johnny, I know." Closer. "I'm sorry." Closer still.

Lucas gritted his teeth and made ready to grab for the gun. Andre kept her gaze locked with Johnny's.

"I was only . . . trying to help . . ." The pain was pounding in his temples now.

"I know, Johnny," Andre said. "I understand. You meant well. I only wanted to apologize. Won't you please give me the gun and we can talk?"

Lucas tensed. Johnny's hand had started to shake. Andre was so close . . . if he grabbed for the gun and the kid tightened his finger . . .

"Please. Give me the gun, Johnny. You don't want to hurt me."

"No," he said, his voice breaking. "I . . . I love you."

Andre reached out for the gun and Lucas felt his heart in his mouth. Her fingers closed around the barrel gently and she took it from him.

"I'm . . . sorry . . ." Johnny said, and Lucas let his breath out in a long sigh of relief. Andre handed him the laser pistol.

Johnny put his hands up to his face and started sobbing. Andre took him in her arms.

"It's all right, Johnny," she said, gently stroking his hair. As she looked at Lucas, he saw that she was crying too. "It's all right. Everything will be all right now."

A moment later, a sleepy Samuel Adams came to his front door dressed in his nightclothes. He had been awakened by voices outside his open bedroom window. He held up his lamp and stared out into the darkness. The street was empty. He grunted, shut the door, and went back upstairs to bed.

The outpost was located in the 2nd century B.C., high in the Alpine range overlooking the Po Valley. Several miles to the west was the mountain pass through which Hannibal would march his forces to meet the Roman consul Scipio at the Battle of Trebia. A short hop from the outpost was a small river. At a spot staked out about fifteen feet from the river's edge, a temporal convergence existed, a confluence point where two parallel timelines intersected.

The temporal range of this particular confluence point was three days and during that time, it was being patrolled by a unit of Temporal Corps Rangers under the command of Major Curtis. The "window" had been carefully chosen and they had only a short space of five minutes, during which time Curtis had been ordered to pull back with his men. He did not know why; he had no need to know. He only knew that something would be happening at the confluence point location during those five minutes that was of a highly classified nature and he had asked no questions.

"How does it feel to be going home again?" asked Lucas.

"It feels a little strange, pilgrim," Hunter said.

"Don't—"

"Call me pilgrim," Hunter finished with him in chorus. He grinned. "All right, pilgrim, I won't." He glanced at Steiger. "No hard feelings, Colonel?"

"No hard feelings, Captain," Steiger said. "But just to set the record straight, if our paths ever cross again—"

"Yeah, I know," said Hunter. "I'd like to say I'm looking forward to it, but then again . . ."

"Go on. Get out of here," said Steiger.

Hunter snapped to and threw him a salute. Steiger grimaced sourly and returned it.

"Take care of yourself, Reese," said Andre.

"You too, kid," he said, shaking her hand. "Delaney . . ."

"Good luck, Hunter." They shook hands.

"Lucas."

Lucas took his hand. "I hope you'll understand when I say that I sincerely hope we'll never see each other again."

Hunter smiled. "Yeah. Likewise. Tell Forrester for me that I think he's a hell of a soldier and he has my respect."

"I will."

"And that goes for you, as well. And give my regards to Dr. Darkness. Fascinating man. I suppose I ought to hate him for inventing that damn warp grenade, but I guess he was as much a victim as any of us were. I wonder if we have anyone like him on our side."

"I hope not," Lucas said. "One of him is quite enough."

Hunter looked around at all of them one last time. "It's been interesting," he said. "I'm still not sure what kind of a report I'm going to make. I suppose I'll have to lie a little. Oh, by the way, I've got something for you." He reached into his pocket and handed Lucas his Liberty medallion. "A souvenir," he said. *"Vaya con Dios."*

He turned and walked straight toward the riverbank without looking back. He passed through the confluence point and disappeared.

"You know, in a funny sort of way, I'm going to miss him," said Delaney.

"Yeah, me too," said Andre. "And if we ever run into him again, we're probably going to have to kill him."

"That's if he doesn't get us first," said Lucas. "But at least we understand each other, which is a lot more than I can say for the rest of this screwed up world."

He sighed and took one last look at the river that led to another flow of time.

"Come on, people," he said. "Let's go home."

EPILOGUE ━━━━━━━━━

The circular letter opposing the Townshend Acts was drawn up by Samuel Adams, with the help of James Otis, Thomas Cushing, and Joseph Hawley of the Massachusetts House, and sent out to all the colonies. While the letter was being circulated and debated, Charles Townshend died in England, succumbing to a fever. In his place as Chancellor of the Exchequer, King George appointed Lord North, a man who felt that the colonists were nothing less than a bunch of mutineers. At the same time, Lord Hillsborough was appointed to a brand-new office, Secretary of State for Colonial Affairs. Hillsborough felt the same way North did about the rebellious colonists. He felt it was time to stop coddling England's "ungrateful children."

When Lord Hillsborough received a copy of the Massachusetts circular letter, he took it to the king and then passed on His Majesty's command to each colonial governor, instructing them to have their legislatures ignore the letter and "treat it with the contempt it deserves." Governor Bernard was ordered to have the Massachusetts House formally rescind the letter. If they refused, the body was to be dissolved.

Bernard passed on his instructions to the House. The members voted. The order to rescind the circular letter was defeated by a vote of ninety-two to seventeen. Sam Adams sent a letter to Governor Bernard, informing him of the decision, and the next day, Governor Bernard dissolved the House, as he was ordered by his king, knowing that by doing so, he played right into the hands of Samuel Adams and the Sons of Liberty. "The Glorious Ninety-two" became a rallying cry in Boston and the names of the seventeen who voted to rescind were posted on the Liberty Tree.

The boycott of British goods was taken up in earnest throughout all the colonies. A worried Parliament took up the question of the Townshend Acts and Lord North spoke before the body. "America must fear you before she can love you," he told the members, urging them not to repeal the Townshend Acts until they saw America prostrate at their feet. In the fall of 1768, four thousand British troops arrived in Boston, nearly one redcoat for every four citizens. The elated Tories set off fireworks in celebration and taunted the patriots with a song called "Yankee Doodle."

> *Yankee Doodle came to town,*
> *a-riding on a pony,*
> *stuck a feather in his hat*
> *and called it macaroni!*
> *Yankee Doodle, keep it up!*
> *Yankee Doodle, dandy!*
> *Mind the music and the step,*
> *and with the girls be handy!*

The song was meant to be derisive. During the French and Indian War, the British troops had taken to calling the New England militia "Yankee companies." The word "macaroni" was London slang for a fop, a dandy, a foolish and superficial young man who hung about in taverns. The song was the Tories' way of making fun of the radicals who met in the taverns on the waterfront, something they felt safe to do now that the British troops were present to protect them. Little did they know that their taunting song would soon be turned around on them, to be used as a marching tune by the Continental Army.

There was trouble with the British troops right from the beginning. The Bostonians refused to house the soldiers, so they pitched their tents on Boston Common and commandeered Fanueil Hall, seizing the arms that were stored there in the process. Governor Bernard also allowed the troops to take over the Town Hall, where the Massachusetts House had lately met. Many of the officers rented quarters in the town from loyalists, while radicals urged the enlisted soldiers to desert. Many of them did. Those who were caught were shot on the Common or whipped in public, the sight of which turned the sympathies of many nonradical Bostonians against the British and gave the citizens a new name to taunt the soldiers with—"bloody backs." Fights often broke out between the troopers and the colonists and the constantly increasing tension made bloodshed inevitable.

On March 5, 1770, a crowd of Boston toughs gathered to taunt a British sentry. A squad of soldiers was sent to reinforce him, or perhaps to bring him back safely to the main guard, but as the soldiers reached the sentry, the gathering crowd closed in behind them, shouting abuse. For some fifteen minutes, there was a standoff, during which the troops stood at the ready while the crowd pelted them with rocks and ice. One soldier struck by a piece of ice fell—perhaps he slipped—but in any event, he fired. His shot set off a volley and when it was all over, five Bostonians lay dead and six were wounded. In the *Gazette*, Sam Adams wrote about the incident with outrage, and news of the "Boston Massacre" soon spread throughout the colonies. The radical cause gained a large number of new converts.

As sympathy for the patriotic cause spread through the colonies, the next major incident occurred when the British schooner *Gaspee* ran aground while chasing a smuggler. The ship was boarded by a party of attackers, the captain was shot in the groin, and the crew was badly beaten. Then the boarders forced the crew over the side and burned the *Gaspee* to the waterline. But as outrageous as this act was to the British, nothing served to ignite their feelings against the colonies as much as the Boston Tea Party.

The man behind it, once again, was Samuel Adams. The East India Company was in serious financial trouble, due in no small part to having been bled dry by agents of the Network. To rescue the company from bankruptcy, Parliament passed the Tea Act in 1773, allowing them to sell tea directly to America without first putting it on public sale in England, thereby eliminating the middlemen and allowing the tea—of which there was a surplus—to be sold more cheaply. More cheaply, in fact, then it could be bought from smugglers. And with a tax on it, as well. When the first shipment arrived in Boston, the colonists would not allow the tea to be unloaded. On December 16, 1773, one hundred and fifty members of the Sons of Liberty, posing as "Indians," their faces blackened with burnt cork, boarded the British ships and dumped three hundred and forty-two chests of tea into the harbor. Among the "Mohawks" were Paul Revere and his apprentice, a young man named Johnny Small.

Still ahead for him lay Lexington and Concord, where he would hear "the shot heard round the world," the bloody battle at Breed's Hill and service with the Continental Army, which would include the near defeat at the Battle of Long Island, the brutal winter spent at Valley Forge, and, finally, the surrender of General Cornwallis after the siege at Yorktown. Eight years would pass from the shots fired at Lexington and Concord to the signing of the peace treaty in Paris in 1783. When it was all over, Capt. John Small would return to Boston as a full-grown man and settle down in Salem Street, near Christ Church, where he would practice his trade as a silversmith. He would meet a pretty young woman named Anne Rafferty and marry, but though they would live a long and happy life together, the couple would not be blessed with any children. He would continue to be good friends with Paul Revere and his family until Revere's death in May of 1818, and with a nice young couple named Jared and Sally Moffat, who were also childless, but he was never very comfortable around Sam Adams, though he never quite understood why.

He would always believe that Anne was the only woman he had ever loved, and yet sometimes, he would dream of a young woman, a blonde just like his wife, with striking features, dressed in male clothing. He would awake with vague memories of those dreams, but when he struggled to recall them, he could not summon up the face, much less the name.

Though his primary trade was as a silversmith, he would often do some gunsmithing on the side. He specialized in pistols. Sometimes, for no particular reason he could think of, he would find himself making drawings of a most peculiar-looking pistol, resembling nothing he had ever seen before, but the drawings never looked practical and something about them always filled him with a strange feeling of foreboding, so that he would crumple the drawings up and burn them, afraid that anyone should see them without really knowing why.

He had one other slight idiosyncracy in what was otherwise a perfectly normal and ordinary life. He had an unusual pet name for his wife, an eccentricity which Anne found both strange and somehow charming.

He called her Andre.

AUTHOR'S NOTE ━━━━

One of the sad things about the way history's taught in schools is that too much emphasis is placed on memorizing names and dates and places and along the way, the *sense* of what happened becomes lost, frequently along with the truth. The Roman historian, Polybius, understood something that most modern history teachers seem to have forgotten, that history—to be truly valuable and interesting—must deal not so much with names and dates and places as with personalities and events.

I recall that as a young student, I found history boring, largely because my teachers were never really able to find a way to make it seem relevant to me. Let's face it, once you've memorized the information for a test, you soon forget it once again, and later on in life, when you're busy trying to make a living and find a place for yourself in this crazy world, it doesn't seem to make much difference whether you know the years during which the Civil War was fought or what specific event triggered World War I. It wasn't until I encountered Col. Rickert that I realized that history could be truly fascinating and that there were lessons to be learned from history that I could apply to my own life.

Col. Rickert taught American History at Valley Forge Military Academy. (V.F.M.A. is the school that Holden Caulfield attended in J. D. Salinger's *Catcher in the Rye*. Salinger called it Pencey Prep. It is also the school where the movie *Taps*, starring Timothy Hutton, Sean Penn, and Tom Cruise, was filmed.) What made Col. Rickert different from every other history teacher I'd ever had before was his approach. He was extremely knowledgeable about his subject and he did not attach as much importance to our memorizing names and dates as he did to our knowing something about the people who made history and what motivated them. He would assign some reading, and then the next day in class, instead of having us sit there and take endless notes, he would kick back and put his feet up on the desk and simply ramble on about people like Andrew Jackson or Abe Lincoln, just talking off the top of his head, sharing stories about them and telling us what kind of men they were. And we'd discuss things, in an informal sort of way, and these people would start to become real to us in a way we could relate to.

Col. Rickert never depended entirely upon textbooks, because textbooks at best are survey works, and they must be written to certain political requirements. You can't really have anything very controversial in a textbook. Witness the recent flap concerning evolution, for example. As a result, there are certain things you're never going to learn from textbooks. You won't learn, for example, that when the U.S. government signed treaties with the Indians, they were promised that the land would be theirs "as long as the sun would shine and the grass would grow," and then the government turned around and gave them blankets infected with smallpox virus in the hope of killing them all off. Chances are you won't learn that as President of the United States, Andrew Jackson once caned a man to death for insulting his wife, Sarah. You won't learn much about Ben Franklin's sexual excesses or the brilliant heroism of Benedict Arnold, because one is supposed to be a kindly, inventive founding father and the other is supposed to be a traitor. You'll learn that Ethan Allen demanded the surrender of Fort Ticonderoga in the name of "The Great Jehovah and the Continental Congress," when the fact is that Allen was an atheist and given to much use of profanity. What he really said was something probably a great deal saltier. You'll be taught that when Nathan Hale was hanged, he said, "I only regret that I have but one life to lose for my country." Not true. According to the diary of a British officer who was there and praised Hale for his courage, he really said, "It is the duty of every good officer to obey any orders given to him by his commander in chief." According to Tom Burnam's *Dictionary of Misinformation* (which I recommend highly), the words widely attributed to Hale probably came from a play by Joseph Addison. And you won't learn that the people who started the American Revolution were in certain ways not very different from the likes of Oliver North, Richard Secord, Admiral Poindexter, and even G. Gordon Liddy of Watergate fame. And yet, those are the *important* things to learn, because only then can you get a proper sense of perspective about historical events. Only then can history become truly relevant and fascinating.

In this book, aside from telling what I hope was an entertaining story, I tried to convey a sense of the people and events that led to the American Revolution. In order to do that, for the sake of the story, certain events have been compressed, but with the obvious exception of those events involving my fictional characters, most of the events that I describe here actually occurred pretty much the way I show them happening. The Hellfire Club depicted in the story is fictional, but there was a real society of sexual libertines called the Hellfire Club in England, headed by Sir Francis Dashwood and John Wilkes. However, the riots in Boston, the destruction of the homes of Thomas Hutchinson and Andrew Oliver, the *Liberty* incident, the sailor Furlong being rescued from the press gang, and the personal history of Samuel Adams are all drawn straight from historical fact. The Sons of Liberty, not to put too fine a point on it, were not a very nice bunch of people. They terrorized the loyal citizens of the colonies, of whom there were many, and after the war, most of the Loyalists lost everything and were forced to flee to Canada.

For a view of this time and these events from a Loyalist perspective, I strongly recommend an excellent and highly readable novel of historical fiction written by Kenneth Roberts, called *Oliver Wiswell*. It is available in paperback or at your local library. Roberts, in particular, perhaps more than any other writer I can think of, makes American history come alive in a very readable and entertaining manner. I can also recommend an excellent biography of Samuel Adams written by Paul Lewis, called *The Great Incendiary*. Esther Forbes wrote a very readable biography of Paul Revere titled *Paul Revere & The World He Lived In*. Other worthwhile books to read are

Patriots by A. J. Langguth, *The Glorious Cause* by Robert
Middlekauff (which is a little heavier reading than the others),
and *The American Heritage Book of The Revolution* by the
editors of *American Heritage* magazine. Another interesting
book is *Sergeant Lamb's America* by Robert Graves (of *I,
Claudius* fame), and George Bernard Shaw's entertaining play
The Devil's Disciple, which was also made into a wonderful
film starring Kirk Douglas and Burt Lancaster, who are both
terrific in it, but Lawrence Olivier as "Gentlemanly Johnny"
Burgoyne steals the show. Watch for it in your local TV listings
and you'll learn how the Battle of Saratoga, the turning point
of the war, was lost because a bureaucrat in London decided to
leave early for a weekend in the country.

There are other fascinating things about the Revolution that
you won't learn from the textbooks. Lord William Howe, for
example, who was Commander in Chief of the British forces,
is often made to look slothful and inept and has been blamed,
probably justifiably, for England losing the war. If he hadn't
hesitated at the Battle of Long Island, he could easily have
captured the entire Continental Army. He allowed them to
escape on several occasions, he has generally been criticized
for being hesitant to commit his troops, and his mistress was a
colonial spy. In fact, although it can't be proven, there might
well be an even more interesting reason for why he acted the
way he did.

Lord Howe was a Whig, a member of the opposition party
to the ruling Tories. What better way to get the Tories out of
power than to lose the war? In a very real sense, the American
Revolution was England's Viet Nam. Many Whigs in England
referred to Washington's troops as "our army" and applauded
colonial victories. It was a war lacking popular support and
logistically almost impossible to fight. Howe knew this very
well and it's entirely possible that his hesitancy and indecision
were politically motivated. In fact, after Howe was replaced as
Commander in Chief by General Clinton, he and his brother,
Admiral Lord Richard Howe, were called before a Parliamen-
tary inquiry to account for their actions. Howe paraded
witnesses before the House of Commons, among them General
Cornwallis and Major General Charles Grey, to testify that the
fault lay not with the commanders, but with the ministry, and
fortunately for him, by that point, Commons was more than
ready to find fault with the ministry. Either way, it is certainly

true that a strong case can be made that we didn't win the war so much as England lost it.

The end result, in any case, was certainly inevitable, but in the early days of these United States, Americans were far from united. There were many people in the thirteen colonies who were against the war and their rights and liberties were thoroughly trampled on. Sam Adams and the Sons of Liberty did some pretty ugly things. The speeches that I have Sam Adams making are entirely fictional, but he probably said things that were very similar. The sort of things he did in the *Boston Gazette* were things that we would call highly unethical today, and in fact, they were highly unethical then, too. It is fascinating to speculate what Adams might have done with the medium of television.

The fact is that if anyone truly deserves to be called the father of our country, it is not George Washington, but Samuel Adams. He was a man of many facets and many contradictions, on one hand so softhearted that he couldn't bring himself to force poor people to pay taxes when he was a collector, and on the other, utterly ruthless and often unprincipled in the pursuit of his goals. He was a man who, in many ways, might have found much to admire in Richard Nixon or William Casey. And if he was around today, he'd probably be torn to pieces by a congressional committee and the media would hang him out to dry.

On the other hand, it's true that for all their violent behavior, the Sons of Liberty are not known to have ever killed anyone and Sam Adams deeply regretted some of the things he felt they were forced to do. He often felt the need to justify his actions and he went to great lengths to do so. He once said, "I have long feared this unhappy contest between Great Britain and America would end in rivers of blood; should that be the case, America, I think, may wash her hands in innocence . . ." It was, perhaps, an unfortunate metaphor, bringing to mind the vision of Pontius Pilate washing his hands after ordering Christ's crucifixion. But in a way, it was also an appropriate one, because if history has taught us nothing else, it is that no one is ever entirely innocent of blame.

Simon Hawke
Denver, Colorado

CLASSIC SCIENCE FICTION
AND FANTASY

___ **DUNE** Frank Herbert 0-441-17266-0/$4.95
The bestselling novel of an awesome world where gods and
adventurers clash, mile-long sandworms rule the desert, and
the ancient dream of immortality comes true.

___ **STRANGER IN A STRANGE LAND** Robert A. Heinlein
0-441-79034-8/$4.95
From the *New York Times* bestselling author—the science
fiction masterpiece of a man from Mars who teaches
humankind the art of grokking, watersharing and love.

___ **THE ONCE AND FUTURE KING** T.H. White
0-441-62740-4/$5.50
The world's greatest fantasy classic! A magical epic of King
Arthur in Camelot, romance, wizardry and war. By the author
of *The Book of Merlyn*.

___ **THE LEFT HAND OF DARKNESS** Ursula K. LeGuin
0-441-47812-3/$3.95
Winner of the Hugo and Nebula awards for best science fiction
novel of the year. "SF masterpiece!"—*Newsweek* "A Jewel of
a story."—Frank Herbert

___ **MAN IN A HIGH CASTLE** Philip K. Dick 0-441-51809-5/$3.95
"Phillp K. Dick's best novel, a masterfully detailed alternate
world peopled by superbly realized characters."
—Harry Harrison

For Visa and MasterCard orders call: 1-800-631-8571

FOR MAIL ORDERS: CHECK BOOK(S). FILL
OUT COUPON. SEND TO:

BERKLEY PUBLISHING GROUP
390 Murray Hill Pkwy., Dept. B
East Rutherford, NJ 07073

NAME_____

ADDRESS_____

CITY_____

STATE_____ZIP_____

PLEASE ALLOW 6 WEEKS FOR DELIVERY.
PRICES ARE SUBJECT TO CHANGE WITHOUT NOTICE.

POSTAGE AND HANDLING:
$1.00 for one book, 25¢ for each ad-
ditional. Do not exceed $3.50.

BOOK TOTAL $ ____

POSTAGE & HANDLING $ ____

APPLICABLE SALES TAX $ ____
(CA, NJ, NY, PA)

TOTAL AMOUNT DUE $ ____

PAYABLE IN US FUNDS.
(No cash orders accepted.)   279